TROUBLED WATERS

HJ WELCH

Troubled Waters
Pine Cove Book Two

Copyright © 2019 by HJ Welch

SCOUT

SCOUT DUFFY HAD NEVER FUCKED ANYONE WHILE BEING watched by a shoal of guppies, but he'd done stranger things on a Tuesday night, to be sure.

He'd also been in far worse nightclubs, especially in small towns. But he had to admit, this Aquarium place was pretty nice, even if the bathroom was home to several breeds of exotic fish that were about to get one hell of a floor show. They'd probably seen it all, but Scout had a feeling the little minx dragging him into the end stall had a trick or two up his sleeve.

Scout honestly hadn't come into Pine Cove's only gay bar with the intention of getting laid. He was there for work, after all, and had an early start in the morning. But after the three-hour drive from SeaTac airport and brief but shitty conversation with his dad over the phone from his motel room, he figured it wouldn't hurt to blow off some steam.

He could have gone to any bar. A big dude as stacked as he was could pass for straight any day of the week. Most days, that was how he preferred it. But as was usual after any kind of interaction with his old man, he'd felt like sticking a finger up to the world and purposefully seeking out other gay guys. On some level, he'd probably known a good, angry fuck was what he was craving.

The thing was, lately he'd found himself so bored of the pretty boys who initially struck his fancy. They had no spice. Scout had known he'd hit gold the second this little minx had stepped on the dance floor.

He was Asian and fucking beautiful with high cheekbones, a slim frame, and eyes that practically screamed how much trouble he was going to be in the sack. He'd slunk his way over to Scout in little more than cowboy boots, denim booty skimmers and a pink mesh top that read 'Butch' in large white letters. He shimmered under the disco lights as he'd began winding his hips, rubbing his ass against Scout's crotch while he twirled his hands above his head.

Scout smirked as he finished his beer, placed the bottle back on the bar, then slid his hands over the minx's hips. They were quite the mismatched pair. Scout was twice his size and dressed in a simple pair of jeans and a tank top that showed off his body art. Whereas the slinky little minx *was* the work of art.

"You look like you're down to fuck," Scout growled in his ear.

The minx gasped and clutched his chest, although he merely glanced at Scout over his shoulder. "She would never. She's a *good* girl."

Scout paused. "Sorry, is that a 'not interested'?"

The minx giggled. "Oh, silly. 'No' means 'yes,' doesn't it?"

"It does?"

In Scout's book, 'no' absolutely meant 'no.' But it was clear this guy was playing some sort of game. Scout wasn't going to make any assumptions, though. "How about you explain the rules to me, then?"

The minx nodded. "'No' means 'yes.' 'Yes' means *'harder.'*"

"So what actually means 'no'?" Scout was all up for a bit of fun and teasing, but in his line of work, safety was the number one priority. He may not have been on the job now, but he still wasn't comfortable unless they were on the same page.

The minx grinned over his shoulder and ground his ass against Scout's crotch. "Ooh, I like you. You ask smart questions."

"Yeah?" Scout slid his hands around, skimming his palms over the deliciously smooth skin of the minx's thighs. Fuck, he smelled good. Like pineapple or something. Scout realized that by pressing his chest against the smaller guy's back he was getting covered in some kind of body glitter, but he didn't care. He'd bought a ticket to this show, and he wasn't backing out now.

The minx bit his lip and wriggled his ass, draping his hands on Scout's shoulders behind him. "'Guppy' means 'no.' Do you want to follow me to the men's room?"

Scout grinned and bit the minx's earlobe. "No," he said, getting into the spirit of this little game.

Sure enough, the minx grabbed his hand and tugged him through the crowd toward the bathroom. The music pulsed all around them as the colored lights swirled overhead. The minx ignored the line and the guys at the urinals as he pushed through the door, heading for the stall right at the end where the whole wall was an aquarium. Luckily there was a brick wall on the other side of the glass tank because he had a feeling they were going to get down and dirty, no matter if there was an audience or not.

He glanced at the guppies as they swished their orange-and-black-tails, hoping they weren't going to mind the X-rated performance about to unfurl.

"There is a line!" one of the guys called out with a tut as

Scout and the minx marched on past. The minx blew him a kiss and winked.

"Sorry, baby. I hope you find an Action Man to play with, too. But I got to get my freak on right the hell now."

The guy rolled his eyes but didn't look all that mad. In fact, he gave Scout an appreciative up-and-down then moaned. "Make it noisy for the rest of us, in that case."

The minx doubled up laughing just as the dude in the end cubicle vacated it. Scout found himself being pulled inside.

He locked the door, his skin tingling at the idea of other guys listening in to what was about to happen. He wasn't usually into voyeurism, but after years spent in the boxing ring, he was definitely a performer. His rock-hard cock straining against his jeans certainly suggested he was into a little bit of showing off.

His minx pressed his back against Scout's chest again, taking his hand and putting it over his crotch. There was no doubt he was just as hard as Scout was in his tiny shorts. For a slim, petite guy, he had a surprisingly tight body. As Scout slid his other hand under the mesh shirt, he discovered lean muscle on his long stomach. Fuck, his mouth was watering. Thank god he had packed protection.

"What do you want to do to me?" the minx asked as Scout kissed his neck.

He noticed that so far, the minx had avoided looking directly at Scout and was keeping his back to him. If that was the way he wanted to play it, that was fine. It had been forever since Scout had experienced a genuinely thrilling one-night-stand. If the minx wanted to keep a bit of mystery to the encounter, that was pretty hot.

"I'm going to bend you over and fuck your brains out," Scout growled. "Does that sound good?"

"Oh, *yes, honey!*" someone hissed from outside. The music was throbbing through the closed door, bursting louder whenever anyone opened it, but aside from that Scout got the impression the guys in the bathroom with them were waiting with bated breath for what Scout and his minx were going to do.

Yeah. That was fucking hot.

"That sounds terrible, you brute." The minx turned his head just enough so Scout could capture his mouth in a filthy kiss. "I hope you've got a big cock."

"Of course I have," Scout said, undoing his pants and shoving them down to his thighs. "I think you should suck it first. Get me wet and hard for that pretty, tight ass of yours."

Someone *fwapped* a fan and groaned. Another guy grumbled about 'fucking exhibitionists,' but Scout didn't care.

The minx grinned, spinning and dropping eagerly to his knees. He avoided looking at Scout's face, but he was staring at his cock instead, which was much better in that moment.

"Oh, dear," the minx said with exaggerated concern as his eyes widened at Scout's hard dick. "How ever will that fit?"

Scout ran his fingers through the minx's thick mop of black hair. "I don't know, but you'd better get to work. I want to fuck your face and your ass."

From outside in the line, one guy gasped over the beat of the music and another laughed. Scout was very much enjoying this little game.

Then he forgot all about everyone else as the minx licked the thick tip of his cock, kissing and sucking on it like a lollipop. Scout groaned and dropped his head back against the stall door, making it bang. "Fuck, you look good," he rasped as the minx bobbed his head further down, swallowing Scout's throbbing dick with little whimpers and moans of pleasure.

Scout's breathing was heavy as he watched through hooded lids, running his fingers through the minx's thick hair, sticky with product. He gave an experimental tug on it and was rewarded with a squeak and a fluttering of eyelids.

It was tempting to just suggest the minx keep sucking him so he could come like that. But this guy was something else. Scout was overcome with the need to claim him, to be inside him. He wanted to hear the noises he uttered as Scout made him come.

So he pulled at his luscious hair. "Come here," he demanded. He didn't care if this guy was avoiding looking him in the eye. Scout wanted to kiss him face-to-face on the mouth properly, even if it was just once. The minx's lips were red and swollen as he scrambled back up to his feet, allowing Scout to seize him by the shoulders. Fuck, he really was so beautiful up close.

Scout tasted himself on the minx's lips and tongue, a slightly bitter musk that thrilled him as their mouths clashed. The minx wrapped his fingers around the fabric of Scout's tank, yanking Scout down to his level. Scout was barely six foot, but that still made him a few inches taller than the minx, and he was far stockier. He liked how their bodies slotted together.

Of course, they could be fitting together even better.

"So we gonna fuck, or what?"

The minx snorted, then bit the side of Scout's neck. "I'm waiting on you, lazybones."

"Oh, you think I'm lazy?" Scout spun the minx around, making him gasp, and pushed him against the aquarium. The glass felt sturdy enough, but several fish swished their tails as they pivoted suddenly, swimming away from the men pressing themselves against their wall.

"Jesus Christ, *yes*," the minx hissed. "Fuck me like you mean it, you barbarian."

"Shut up," Scout growled, not meaning it in the slightest.

The minx smirked over his shoulder. "Make me."

Scout fished into his jeans pocket for the condom and single-use packet of lube, dropping them on the shelf behind the toilet. The minx still had his hands resting on the glass wall, waiting for Scout. Ordinarily, Scout would be annoyed if the guy he was fucking was expecting him to do all the work, but there was a challenging look in the minx's eyes. Like he was daring Scout to tell him off.

Instead, Scout got kind of a rush being in charge of this whole thing. He chose what happened and how it happened. So he reached around and unzipped the minx's booty shorts, staring at his eyes the entire time as he shoved them down, freeing his cock. The minx wouldn't return his gaze directly, staring at Scout's mouth instead before leaning over to bite his bottom lip.

The minx was wearing a chunky red thong with a snug pouch for his not-so-small cock. Scout's own length strained at the tantalizing sight. He wished he could take his time to admire the underwear, but if he didn't fuck this piece of ass right the hell now, he was going to explode.

So he pushed the thong down around the minx's thighs along with his shorts, then grabbed the condom, tearing it open with his teeth and rolling it hastily down his throbbing dick. It had a little lubrication, but he sensed neither of them wanted to spend a lot of time stretching out, so Scout was appreciative of the extra lube he'd brought.

Within seconds, he had it smeared along his cock and between the minx's pert ass cheeks. He rubbed against his hole, probing with his middle finger, making the minx moan. There might have been more snickers and disapproving grumbles from guys waiting for the other stalls, but Scout could hardly tell over his own racing pulse.

"Is this what you want?" he rasped as he angled the tip of his cock and pushed against the tight ring of muscle. "Is this what you like, beautiful?" The minx gasped and nodded, scrambling his hands against the glass as Scout pushed inside him. He could feel the minx relaxing, even as he gritted his teeth and groaned. "God, you do, don't you? Being fucked in a goddamned public toilet."

"Less talking, more fucking," the minx snarled through a grin, his eyes sparkling as he captured Scout's mouth for a filthy kiss. He whimpered and flinched, then turned away to press his forehead against the glass wall. "That's it. Take me. I want to feel you all the way."

Scout grunted, pulling the minx's ass cheeks apart to allow him easier access, pushing his cock further inside the minx's tight, hot hole. "Fuck, you feel so good." Scout bottomed out, taking a moment as both of them panted, sweat running down their backs. Scout paused to use his trembling hand to reach around and squeeze the minx's cock, making sure he was still hard. "Do you want me to fuck your sweet little ass now, pretty boy? Would you like that?"

"God, your ego." The minx rolled his eyes. "Just hurry up before I do it myself."

Scout bit his earlobe and grabbed his hip with the hand not holding his cock. "I should leave you high and dry. Fill you with cum and let you sort out your own blue balls. Lucky for you, I want to hear you scream."

A guy out in the line moaned. *"Yes.* Get that ass." From another cubicle, Scout swore he heard a guy growl, *"Like that. Harder."* He snickered to himself. They were inciting an orgy.

As much as Scout was enjoying their fun, he didn't actually want to hurt his little minx. So he slid his cock out slowly before easing it back inside the tight, perfect hole, gradually building up a rhythm. The minx rolled his hips in time, matching him thrust for thrust as Scout squeezed and stroked his juicy cock. Fucking hell, it wasn't going to be long before he climaxed.

"Yes, yes, yes," the minx was whispering. "Holy shit, I'm gonna come. Don't stop, don't stop."

The stall was rocking where Scout kept banging into it. The minx's damp hands squeaked as they inched up the glass. The air in the cubicle was thick with the sounds of their grunts and gasps and the smell of their masculine musk and sweat. Scout's cock pounded inside the minx's ass while he jerked off his rock-hard length.

Cum splattered on the side of the aquarium without warning, startling any fish that had floated back their way. The minx wailed and gnashed his teeth, pushing back against Scout's cock as he chased his orgasm, thrusting the last few times while the minx shivered in the wake of his own climax.

Scout's release hit him like a wrecking ball, snatching his breath away as he fired his load into the condom deep inside his lover's ass. He wrapped his arms around the minx's body as his vision blacked out for a few seconds, breathing deeply and inhaling the minx's sweet pineapple scent mixed in with the delicious tang of cum and sweat.

He kissed the side of the minx's neck and ran his hands along his chest and arms. "Thank you for that," the minx said, then hummed. He glanced over his shoulder, looking more at Scout's stomach than his face, but Scout could still see the contented grin tugging at his plump lips.

The minx eased himself off Scout's softening cock ,and Scout set about carefully pulling the condom off and tying the top so he could throw it into the trash. When he looked up, the minx had already mopped himself up with a ball of toilet paper and pulled his thong and shorts back up. Before Scout could react, the minx stood on his tiptoes, kissed Scout on the cheek, then unlocked the cubicle door.

"Enjoy the rest of your night, gorgeous."

With that, he swung the door open and sashayed back out

into the main area of the men's toilets, only just giving Scout enough time to tuck his cock back into his jeans.

The line gave the minx a round of applause as he strutted out. Scout stuck his head out in time to see him blowing kisses at the men at the urinals, washing their hands or waiting for the cubicles. Then the minx pushed his way through the door, back onto the dance floor.

Scout blinked. His heart was still racing, and his body was still slightly trembling as he came down from his high. He hadn't expected to be abandoned quite so fast.

"Are you done?" the guy at the front of the line asked impatiently.

Scout glanced back into the stall. His minx had even wiped down the glass and put the two wrappers in the trash.

It was like they had never even been there.

"Uh, yeah. All yours." Scout walked back out to a mix of appreciative and jealous looks. He half smiled and nodded at the line, then walked down to the sinks to wash his hands in cold water, rubbing his wet hand against the back of his neck to cool him down a fraction after his encounter.

His head was spinning. He prided himself on having had a lot of sex in the years since he'd come out of the closet. But that had to rank as some of the best he'd ever had.

Except, he couldn't help but feel like something was missing. He dried his hands on his jeans and shouldered through the door, the music from the club hitting him like a wave as he navigated his way through the throng on the dance floor. It didn't take him long to scan the crowd.

The minx wasn't there.

He wasn't out the back in the patio area with all the fairy lights and seashells. He wasn't out the front with the smokers either.

He was gone.

Scout couldn't remember the last time he'd asked for a

phone number after a hookup. But with a pang, he realized for this little minx he would have made an exception.

Hell, he would have settled for a damn name.

Deflated, he didn't feel like hanging around any longer at the bar, and he wasn't one for dancing anyway. He did order a shot of whiskey for the road, warming himself and chasing the buzz from his post orgasm high. Then he stepped back out into the night, opting to walk back to his motel instead of grabbing an Uber.

He wanted to reflect on his spectacular encounter for a little longer in the dark where it still seemed real, before he woke up to reality tomorrow, and it all felt like nothing more than a dream. The longer he walked, the more his loneliness consumed him.

Yeah, for once, he maybe wouldn't have minded sharing his bed.

2

EMERY

Emery Klein only stumbled once on the short walk
from his Uber to unlocking the front door of his apartment
building. All right, maybe twice. But he definitely didn't
bump off the wall of the lobby or hiccup as he slowly made
his way up the stairs. He might have giggled, though.

He wasn't drunk, but he was certainly a little more than
tipsy. However, it was the deliciously sore and full sensation
in his ass that was making him giddy as he swayed in the
stairwell. Christ, when was the last time he'd had a truly
good fucking like that?

It was a shame to leave his brute right afterward, but
those were the rules. No looking, no lingering. Although he'd
seen enough to leave a reasonable impression, particularly of
the lone wolf tattoo on his bicep that had drawn Emery over
the dance floor in the first place. It had glistened under the
swirling disco lights, making Emery think maybe it was new
ink that the barbarian had oiled up to take care of it.

He'd certainly taken care of Emery, all right.

Emery would have been a dirty liar if he didn't admit he'd
been sorely tempted to sneak a photo or even one last kiss

before he scampered from Aquarium. Because the irony of it was the brute had actually been quite the gentleman. It just amused Emery to refer to him like that, as a brute or a barbarian, with his big muscles, dark hair and light eyes. Jesus, the ways he'd manhandled Emery and fucked him hard against the fish tank…it made him shiver at the mere memory.

Emery leaned against the wall in the stairwell on the second floor, clutching his phone to his chest. He'd been using the cab ride to catch up on whatever replies or admin tasks he could cope with after so much vodka, but now he just wanted to stop and revel for a moment. He touched his lips, chasing the sensation of the brute's mouth on his, the taste of his sweet beer lingering like a ghost.

Over the years, Emery had become quite skilled at not committing details of his lovers to his memory in the first place, let alone evoking them afterward. He had a naturally terrible memory for faces in any case, something he'd had to work really hard on to improve in his professional life, but generally aided him with string-free hookups. So the brute's image had already blurred into a mashup of dozens of different guys. It was safer that way.

But Emery had a feeling that it would be harder to shake the recollection of the way his big strong hands had gripped and pulled at Emery's body, the way his teeth and lips had felt nipping and kissing Emery's skin. Even more than that, the way his voice had lilted with excitement as he and Emery had teased each other.

Emery loved a good tease.

Well, there was no sense dwelling on anything. It had been a spectacular moment, and now it had passed. There was nothing stopping Emery from treasuring it in his spank bank, but for now, he really should take himself upstairs to bed and get some rest. He'd been working since around five that morning, and now it was past midnight, so exhaustion was creeping into his bones.

He forced his phone into the tight pocket of his shorts. Then he unlocked the door on his floor by tapping his key fob to the panel on the wall before fishing out his apartment key.

Except, when he turned the corner on the fourth floor, he realized he didn't need the key to his apartment.

His door was already ajar.

Fear lanced through his chest, making his heart stutter in panic as he pulled himself back around the corner. *What the fuck?*

Several thoughts raced through his brain while he carefully glanced back down the hall. The first was questioning if his best friend, Ava, had mentioned staying over. But no, Emery might have been tired and a little drunk, but he was sure they hadn't made any sort of arrangement. He knew he'd never leave it open. He always doubled-checked the lock before he left his home, sometimes even triple-checked. His cleaner had a key, but she came on Thursdays. Also, she came during the day. In his panic, he wasn't thinking clearly at all.

Because the only logical conclusion was that someone was in his home who really fucking shouldn't be.

"*Shit,*" Emery hissed, tears of rage and desperate fear pooling in his eyes.

Oh, god. This wasn't anything to do with *those* messages, was it?

Being vaguely internet famous left anyone open to getting harassed, especially when they were an outspoken LGBT activist like Emery was. He'd seen his fair share of hate over the years. But lately he'd been inundated with anonymous messages that all looked to be from the same person, judging by the tone and the language used. They all said the same sort of thing.

You took what's ours. We're coming to take it back.

Homos like you are fucking AIDS filth! You don't deserve any of it, you thief!

We know where you live. The world won't miss you.

Emery didn't have to be an FBI profiler to know that this stalker, whoever they were, had some serious issues.

But he never thought it would come to anything like this. Someone had broken into his *home*. What the hell should he do?

He should call the police. They probably wouldn't arrive for several minutes, though. In the meantime, whoever the intruder was could very well get away.

Emery shouldn't be out here lingering when they came back. He should run and figure out how the hell these motherfuckers could have gotten through the secured front door as well as the door to his floor later. When he was safe.

But he was furious at the idea that some asshole was rummaging through his stuff! Who knew what they were putting their filthy hands all over, what they were trashing or bagging up *right now*. As his heart raced and he clung to the corner of the hallway, he tried to reason with himself that everything could be replaced.

Except…

"No!" he gasped, the tears spilling from his eyes. "No, no, no, *no!*"

Everything could be replaced. His laptop, his clothes, his shoes, his precious keepsakes from all around the world. They were just material things, and if he lost them, it would be okay.

But not Sonic.

A wave of dizziness rushed over Emery, and he tried to use the wall to keep him upright. He'd never, *ever* forgive himself if that bastard harmed his Sonic. Emery couldn't leave him. He couldn't even risk waiting for the police to arrive. Some people were sick bastards who wouldn't miss the chance to hurt an innocent creature.

Emery unfortunately knew far too many sick bastards these days. He had to save him.

He scrubbed the tears from his face, his throat clamping and his heart thumping so fast in his chest he thought he was going to be sick. But somehow he made himself put one foot silently in front of the other, creeping toward his open door all the way down the hall.

Whoever the intruder was, they weren't making a sound. Even as Emery reached the threshold of his apartment and hovered by the door, he couldn't hear a thing. He moved as close as he could to the crack in the doorway and glanced inside his living room. He couldn't see anything moving.

At least, anything that wasn't supposed to be.

Emery's eyes went directly to Sonic's large cage, focusing on it intently. Yep, there he was, his little hedgehog, wide awake and snuffling around in his wood shavings. Luckily, he wasn't inside one of the many pipes or using his squeaky wheel. It didn't look as if the intruder had disturbed him in any way.

For a fleeting second, Emery wondered if whoever it was had already been and gone, not bothering to close the door behind them. But then the faintest bump and rattle came from the direction of the bedroom, and Emery's adrenaline surged once again.

His bedroom was *sacred*. His blood boiled to think of some asshole rummaging around in there. But that also meant there was only a partially closed door between whoever was in there and Emery and Sonic.

He had to act, *now*.

Steeling himself, he took a few breaths as silently as he

could. It was amazing how fast he'd sobered up in the face of real danger. This was his responsibility, though. He had to get both himself and Sonic out of there safely.

He pushed the door as quietly as he could, padding over the wooden floorboards in his open-plan living room. It didn't look as if the intruder had disturbed that much in here, except there were several drawers left open, their contents scattered over the floor. But the TV was still straight on the wall, as well as his artwork.

For now, it sounded like the intruder was preoccupied in the bedroom, probably busying themselves with Emery's safe. After all, they might have intended on stealing his laptop to get into his private affairs, but he wished them luck physically getting to it.

On the other hand, that meant they could give up and come back out here at any time. Emery swallowed his fear and scuttled as fast as he could over to Sonic's cage.

"Come on, baby," Emery whispered so softly it was barely louder than a breath. His gaze was flicking frantically between his bedroom door and the top of the cage as he opened it. "Come on, sweetheart. Time for an adventure. We're going to see Auntie Ava. It's okay, it's okay."

But Sonic could tell it was very much not okay. By the time Emery had slipped on the oven mitts he used to protect his hands from Sonic's pointy spines, the hedgehog had backed himself into the corner he knew was the most difficult to retrieve him from.

Emery could have screamed.

Instead he reached inside the cage, angling his arm awkwardly like he had a hundred times before. This was fine. He could do this. He just had to make sure he scooped Sonic up without hurting him. He didn't even care if he stabbed his fingers at this point. They were running out of time, and the intruder was still lurking in the bedroom.

If they came out, what would they do? Would Emery have time to escape?

What if they had a gun?

He wasn't going to find out.

"Come on, my darling, it's time to go. Come on. *Come on.*"

Sonic trembled and scrambled away from the oven mitt, kicking up the wood shavings. He could probably sense Emery's terror and desperation to get them out of there. It was natural his instincts would tell him to run, but Emery was making himself dizzy looking between his baby and the bedroom door. Was that a slightly different sound he'd heard? A leg hitting a bed in the dark, perhaps? A hip catching an open closet door?

He'd wasted too much time.

He changed his angle, scooping up a handful of shavings but also one frightened and stubborn hedgehog. He could have cried in relief as he pulled his arm back, cradling Sonic to his chest.

Just as the bedroom door swung inward.

Emery didn't think. He didn't hesitate as his feet kicked into gear, sprinting for the front door he'd left ajar.

Whoever had been in his bedroom roared, a terrifying animalistic sound that must have woken half the neighbors on Emery's floor. But Emery didn't even pause long enough to glance back.

He just fucking ran.

Tears streamed down his face as his feet pounded on the hallway carpet toward the door that led out to the stairwell. Mercifully, this side didn't need a key fob to open it. He had Sonic bundled up in the mitt. Some of his spines were scratching Emery through his mesh shirt, but at least Emery had a hand he could slip free from the mitt. He slammed his hand on the button to unlock the door. It felt like it took forever to hear the click. But it was only a second before he was able to haul the door open and escape into the stairs.

He didn't even know what smacked into the back of his head, but it was heavy enough Emery was thrown forward, his forehead catching the edge of the door.

What the shit? It was a heavy object, not anyone's fist. The intruder had thrown something – he was still twenty feet behind him. That was a little comfort as pain exploded through Emery's head. The bastard hadn't caught him yet, though, and he wasn't going to. Another surge of adrenaline assaulted Emery's already ragged nerves.

Run, run, run! his brain screamed.

So that was what he did.

With Sonic clutched to his chest, he dashed down the steps, unsure if it was blood or sweat running down his back. He kept to the outer edge of the stairwell so they were out of sight from anyone looking down the middle. But Emery heard the bang of the door soon enough and the clatter of footsteps behind him. The intruder hadn't called out again after the initial, wordless bellow, but it was as if Emery could feel the loathing radiating off him.

There was no doubt in Emery's mind that this was personal. This fucker knew him. He was probably one of the faceless assholes who had been tormenting Emery for months, years. Could it be 'ekleinhater'? The one who seemed to think Emery owed him something. The one who had been so confident when he'd gloated that he knew where Emery lived.

His legs felt like jelly, and his head was throbbing as he reached the front door, but he pounded on the release button, slamming his way back out into the night. His apartment building was on a relatively well-lit main road, but this was Pine Cove, not a major city. At this time of night, the whole area was pretty deserted, and Emery didn't trust that a few streetlamps would be enough to stop his attacker from trying anything further.

So instead of running down the sidewalk, Emery pelted down the alleyway, past the dumpsters, sending a couple of lurking cats scattering in surprise. He hoped them fleeing didn't give his direction away, but he didn't even have a second to spare worrying about it. He had to get out of the alley before the intruder reached the other end and saw which way he'd gone.

"Go, go, go!" he gasped, begging his wobbly legs not to trip him up. Just a few more seconds…

He rounded the corner and released a tiny cry of ecstatic relief without pausing at all in his desperate pace.

"You can do this! Run!"

In the end, he wasn't sure how long he made his frantic dash for. But he didn't stop until his legs gave out and he crashed his shoulder against the brick wall of a fishing tackle shop, dark and closed for the night. Several glances behind Emery's shoulder had told him he wasn't being followed anymore.

Sonic looked up at Emery, wiggling his little nose as he scratched anxiously at the oven mitt. But Emery grinned down at him, wiping the tears from his face, then very carefully stroking the top of Sonic's head with his finger.

"We did it," he whispered, giddy with joy. "Let's get to Auntie Ava's, huh? She'll look after poor Daddy and Baby Sonic, won't she?"

Emery's hand was trembling so badly it took a while to open up his phone and order an Uber. But luck was on his side, and there was a car only two minutes away. Hopefully, even if his attacker had somehow managed to work out what route Emery had run, he'd be gone by the time he got here.

All the same, Emery didn't truly rest easy until he and

Sonic were in the cab, speeding toward Ava's apartment across town.

Only then did Emery take a slow, deep breath and start to wonder exactly which of his online psychos had taken their abuse one step further, going from cyber stalking, to real-life aggravated assault.

3

SCOUT

Scout had seen a great deal of America in his time. Lots of big cities and small towns, some with charm, some with style, some he would never care to see the likes of again. He had to admit, this Pine Cove place had something going for it.

For a small town, it felt like it had a lot of pride. Some places never got big enough to really claim their own sense of identity, Scout felt. But here, he felt welcomed by everyone he saw. The views over the enormous lake from the boardwalk at the end of the main street were breath-taking. The stores felt modern as if the people here weren't letting themselves get left behind in the previous century like other places Scout had been.

But in other ways, it clung on to an other-worldly charm. Like his motel. Unlike many of the countless soulless, sticky rooms he'd found himself in over the past decade, the Pine Cove Lodge was more like a log cabin than a cheap pay-by-the-hour joint.

Yeah, as much as Scout appreciated the hustle and bustle of city life, he could see why folks chose a small town like this as he parked his rental car along the main street. There weren't many chain stores he could see on either side of the road. But as he walked down to the diner near the lake, he spied a mom and pop grocers, a Turkish barber, a secondhand book place and a bakery that smelled utterly divine. If he hadn't been on his way to meet Christopher, he probably would have swung in there for a bear claw and a latte. Perhaps another time.

Christopher Oakley had been Scout's boss these past few years, ever since he'd traded in his pro-boxing gloves at the end of his twenties for the private security business. Christopher was in his late forties, a former Military Policeman, who decided to settle down once he became a father. Usually, he briefed Scout over the phone or at his office in San Diego. But occasionally he'd fly out and meet his agents when they had a particularly tricky client.

'Tricky' could mean all sorts of things. In this case, Scout was under the impression this new guy was some sort of minor celebrity. It was also mildly unusual in that they hadn't been hired directly by the guy they would be protecting but by a friend who was acting on his behalf.

Apparently, the client didn't want any protection. Those were always the most annoying, and Scout had to work hard not to build a resentful image of who this jackass would be. But if Scout was getting paid, then he was going to damn well do his job and keep whoever the client was safe.

Whether he wanted Scout to or not.

Christopher waved at Scout as he walked inside the Sunny Side Up diner. Scout nodded at the waitress who caught his eye, letting her know he didn't need help being seated, then strolled down the aisle to go sit with Christopher in one of the booths.

"Hey, man, how's it going?" Scout slapped his hand to Christopher's, then shook it before sitting down.

Christopher nodded as he inched a manila file over the table toward Scout, then signaled toward the same waitress Scout had made eye contact with. She smiled and held up a finger to let them know she'd just be a minute. Christopher nodded, unconcerned, and turned back to Scout.

"I'm not bad," Christopher said, answering his question. "But it's a good thing I came to start you off on this job. I had a hunch it would be a little complicated."

Scout raised his eyebrows as he spun the file around so it was the correct way up for him. 'Emmerich Klein,' read the name on the top. "Has something developed?"

Christopher paused as the waitress approached them. He ordered them two coffees and some grapefruit for himself. Scout was still slightly tired and hungover from his escapades the night before, so he ordered a stack of pancakes, bacon and hash browns. Back in the day, he'd been pretty obsessive about his weight so he wouldn't move up or down a class, but also so he looked good when he stepped into the ring. It had taken him a while to realize that with the amount he worked out still, he could afford the occasional indulgence.

"There was a home invasion last night," Christopher explained once the waitress bustled off to her next table. "Mr. Klein suffered a mild concussion as he fled the scene, and it appears there was some damage to his property, according to the police that went back there this morning. The woman who contacted us for the initial consultation – a Ms. Coal – already called me advising that Mr. Klein might want to jump right ahead to a protection detail after this development."

Scout was about to open Mr. Klein's file when the waitress returned with their coffees, so he paused to smile and thank her. "This Ms. Coal, is she Mr. Klein's girlfriend?" he asked once they were alone again. There were around a dozen other tables currently being occupied in the diner, but none near them. Christopher had an impressive scar on the left side of his face that he was an expert at wielding when he wanted people to keep their distance. Little did they know he was just a big old pussy cat, really.

He sipped his coffee and considered Scout. "Not his girlfriend. Best friend, I believe. Mr. Klein is gay."

For a moment, Scout just fixed Christopher with a stare. "Right," he said, then took a mouthful of his own coffee.

As much as Scout liked Christopher, he employed a lot of macho ex-military types. Real alpha males.

Not the kind of guys usually interested in protecting a queer client.

This wasn't the first time Scout, as a gay man himself, had been asked to work for someone in the LGBT community. He didn't mind – in fact, he took great pride in it. But it kind of pissed him off that the other guys weren't called out on their bullshit. Why should their beliefs stand in the way of their work? Or even go so far as to endanger anyone's life?

Scout was Catholic, and he'd protected people of all religions. He'd also protected a couple of people whose politics he had disagreed *strongly* with. But he didn't get to put a value on their life. His job was just to keep them safe, no matter what, and he took that very seriously.

In any case, Scout was here now, and he already liked the town, so there wasn't any reason to get mad. But perhaps sometime soon he should explain to Christopher just what his grievances were.

In the meantime, he was pacified by a large, shaggy dog that had ambled over to their table to say hello. Scout couldn't help but laugh and scratch between the big guy's ears. "Well, hi there. Aren't you beautiful?"

"Sorry, sorry." An older Native American guy came rushing over, waving his hands. "Peri is friends to everyone.

But you might not want a side of slobber with your pancakes."

Scout chuckled. "Not really, no. But I do love dogs."

The older guy – who Scout assumed was a manager here or one of the owners – placed his hands on his hips and sighed as Peri flopped down by Scout and Christopher's feet, clearly settling in. "Well, it's a good thing because it looks as if he likes you." He held out his hand. "I'm Tyee Perkins. Sunny is my husband. Are you guys visiting town for business or pleasure?"

Wow. He obviously recognized Scout and Christopher weren't locals. Ordinarily, Scout would have found it kind of creepy that someone was keeping tabs on everyone like that. But Tyee Perkins reminded Scout of his childhood boxing coach, the one who'd taken him under his wing. If Scout knew people (which he invariably did), he'd guess that nothing was too much trouble for Tyee when it came to his community.

A theory partway proved after Christopher answered they were in Pine Cove for business. The waitress who had been serving them so far came rushing over to Tyee with a cordless phone clutched in her hands. She looked like she might still be in school or have just graduated.

"Grandpa Tyee," she said anxiously, glancing between him and the table. "Sorry to bother you, but…it's Uncle Micha. It sounds like – well – could you take this?" She thrust the phone at him, obviously hoping he'd talk to the person on the other end of the line.

Yep, that looked like trouble. And sure enough, Tyee rolled his eyes and sighed, but there was clearly sadness and empathy there too. "You guys got kids?" Scout shook his head while Christopher nodded. Tyee gave him a sympathetic look. "You never quit worrying. Not ever. Okay, Rona, I'll take it. You fellas don't mind if Peri stays with you, do you? If he becomes a bother, just give us a shout, okay?"

Scout promised he would, although he didn't imagine a big old fluffster like this would be a bother. As Tyee and Rona walked away, he reached down and petted the big dog between his ears again, smiling as Peri yawned and wiggled a little at Scout's fussing.

Scout loved dogs. He wished he could have one, but his lifestyle would never permit it. It was one of the reasons he'd gotten a wolf as part of the sleeve tattoo currently hidden under his suit. He felt a kinship with wolves and dogs in a way he couldn't really explain. Just that they made him happy.

"So," he said, nodding at Christopher. "Back to business."

"Indeed. That's all we have so far." He tapped the manila file with the client's name written on the front. "I've only spoken with Ms. Coal twice. I was hoping you could get up to speed this morning. Unfortunately I have to fly back to California shortly, but at least I can brief you now in person."

Emmerich Klein. Scout would have said before even opening the file that he sounded like an older German guy, but then he saw the scribbled note on the front that said the client preferred to be called Emery. That made him sound younger.

Rather than sit there guessing who he was going to be working for all morning, Scout took another sip of his coffee and opened up the file to leaf through the few sheets of paper they already had detailing Mr. Klein's needs.

Except Scout stopped before he could read a single word.

Because there was a photo.

Holy Mary, Mother of God, Scout cursed silently as horror filled his veins. What were the fucking chances? Of all the guys he could have hooked up with last night, how the hell was it the same face staring back at him now?

Emery Klein may not have looked that closely at Scout, but Scout had burned his face into his memory. It was definitely him.

Shit.

"Is there a problem?" Christopher asked, clearly detecting whatever expression had flitted across Scout's face before he'd been able to school it.

He shook his head before he could think. "Just younger than I expected. Didn't you say this guy was a high-roller?"

What the hell? He should tell Christopher right now this was a conflict of interest. Scout had fucked this guy senseless mere hours ago. How could he protect him objectively now? He needed to be a professional about this.

Except, his unprofessional side was just about winning over logic. Scout had tossed and turned all night, unable to get the little minx out of his brain. He'd almost been tempted to swing by the bar sometime today and ask around to see if anyone knew who his hookup was.

Now he had been dropped into Scout's lap.

The thing was, if Scout demanded one of Christopher's other guys took the job, there was always a chance he'd be assigned someone who wouldn't take the work as seriously. Emery wasn't just gay, he was flamboyant and sassy and a load of other things many insecure men would call 'too gay.' He was the kind of guy Scout had heard other dudes complaining about, saying how they weren't exactly *against* gay marriage, but did 'they' really have to behave like '*that*'?

It would probably be the right thing for him to confess to the hookup and try to find Emery someone responsible. But on the other hand…would it really hurt for Scout to reach out first? There was a disgraceful, selfish part of him that just needed to ask the question: was there anything between the two of them beyond last night?

It was wrong, but Scout also argued with himself that it

was the safest option at this point rather than throwing one of Christopher's other guys in with an LGBT client for the first time when there was a chance prejudice could interfere with their work.

Just the thought of anyone hurting Emery made his blood boil.

"You said he had a close call last night?" Scout prompted, flicking through the various forms the head office had filled out on Emery's behalf.

Christopher nodded. "Mr. Klein disturbed an intruder when he returned home at just past midnight. He didn't see anything as he fled immediately, but he said the suspect appeared male and of a medium build. A hooded sweater was covering most of his face. As Mr. Klein ran, the intruder threw a ceramic mug at his head. He received a mild concussion that was treated at Ms. Coal's home."

Scout was grateful for the arrival of their food so he could take a moment to compose himself. He was irrationally angry at himself for not walking Emery home, then at Emery for ditching him before their cum had even cooled down. But then, they'd had no idea this was going to happen.

Except, wait. Yes, they *had.* Ms. Coal had already contacted Christopher regarding an initial security assessment. Scout absently snapped one of his bacon rashers, eating half as he held the other half down for Peri. The old dog chomped it down as Scout skimmed Emery's file. "So Mr. Klein has been receiving increasingly detailed and menacing death threats?"

Christopher nodded. "Apparently, he's a social media influencer."

"What's that?"

Christopher scoffed and rolled his eyes. Not perhaps the most professional reaction. "Someone who gets famous for being pretty on Instagram, as far as I can tell. A real Einstein.

Anyway, it's homophobic from what we can tell, but more than the usual 'you're going to hell' messages. There's apparently one series of messages they reckon are from the same person, although they're all anonymous. They keep saying Mr. Klein stole what was rightfully theirs, and they claimed to know where he lived."

Scout was rapidly losing his appetite as he combed through the messages and comments that had been copied into Emery's file. Plenty of these people had felt brazen enough to reply openly to Emery's social media posts on the likes of Instagram with their own usernames, using all kinds of homophobic and racist slurs, wishing him harm. But the private messages Emery and his friend had strung together and assumed were from the same person were the worst.

Scout was a bit of a Luddite when it came to technology and could barely work his old smartphone for calls. But he had a feel for people, and as he skimmed through the language and grammar patterns, he had to agree these messages did appear to be penned by the same person.

Whoever this was, they really hated Emery and were clearly fantasizing about harming him. Whether or not that meant they would actually do such a thing was for the police to investigate. Or…

"Why not contact the FBI? There is more than one death threat here." As much as Scout had to admit he was feeling stronger about being the one to take care of Emery, death threats were no joke. Especially now it had escalated from online bullying to an actual home invasion and assault.

But Christopher shook his head. "In Ms. Coal's words, Mr. Klein is being 'a stubborn ass mule' about the whole thing. He swears it's nothing and will all blow over. She thought if she contracted someone like us, he'd finally see the threat was serious. But from the sounds of it, even after last night, he doesn't want anything more than the cops getting involved. She said he almost didn't even call the police to report the attack. It was only when she pointed out his neighbors were at risk too that he relented."

Why didn't that surprise Scout? He held back a chuckle. Fucking brat.

But even as he mentally admonished Emery, whose character he felt he knew even after such a brief encounter, Scout's heart also ached. Jesus Christ, he must have been so scared. And he cared about his neighbors, so he wasn't selfish.

In any case, no one deserved to have their life threatened. Scout had protected some real douchebags in his time, and every one he had done so to the very best of his ability, without complaint. Out loud, at least.

But Emery would get his best service, no doubt about it. And they were both adults. Scout was sure they would be able to keep things strictly professional, especially if Emery's life was in danger.

But Scout was only human. He couldn't help it when his mind drifted once or twice as he finished his breakfast briefing with Christopher. Because there would come a point where the job would end, after he and Emery had spent however many days or weeks together. Some jobs even took months. That was all time in which Scout could possibly get to know the fiery minx who'd manage to steal his heart in only one night.

Was it wrong to hope that when the dust settled, Scout might be able to see if the chemistry he'd felt between them was real after all?

4

EMERY

"Are you sure you're okay?"

Emery glared at one of his other best friends, Ava's brother, Robin. "If you ask me that again, I will choke you on your own ugly-ass tie."

Ava cocked an eyebrow. As usual, she was wearing black jeans and a black tank with her dark curly hair falling to just above her shoulders. She shared a look with her brother. "Oh yeah, he's fine."

The group didn't look convinced. They were all hovering around Emery, who was sitting on the couch in Ava's living room where he had slept the night. "Emery," Dair, Robin's boyfriend, said patiently. "You've been through a hell of an ordeal. It's okay not to be okay."

Logically, Emery knew that Dair was a former Marine and he'd seen a fair bit of active service as a mechanic. He probably knew a lot of people with PTSD. But every second his loving, well-meaning friends fussed over Emery was making him want to scream.

This was his fault. He'd brought this attention upon

himself, he knew that. If he wasn't who he was, who he'd been born as, people wouldn't want to kill him all the time. All his friends' fretting was doing was reminding Emery of what a problem he'd been his whole entire life.

He just wanted to forget it all. Ava had said he could crash here as long as he liked, but Emery had a work trip coming up in a couple of days that would take him out of town anyway. The police had sent the forensics team over to his apartment (despite his protests) and dusted for prints. He needed to assess what, if anything, was missing. But a detective Padilla, who was apparently looking into his case, had assured him that the intruder hadn't managed to get into the safe.

So Emery's laptop, video equipment, most expensive jewelry, and emergency cash were fine. More importantly, he and Sonic had escaped unscathed. More or less. The back of his head was still tender to the touch. But everything else was just material or aesthetic that could be cleaned, mended, or replaced.

All this fuss was grating on his nerves like nails on a chalkboard. He could take care of himself. Quite frankly, what would help him the most right now would be a good meal, loud music, and a shit ton of booze.

"Alasdair," he announced, cutting off his friends' discussion around who could perhaps pop over to Emery's apartment and collect some of his things. It was cute, but Emery had already ordered a bunch of clothes and toiletries to be delivered to Ava's place first thing in the morning, not to mention a temporary cage for Sonic, who had been the bravest boy and slept on Emery's lap most of the day.

Dair blinked and looked down at Emery. "Yes?"

"If I asked extra super nicely, would you make us green curry this evening? The one with the sweet potato?"

Dair glanced at Robin. They had been dating the last couple of months, since Robin and Emery's high school reunion, and already spent most of their time in Pine Cove. They were looking to move here now that Robin was getting his cyber security business off the ground, and Dair had been offered a job with one of the local mechanics. Therefore, they were spending most of their spare time back in Pine Cove, along with their adorable fluffy puppy, Smudge.

Emery had to say he was thrilled that Robin was back in his life and had brought such a charming boyfriend with him. But he was still working out the best way to handle them both. It seemed asking for exactly what he wanted was a step in the right direction.

"Uh, sure," said Dair happily. "Anything you want."

"In that case, I want puppy cuddles. Robin, fetch me the Smudge monster. And, Ava, I know you've got a fresh bottle of vodka in the fridge because I put it there."

He knew the way all three of them narrowed their eyes at him meant they weren't convinced by this particular solution. But it was the way Emery wanted to cope with the fact that his life had briefly been turned upside down.

"Look," he said as patiently as he could. "If I sit here crying, this asshole wins. If I allow myself to get so scared I never go outside again, he wins. I don't know who this person is or what he wants. Maybe he *is* that prick who's written me all those messages telling me they want to kill me. But I won't let him win. I *won't* let him terrorize me into being anything less than I am. And I am *fabulous.* So I want booze and laughs and lots of cuddles, of both the human and canine variety. Is that okay?"

Robin's lip wobbled as he dropped onto the sofa beside Emery and threw his arms around his shoulder, careful not to disturb Sonic in his lap. "We just want to make sure you're all right," he mumbled into the T-shirt Ava had lent him.

Emery sighed and hugged his friend back. "I know, sweetie. And you're all doing a wonderful job. But this is the best thing for me, I promise. Indulge me, my darlings. Don't give the bad man a second thought."

Dair rolled his eyes, but then he smiled and leaned over to squeeze Emery's shoulder. "I'll head out to the store and get what we need for curry. I'll also get some mixers for the vodka."

"I'll go find Smudge," Robin added, kissing Emery's cheek before he stood back up. "He's probably under Ava's bed, chewing shoes."

"Again," Ava lamented with a quirked eyebrow. Emery knew, though, that she would have lifted anything she didn't want being eaten, so she couldn't really mind. But she had a look in her eye that suggested there was something else troubling her.

Robin seemed to sense it too, as once he deposited Smudge on the sofa, he announced he was going with Dair to the store. Smudge sniffed uncertainly at Sonic as the little hedgehog snuffled and wriggled around on the cushion Emery had gotten for him to sleep on. Ava sat herself on the other side of him on the couch and petted Smudge's golden fur, looking at Emery seriously.

"What?" he asked gently once he'd heard the front door close.

She tilted her head, not breaking eye contact. "You know how I suggested contacting a private security agency if you weren't going to report death threats to the FBI like a sane person would?"

Emery sighed. "No, Ava," he said heavily. "I'm not interested. I'll see what the police say and discuss the door thing with the building superintendent. They should have footage from the cameras in and around the building. I'm sure we'll work out what happened and make sure it doesn't happen again."

"Yeah, that's all great," Ava said all deadpan, not missing a beat. "Except I already had a security company booked to come out here to assess the situation, and now you'll be meeting your new bodyguard in about fifteen minutes."

"What?" Emery exploded so violently poor Smudge jumped off the sofa and hid under the coffee table. Emery wanted to pick him up again and assure him everything was going to be all right, but he was too livid to think straight. "Ava, you had *no right* to do that! No, I don't want that! I refuse!"

Ava didn't even flinch at his outburst. She just glared at him. "Boo-hoo. You've got it. Get over it and let us look after you, you stubborn little princess. Or were you lying about the DM you got this morning?"

Emery ground his teeth and stared back, regretting showing Ava that in a moment of vulnerability. But he'd gotten another message from what they assumed was the same anonymous account. Emery blocked them each time, but they just created a new account with a different number. 'ekleinhater1,' then 'ekleinhater2' and so on.

'ekleinhater23' had asked, *"How's your head?"* Which meant they had to be the intruder who had thrown the mug at Emery last night.

He growled out a huff and flopped back against the back of the sofa. *"Fiiiine,"* he complained, making the word last as long as possible. "I'll meet this knucklehead. But I reserve the right to fire his ass the second he turns out to be a closed-minded douchebag, which he will be."

Ava's mouth twitched on one side. "Good boy. Now you get vodka."

Emery sighed as he was left alone while she went to the kitchen. He at least managed to coax Smudge back on the couch with him. He felt like a bit of a Disney princess, surrounded by his animal companions.

He hoped that meant he would get a happy ending.

Fuck, he could throttle Ava. He knew she was only trying to help. But the mere thought of trying to explain his life and his problems to some straight, tough macho man was already making Emery cringe.

People had always meant him harm for being born different. He had been a petulant child, so fabulous and effeminate. There had never been any doubt to anyone that he'd not only grow up gay but one of *those* gays. The walking stereotypes who brought shame on the guys who could pass for straight. Emery knew that was exactly what everyone thought, even his friends who loved him the most.

But he didn't fucking care. He *was* fabulous, and there was absolutely nothing wrong with being effeminate. If anything, being pushed into a corner like this made him extra of everything he was naturally. If someone thought he was too loud, he was louder. If someone thought there was something embarrassing about being camp, he pulled out the confetti cannon and started prancing around the room to fucking Barbra Streisand.

No one was going to rain on his parade. Not some homophobic rednecks who could barely spell his name. Not some uptight bodyguard. Not even Emery himself.

Ava was his best friend precisely because she brought him a raspberry vodka and lemonade, punched his arm, then went to go busy herself in the kitchen, leaving him alone again. She even put some very loud Britney on. Emery gave a shaky sigh as he sipped his drink, letting the buzz go to his head as a tear or two escaped his closed eyes. Just because he didn't want to talk about the attack didn't mean he was done processing it. He was allowed to wobble for a moment, he was sure.

It was crazy stupid, but for a fleeting second, Emery couldn't stop himself from thinking of his handsome gentleman from last night. If that brute fought like he fucked, *he* would keep Emery safe from harm. Shit, Emery might even let him.

But that was dumb as all hell. Emery didn't need a single other person fighting his battles, let alone a big strong guy. Emery was big and strong in different ways, but more importantly, he'd listened to Destiny's Child growing up. He was a god-damned independent woman, and he was standing up for himself, no matter what.

Well, maybe not literally.

When there was a knock at the door, Emery dropped his head back and pouted, even though there was nobody there to see him do it. *"Avaaaa!"* he whined. *"Dooooor!"*

She made some sound of protest over the Madonna track that was now playing, but Emery just grinned, knowing that was her way of telling him that she loved him. Besides, it was either Dair and Robin back already with dinner supplies, or...

At first glance, the bodyguard looked exactly like Emery had assumed he would when he stepped into the living room. He was suited and booted at around six foot – so not too tall but a few inches taller than Emery – with a stocky build that suggested he could bench-press some serious weight. Emery wasn't sure, but he guessed he was wearing a gun holster under his suit jacket, and that made Emery nervous. However, it was to be expected in his line of work.

But...god, he was fucking gorgeous. He radiated power in the way he stood with his hands clasped in front of him and his feet shoulder-width apart. And that smell – *urgh.* There was a spicy aftershave that reminded Emery of the sea as well. It screamed masc in a way that usually pissed him off, but on this guy, he had to say it made his mouth water. His hair was dark brown and just long enough to get a good handful. As intimidating as he was coming off, though, his green eyes had a kindness to them. Or maybe Emery was feeling so fragile he was imagining that.

Was he also imagining that he seemed vaguely familiar? No. He probably just had one of those kinds of faces that Emery was so good at blurring together. But he was looking at Emery strangely, too. Perhaps he'd seen him online and was wondering who this small, exhausted-looking creature was before him. Emery had to admit he hadn't been caught out in public without glitter or lip gloss in years.

Ava followed him into the room, glaring at Emery as if daring him to protest. But Emery was prepared to behave himself for now. Mainly because he wasn't the only one judging this guy.

"Good afternoon, Mr. Klein," the suit began. But then he stopped and looked down at the ball of fluff that had just launched himself at his knees.

"Oh, no!" Ava cried. "Get down, Smudge! I'm so sorry!"

The suit smiled, though, and leaned down to pet the overly eager Smudge. "Oh, that's fine," he murmured, his voice rumbling right through Emery and waking his cock up. God fucking damn it. That wasn't attractive. It *wasn't*. Okay, yes it was, but this guy was clearly straight, and Emery was about to employ him, so he needed to get a grip. "Hi, Smudge. Do you belong to Mr. Klein?"

"It's just Emery, actually," he corrected. "My friend Ava called you, not me. And the adorable dog is sadly not mine. But my friends will be happy you like him." He offered the guy a small smile. Emery didn't have to be a *total* ass to him, he supposed.

The suit nodded. "Ms. Coal contacted us with good cause. I'm sorry to hear about your troubles. But Oakley Security is fully prepared to assist you in all your protection needs. If you like, we can discuss your needs and our course of action this evening. I'm Scout Duffy, by the way."

"Actually, we're going to be having dinner-" Emery began.

"Which you should join us for," Ava interrupted loudly. She folded her arms and narrowed her eyes at Emery. "Emery wants to keep this all super casual and ensure minimal disruption to his life. So, dinner. Yes?"

Emery glowered at her. *What the fuck?* No, he didn't want Scout fucking Duffy to join them for what was supposed to be Emery's recovery-blowing-off-steam evening. And why was Duffy still looking at him like he was expecting him to jump up and tap dance or something?

However, Emery wasn't stupid. If security was this guy's business, then perhaps they should actually discuss what Emery could do to protect himself until the cops caught the intruder. Maybe it was smart to have him stay a bit longer.

It didn't matter if Smudge liked him…or that he was nice to Smudge. This was purely business, and Emery couldn't afford to let himself forget that a guy like this probably didn't understand someone like Emery at best and probably hated his guts at worst. However, if he was being paid, then hopefully he'd keep any prejudice he had in check.

So Emery might allow him to have some curry. But that was it. He didn't have to play nice beyond that, and he reserved the right to kick this straitlaced goon out of Ava's apartment the second they were done talking.

A traitorous part of Emery's brain informed him he wouldn't kick this guy out of *bed* in a hurry, but that kind of thinking was entirely unhelpful. Someone like Duffy would most likely rather punch someone like Emery rather than kiss him. What a waste.

But Emery decided he was going to be the bigger person here. He'd show Duffy that a weak little queer boy could have manners and wasn't as dumb as the gloss on his lips.

He'd prove to him that he was a fighter and he'd listen and learn from whatever Duffy wanted to tell him.

And then he'd get the hell away from him. Emery didn't need his judgment, and he certainly didn't need what he was doing to Emery's poor confused cock.

5

SCOUT

SCOUT THOUGHT HE WAS DOING A VERY GOOD JOB OF KEEPING a professional demeanor going. Because internally, he was raging.

Emery didn't fucking remember him.

Either that or he was a phenomenal actor. But seeing Scout had to have come as a total shock. There was no way he could have anticipated it. Yet he hadn't flinched or gaped or shown a single sign that he recognized Scout as the man he'd had sex with less than twenty-four hours ago.

Scout was fully aware that the more pressing concern at that moment was Emery's safety. But had their encounter meant so little, been so forgettable, that Emery hadn't even bothered noticing anything at all about Scout whatsoever? Scout had been up half the night, in knots about what he thought was a once-in-a-lifetime encounter. Had he just been the next guy in a long line of faceless toilet hookups?

Scout didn't need telling he wasn't anything special. But it was another thing entirely to be as good as told he was nothing. That he didn't matter.

What a brat. Well, if he went around using people like

that, maybe Scout didn't want anything to do with him anyway. He wasn't sure he'd ever been made to feel like such a piece of meat. Was that all he'd been to Emery – a cock to ride?

Scout's anger was conflicted, though. He was torn between his own outrage, which he knew was pretty selfish, and anger toward the person who had attacked Emery after they had parted ways. Because, as mad as he was at being so thoroughly rejected, there was still a stubborn piece of his heart that was carrying a torch for what he and Emery had shared.

It was heartbreaking to read the more in-depth files the head office had sent over, which detailed message after message of hate toward Emery. This 'ekleinhater' didn't know Emery. They just had an idea of what he represented. Yet that was apparently enough to loathe him, to wish him harm.

To want him dead.

It was sickening. Would these trolls say that to Emery's face, or were they only brave behind a computer monitor?

Would they say those things to Scout? Scout strongly suspected he didn't count, because he didn't 'look gay enough.'

As irritable and aggravated as he was, he still had a vested interested in this case, as he would for any client. But Emery deserved to be safe.

Ultimately, Scout needed to acknowledge the fact that Emery hadn't recognized him for the blessing it was. They didn't need that complication interfering with Scout's work, because that would only jeopardize Emery. Yet he couldn't quite let go of the hurt that lingered. It was childish, but he'd *wanted* Emery to think he was special. Not just another notch on his bedpost.

It would help if Emery wasn't glowering at Scout with his

arms crossed, like he was offending him just by walking in the room. It would *also* help if Emery didn't look so different in a simple T-shirt and pair of sweatpants. With his body covered up and no makeup around his eyes, he looked younger. More vulnerable. Scout was torn between being fucking furious and painfully sympathetic.

There was one thing he could say about his new client, he supposed. He wasn't boring or predictable.

As much as he could sense the atmosphere radiating off Emery at Scout's intrusion on their evening, he didn't cave in to the temptation to leave. Now that he was here, he had a job to do. A couple of Emery and Ava's other friends arrived not long after Scout had before going to make themselves busy in the kitchen. But Scout got the impression these guys approved of Scout being there to protect Emery. He also picked up very fast that they were a couple.

Scout couldn't remember the last time he'd been in a group of queer people that wasn't a bar or a club. He didn't go to any queer events, not even Pride parades, and he didn't have any queer friends.

He didn't have any friends, a mean-spirited voice in the back of his head reminded him. But that was just a fact of life when you spent your life on the road. Scout wasn't going to go feeling sorry for himself for the career choices he'd made. He still had a few old boxing buddies from the circuit, after all. They were just more Facebook friendships these days.

But he did take a moment to appreciate being in someone's home, filled with people, where they didn't have to pretend or hide away. It was also Scout's choice in life to remain private about his sexuality. He wasn't closeted, but he also didn't see that who he slept with was anyone else's business other than the man in his bed. It certainly didn't affect the kind of guy he was or his ability to do his job. But he very much respected those who were loud and proud about their sexual and gender identities.

"What are your current plans for living arrangements?" Scout asked as he sat in an armchair adjacent to the sofa Emery was taking up with a small fluffy dog and – surprisingly – a hedgehog. Although it wasn't that odd when Scout considered it. A prickly, un-huggable pet did seem to suit what he'd learned of Emery's personality so far.

Ava marched back into the room and thrust a glass of lemonade into Scout's hand before Emery could answer. "Don't let him give you any shit."

Scout looked between her and Emery, but Emery just rolled his eyes, evidently not minding her words.

Scout inclined his head at them both. "Mr. Klein is aware I'm here for his protection and has been most attentive, so far."

"Emery," Emery grumbled, giving Scout a surly look.

Scout knew he'd asked to be called that, but it felt deeply unprofessional to Scout. Particularly when he wanted to put as much distance between them and their rendezvous the night before. Still, he wanted to respect Emery's wishes, and he clearly didn't remember there was any special reason they should be professional.

"My apologies, sir. It's just protocol."

"Oh, dear god, no, not 'sir' either," Emery cried, slapping his hands on the couch. "Just Emery, okay? Like Emily, but an 'r' not an 'l.'" He shook his head. "Let me guess. You're ex-Military."

"Ex-boxer, actually," Scout corrected.

"Dude, let the man work," Ava interjected and folded her arms. That appeared to be her default stance. It would be tempting to call her intimidating, but Scout felt like under that austere façade she very much cared about her friend.

Scout liked her. "We figured Emery would stay with me for now," she told him.

"I have a work trip on Friday, as well." Emery didn't look up at Scout as he spoke, focusing instead on gently petting the tip of his hedgehog's nose.

Scout immediately saw two large issues there. Ordinarily, he wouldn't hesitate to be straight with his clients, but there was still a tiny, frustrating part of him that wanted Emery to like him.

Well, he better suck it up fast. He wasn't here to be anybody's friend.

"If someone has been watching or keeping any electronic tabs on you, it wouldn't be a huge leap for that person to follow you to your best friend's house or to that of your family members."

Emery scoffed. "I'm not going to stay with my folks," he said. Then he seemed to compute what Scout had actually said. "Hang on. Are you saying Ava is in danger now from that asshole last night?"

Scout licked his lips and glanced between Ava and Emery. "Potentially," he admitted. "I don't want to alarm anyone. I'm just trying to be vigilant."

"Okay. I'll go to a hotel," Emery said without pause. "But Ava might already be on this person's radar, right? Is there anything you can do to help her?"

Scout was impressed at Emery's immediate concern for his friend's safety and proactiveness to find a solution. He held up his hands in what he hoped was a reassuring manner. "Of course. I can inspect the property and speak with the building's doorman. But the chances are your attacker won't be interested in her. You are their target. If you leave, she should be safe, especially if we take some precautions."

Emery arched an eyebrow. "Yeah, fine. I'll just book a hotel room right now. No big deal."

This led to Scout's second concern. Well, he couldn't let his reservations show on his face, and he had to do his best not to let them come through in his tone either. But he wasn't willing to let Emery out of his sights, for more reasons than he cared to admit.

"I don't believe you should be on your own right now. I'm proposing twenty-four-hour surveillance until we – my company, the cops, or the FBI if we chose to involve them-"

"No FBI," Emery interjected firmly.

Scout inclined his head. "In that case, until we or the police make any headway with identifying the attacker, I strongly believe you should be under twenty-four-hour watch."

Emery looked at him in horror. "You can't be serious?"

Perhaps Scout was being fractionally overdramatic, but he couldn't seem to help himself. Also, there might have been the tiniest part of him that wanted to punish Emery for forgetting him so damn easily.

"I don't want to be getting in your way. I'm sure there will be times I can manage surveillance from afar. But right now, with the attacker still at large and likely to try and get close to you again, I'll need to make sure I'm at the top of my game."

Emery narrowed his eyes at Scout, then glanced at Ava. "So what are you suggesting?"

Scout resisted the urge to clear his throat or rub his hands or fidget in any other way. This was strictly business. He would suggest this no matter who the client was. "Adjacent, preferably joining rooms for the two of us. For the next two nights, at least, while the police are working. And where is your trip to?"

Emery gave him a cold, hard stare. "Hawaii. It's business, not pleasure."

That wasn't what Scout had been implying, but he

allowed Emery to have his little dig anyway. Because, *damn.* It couldn't have been Seattle? He would have suggested he accompany Emery somewhere not too far away, but Hawaii was a bit extravagant.

Would he really expect anything less from Emery Klein?

"Have you been public about your itinerary?" Scout asked.

Emery shook his head. "I never tell people where I'm going. I only post content about it afterward. It's safer that way."

Ridiculously, Scout felt proud of him. "That's right. Good. Unfortunately, though, we have no idea how closely you're being monitored. There's a chance your attacker could know where you're headed from your online bookings."

"And there's a chance they don't," Emery countered. "I'm not canceling work."

Scout nodded. That was fair enough. He wanted to know exactly what it was Emery would be doing in Hawaii, but it wasn't strictly relevant. "I think you should at least consider going with someone and keeping them close."

Emery looked smug. "I travel with my VA. He's more paranoid than you are. He has this thing about making sure fans don't get too enthusiastic or try and get a piece of me just because they have this misconception they know me. He books our travel through a secure agency, and the rooms are under pseudonyms."

Scout had to say he was impressed, both with Emery's level of success and the apparent resulting fan attention, as well as his virtual assistant's professionalism. "Good," he said again, meaning it. "In that case, I strongly urge you to consider my offer of surveillance until you embark on your trip. Then we can reassess the situation once you return to Pine Cove."

Ava had been quiet for the past few minutes. But at that, she raised her eyebrows at Emery, then turned to Scout. "I like it. Let's do it. You want to look around my place before dinner?"

Scout flicked his gaze between her and Emery. Emery caught his eye, then nodded with a huff. Scout took that as permission to proceed.

"Excellent. Yes, Ms. Coal. I'll assess your needs first. Then we can address Mr. – uh, Emery's. But I'll quickly call the motel and see if the room next to mine is available. If not, I'll see if they can switch me to somewhere we can be side by side."

"What? No!" Emery spluttered. "Did you say *motel?* No. I have no desire to catch bed bugs. I'll book a hotel. A *nice* one. There are a couple on the outskirts of town."

"If staying at a motel is out of character, then all the better to go there," Scout countered, ignoring the disdain in Emery's voice. Scout spent most of his life in motels these days and was a little stung by the barb. "It's also a good idea for me to make and pay for the booking in my name, and unfortunately the company won't cover the cost of a luxury five-star place."

That was a bit of a white lie. If Emery really wanted, he could cover the cost and Oakley would reimburse him for any place he wanted. But Scout was hurt by the idea that Emery thought he was staying in some sort of rodent-infested hovel. He wanted to show that motels – especially nice ones like Pine Cove Lodge – weren't actually all that bad.

Because if Emery looked down on the kinds of places Scout stayed in, that meant he was looking down on Scout. He could deal with Emery not even bothering to remember what he looked like, but his dignity demanded he gave his lifestyle choices at least a minute's consideration.

"The motel is nice," Ava said. "Don't be a brat."

Emery scoffed. "I'm not a brat. I'm a princess" he shot

back, more or less proving Ava's point. "I'm suffering enough. I shouldn't have to be subjected to this."

"You're a brat and you know it," Ava said with a quirked eyebrow. "Dude, it's not a war zone. You said you didn't want us fussing, so this is no fuss."

Emery scowled. Scout sensed she'd outwitted him there. But then his eyes widened. "What about Sonic? I doubt they accept pets."

Ava shrugged. "I'll keep him here. I was going to look after him while you had your trip anyway."

That was apparently not what Emery had been wanting to hear. He ground his teeth and picked at his nails. "Fine," he snapped, glaring at Scout. "But I actually have to work tomorrow. I've wasted enough time in losing today. I'll stay in your little motel. Then you can take me back to my apartment tomorrow to retrieve my equipment and pack for the trip. We can make a pen here for Sonic to keep him safe until his new cage gets delivered tomorrow. And any work you do here to make sure Ava is properly protected you can add to my bill. Deal?"

For a second, Scout seriously considered whether this was ethical or not. If Emery didn't remember him from the bar last night, was Scout morally obliged to inform not only him but his boss, Christopher, as well? He should take himself off the job and give it to someone else.

Because this version of Emery was as annoying as hell and was clearly going to do everything he could to be difficult for Scout.

But if he gave in now, that felt like he'd be letting Emery win all over again. Scout wasn't important enough for Emery to even bother getting a good look at his face, but he was going to damn well show Emery he was good at his job. It wouldn't be the same as earning his respect as a lover, but it would have to do.

Scout was one of Christopher's best bodyguards, so he was going to make sure no further harm came to Emery Klein or anyone he cared about.

Even if that didn't include Scout.

He nodded at Emery and held his hand out. "Deal," he agreed.

Hopefully, he wouldn't regret it.

6

EMERY

"HOLY FUCK," DUFFY RASPED THE NEXT MORNING AS EMERY let him into his apartment. "They really trashed the place, didn't they?"

Emery gritted his teeth, refusing to let some meathead make him feel bad. He'd been good and played along by sleeping in the motel last night. It hadn't actually been the disaster he'd imagined it would be, but he didn't want to admit that out loud. Especially not after that comment.

"Actually, the mess is mostly mine. They just tipped a few stacks of crap over. But they didn't actually break anything."

He looked sadly at the dust the forensics team had left all over the doorframes and handles, knowing there would be more around the safe too. They wouldn't learn for a while if there were any prints other than Emery's own, but he was pretty sure the intruder had been wearing gloves when he'd chased Emery down.

"Oh," said Duffy.

No doubt he was taking in the crumbs, the clean and dirty laundry scattered about, and piles of old photo frames, takeout menus, electricity bills and theater programs. To be fair, the few drawers that had been tipped out really didn't help improve the image the living room was projecting right now. There was all kinds of shit scattered all over the floor, from half-empty packets of batteries, to old birthday cards, to the make-your-own sushi magazine that his mom had gotten him a subscription to one Christmas, even though he never cooked anything.

"Yes, I live like a pig," Emery said tiredly. He didn't have the energy to try and explain how cleaning aggravated his mental health. A lot of people just saw it as lazy. Sometimes he attempted to justify how a creative job that he worked twenty-four-seven left little room for caring about vacuuming, but today was not one of those times. "I normally have a cleaner in on Thursdays. She's wonderful, but I postponed her for now. She shouldn't have to deal with a goddamned crime scene. I'll see what I can do first."

He sighed, not knowing when that would be, seeing as his trip was starting tomorrow, but he'd make time for Lola. She honestly kept him sane with how lovely she made his home.

Duffy finished looking around the living room and kitchen. "Oh, well, that gives me something to do while you pack, then."

Emery blinked. "Huh? Oh, no. You don't have to clean, honestly. I'd be so embarrassed."

"Why?" There was no hostility to the word. In fact, Emery could have sworn he detected kindness. "You've had a home invasion. Most people don't really consider what a violation that is. But it's awful. Besides, my ma would never forgive me if I sat around while there was work to be done." He pointed his thumbs at his chest. "Catholic," he said by way of an explanation. "I'd be happy to roll up my sleeves. I've always been good with my hands.

Fucking hell, I bet you are. That conjured up all kinds of filthy things in Emery's mind. What he wouldn't give to suggest they forget the apartment and get straight to work in the bedroom. But that was a dangerous thing to even think around a straight man, let alone one in Emery's employment.

It was tempting to indulge in an idea that because Duffy wanted to assist with cleaning up, that meant he understood Emery's needs when it came to housework. But most people judged him for having terrible domestic skills, so why wouldn't Duffy? It was why Emery always hung out at his friends' places and never brought hookups back. If a place had nice public bathrooms, it was preferable to asking any guy to kick his way through dirty socks and discarded feather boas.

The only thing Emery was really good at keeping clean was Sonic's cage. The place felt so lifeless without him here. He hoped he was getting along okay with Auntie Ava and that his new cage and supplies had been delivered all right.

Emery had woken up screaming in a cold sweat last night, having dreamed that he hadn't gotten to Sonic in time during the invasion. Even though he'd been next door, Duffy had come running at Emery's scream. He'd banged on the door, demanding to know if he was all right. As Emery's racing heart had started to calm down, he'd had to admit that had been fucking hot.

He bit his lip as he led Duffy into the kitchen to start dealing with the dishes. That seemed like an easy task he could give him that wouldn't require knowing where anything was supposed to live. He just had to rinse things, then load them into the dishwasher. Emery was going to start wiping down the forensics team's residual dust.

He had expected Duffy to make him feel dumb and worthless. Most people didn't understand why his work was so important, and just saw him as some wannabe model that got paid to go on vacation. That wasn't it at all, but most of the time, Emery didn't have the strength to try and convince people otherwise. Especially not straight white cis dudes.

But – although Duffy was certainly a pain in his ass making mountains out of molehills, and they would never have anything in common – so far, he hadn't made Emery feel like a worthless piece of shit. Hadn't made him feel like the people relentlessly telling him they were going to lynch him or give him AIDS didn't sort of have a point.

Was he just being professional? He probably had to be polite to whoever he was protecting. Emery hated fake people, though, and didn't want Duffy to pretend. As much as Emery would like the person he was suddenly being forced to spend all his time with to genuinely like him, he'd actually rather know if he secretly was offended by Emery and everything he stood for.

"So," he said as he ripped open a packet of disinfecting wipes and began to rub down the door frame into the kitchen.

Duffy glanced over his shoulder. He'd swapped his suit for a much more casual jeans and hoodie, of which he'd literally rolled the sleeves up to do the dishes. Huh. He had tattoos. Emery told himself that wasn't attractive, but it was a weak lie at best. The ink practically glistened on his skin, bringing the beasts and mythical creatures to life.

What was he saying? Oh, yeah. He wanted to find out a little more about Scout's background.

"Am I the first queen you've been stuck with? Must be a bit of a shock." He deliberately ran his hand up and down the wooden frame as provocatively as he could manage. As if it was a stripper pole or, even better, a large cock.

Duffy merely raised an eyebrow, then turned back to his sink full of suds and dishes. "No."

"No?" Emery repeated, but Duffy didn't seem inclined to elaborate. Did he mean Emery wasn't his first queer client or was he telling him he wasn't going to discuss other clients' information with him? He decided to try a different angle. "Do you know what I do for a living? Why this guy and other people are going after me?"

Duffy nodded, but this time he didn't turn around. He just kept his focus on the plates he was rinsing under the faucet. "You run a YouTube channel and have been producing videos for several years. But it wasn't until you honed your Instagram account that you streamlined your brands. You started out with LGBT opinion pieces mixed with drunken lip syncs. But now you appear in official artists' music videos and reality TV shows. Your most notable achievement, though, is probably your Over The Rainbow Foundation, raising thousands of dollars for education, housing and legal aid for LGBT youth in America."

Emery realized he had stopped cleaning and was standing with his mouth open, staring at Duffy's back.

Okay, all right. So he'd memorized his client's résumé. That wasn't all that impressive. And just because he didn't sound like he was rolling his eyes didn't mean he wasn't. Emery couldn't see his face, after all.

"Uh, yeah," Emery said, trying to compose himself. "That's me."

Duffy nodded. "It's good work. My old man and I don't ever really get along. But he taught me the value of a self-made man. You started making videos on your phone in your bedroom. Now you're rehoming vulnerable kids and sending them to college."

Emery bit his lip as a lump rose in his throat. *No, no, no.* He didn't need approval from anyone, let alone a guy like Duffy. It shouldn't matter what he thought either way. Emery's emotional response to his approval was just relief at not getting chewed out yet again. That was all.

"Yeah, well. Most people just think I squawk a lot and make drama and the world would be a better place if I were dead."

Duffy arched an eyebrow as he looked over his shoulder. Emery quickly started rubbing down the doorframe again. "A couple of neckbeards aren't 'most people.' Fuck those guys. For every tool out there, you've got a hundred kids whose lives you've made better. Even if it's just watching someone like them online."

Emery had to agree with that. "Yeah," he said absently. "I bet you had a ton of role models growing up. I had precisely zero."

Duffy grunted, dropping another plate into the dishwasher with a loud clatter. Oh, he didn't like that. Emery narrowed his eyes. Maybe he was one of those guys who didn't like to be told he'd been born with privilege? How many arguments had Emery seen from straight white middle-class, able-bodied cis men who loved to gnash their teeth and decry that they shouldn't have to apologize for who they were? That they'd earned everything they had.

Emery would never tell anyone they hadn't worked hard for their life. But it made him so mad when those same people chose to ignore the struggles of those in different walks of life who had been forced to overcome challenges they'd never even had to dream of.

Which was exactly *why* he'd put himself on the internet. Because several years ago, he couldn't find anyone speaking for him, telling stories of a similar life lived. He just wanted to go online or switch on the TV *once* and see someone that made him go: Oh my god. That's *me.*

So let 'ekleinhater' send their fucking death threats. Let them and all the others try and troll his posts with vile comments. Let them tell themselves that Emery was the worst thing they'd ever seen.

Emery was never going to stop.

Because Duffy had gotten something right. Those hateful comments didn't mean shit. Little did he know that Emery had a shoebox under his bed, filled with printed-out PMs and DMs and emails and honest-to-god letters, all from kids who told him they'd saved their lives. That he'd kept them going when everyone else around them was telling them they were wrong. When they were kicked out of their homes. When they were going to school every fucking day to be beaten on and spat at and bullied relentlessly.

Emery Klein was a symbol for little boys who felt bad for joining the drama club or the cheerleading squad. For the queer kids who didn't know where they belonged. For anyone gender nonconforming having to listen over and over that they were wrong and had to pick a box. He was something bigger than himself, and he damn well knew it.

It wasn't like he wanted to be scared. He definitely didn't want to fucking die. But if he was gone, the legacy he was already building would live on. Of that, he was sure.

So someone like Scout Duffy – a blue-blooded all-American male – could scoff at the idea that the world needed role models like Emery. That was fine. Emery didn't need to prove anything to him. He just needed to keep working his ass off and getting his name and his face and his message as far and wide as he could.

The hard work started in that moment with getting the goddamned forensics dust out of his apartment. It looked like the Pillsbury Doughboy had shot his load all over the place.

"You know, I'm fine here," Emery piped up, not looking at Duffy as he continued to rub down his doorframe. "If you want to go wait in the car or something, I'm good."

As if on cue, Duffy closed the dishwasher door and pressed the on button to start the load. "It's fine," he said.

"Many hands make light work. I learned *that* from my ma. I'll clean the rest of the doorframes if you like? That way you can start packing."

God fucking damnit. Why did he have to be so calm and easygoing about everything? Emery just needed some space to go through all of this crap alone. Without his well-meaning friends fussing or some goon paid to watch over him.

"You know, if you're going to boss me around, we should at least discuss a safe word." Emery smirked, hoping to freak Duffy out with talk of kinky gay sex. "Did you know I'm a sub? I like big tough guys pushing me around and taking charge. I don't imagine you've had much experience of that, have you? You're a *good* boy."

Sure enough, that did the trick. Duffy's face was definitely stormy as he angrily dried his hands on a dishcloth. "I'll go wipe down the front door," he said gruffly. "On the *outside.* Let me back in again when I knock, please."

Victory. Emery preened as Duffy stalked past, snatching a couple of wipes from the packet. "Of course," Emery said with barely contained glee. "And then, when I've tidied and packed, I have several errands to run in town. You don't mind driving me around for those, do you?"

"Whatever you say," Duffy grunted. Then he slammed the door behind him.

Emery grinned, telling himself he had won.

It wasn't until a while later that he realized he wasn't even sure what it was he thought he'd won or why he thought it even mattered.

7

SCOUT

Just when Scout had thought he and Emery had been making progress, Emery went and pulled crap like that. Scout tightened his grip on the steering wheel as he navigated the winding roads toward Pine Cove's main street, determinedly not looking his client's way.

Talk about adding insult to injury.

Scout didn't generally care what other people thought about him, and he figured he'd done pretty okay for himself so far in life. But it was difficult not to feel worthless when someone had so thoroughly wiped you from their memory. Especially when you'd been under the mistaken impression that the time you'd spent together had been pretty damn meaningful.

The joke about the safe word had been some kind of sucker punch. It hurt so much. Scout hadn't tried that kind of thing with anyone else. However, Emery did it all the time, apparently.

He needed to get over this. He was acting like a high schooler, pining over an unrequited crush. Whatever had attracted Emery to Scout in the bar that night had obviously been a one-time thing. He needed to shake off this stupid preoccupation he had with his client and do his damn job.

But that was easier said than done when Scout's heart betrayed him whenever Emery was around. It seemed to speed up or skip at the mere sight of him or sound of his voice. Scout couldn't remember the last time he was this infatuated with a guy. It was infuriating and heartbreaking, all at once.

He was used to accompanying clients to all kinds of places. Shopping was pretty run of the mill when he'd witnessed other people negotiate million-dollar deals in strip clubs, skied after them down mountains, and smuggled them into A-lister after-parties.

Neither he nor Emery seemed keen to get in each other's hair after the slightly tense atmosphere lingering from Emery's safe word teasing. So Scout mostly spent the day hovering by store fronts, looking like he wasn't watching Emery at all. He'd perfected the technique of inconspicuous observation, dressed in a more casual attire of jeans and a hoodie so as not to attract attention to himself or his client.

Scout had spent his twenties making a career out of being watched. The thrill he'd gotten from boxing hadn't just been the fights. It had also been the roar of the crowds, knowing that every match he had hundreds – sometimes thousands – of eyes on him, taking in every move he made.

After a childhood of being forced into trying to make himself invisible, he'd found that pretty rewarding.

But then he'd hit thirty, and it was as if the appeal had suddenly switched off. What did being noticed by thousands of people matter if all those people were strangers? They knew Scout, but he didn't know them. Overnight, stepping in the ring went from validating to the loneliest thing imaginable.

And now he made a career out of being invisible. Most

days, he liked it like that. But today he was getting itchy feet.

Emery seemed determined to keep Scout in the dark about where they were going and what they were doing. "It would help if I knew how many more places you wanted to visit," Scout said as calmly as he could as they finally left the Turkish barber. At least there had been another adorable fluffy dog there who had been excited to keep Scout company while Emery got his hair cut.

Emery batted his eyelashes at him. "Why? Are we getting bored?"

Boredom wasn't an option in Scout's line of work. He'd gotten very good at training his mind to remain attentive of his surroundings while not drifting off on wild trains of thought. "I understand that the situation isn't ideal, Mr. Klein – sorry, Emery. I'm just trying to make things go as smoothly as possible in the hope that your life can return to normal as soon as possible. If I know where we're headed, I can do my best to remain so out of sight you won't even know I'm there."

He felt Emery looking at him as they walked down Main Street, but Scout kept his gaze forward. "What if I want to see you?" Emery asked. There was a hint of playfulness in his voice. Christ, Scout couldn't figure him out at all. Did he like Scout or didn't he?

It didn't matter, Scout scolded himself.

At least, it shouldn't.

"You're used to getting what you want," Scout said. It was a statement, not a question. It was probably unprofessional as well, but the words had left Scout's mouth before he could consider their full implication.

Again, he didn't look at Emery directly, but he could almost physically feel the way he looked Scout up and down, fluttering his eyelashes. "Oh, you bet," he said provocatively.

These mixed signals were infuriating. One minute,

Emery's every word was dripping with disdain. The next, he was outright flirting, talking about kink and almost daring Scout to cross some sort of line.

Was he playing chicken? Perhaps he thought if he pushed Scout enough, he would want to leave. Maybe that was why he'd asked if Scout had ever had an LGBT client before.

If only he knew.

Oh, shit. If Emery truly didn't remember Scout, then he probably assumed he was straight. The realization dragged Scout's mood down again. It was his choice not to be vocal about his sexuality, but to think Emery more than likely presumed Scout was nothing like him was more distressing than Scout would have guessed.

Well, it was up to him. He could divulge that he was gay. But at this point, it felt like he was scoring points for the sake of it, which was kind of cheap. Besides, unless it would assist Scout in protecting Emery from his stalker, there was no reason to get that personal.

Emery huffed when Scout didn't respond to his comment about always getting what he wanted. Scout didn't even know what the hell he *actually* wanted, and even if he did, he wasn't about to jump through hoops to give it to him.

If it wasn't for their ill-fated encounter at Aquarium, Scout could probably handle a bratty client with more grace than he felt he was mustering at present. But he was starting to think that if Emery wanted him gone, that might not be a bad idea.

Except Scout had a job to do. He had never bailed on a client before, and he wasn't about to start now.

He checked his watch. It was mid-afternoon, and he didn't need to take Emery to the airport until tomorrow morning. They hadn't heard anything from Detective Padilla at the police department yet regarding the break-in, so Scout was determined to keep up his round-the-clock surveillance.

That meant several more hours at the mercy of Emery's whims.

Food would improve his mood, he was sure. "Are you hungry? It's been a while since breakfast."

Emery frowned and checked the time on his phone. Scout was starting to think he was one of those highly driven people who needed to be reminded to eat and sleep. "Oh, yeah. Sure, let's feed you, big boy."

Scout opened his mouth to protest that he hadn't been thinking of himself. But then Emery turned around and made a beeline for the bakery Scout had spied yesterday morning. Well, if his client was going to stop for lunch, then it was okay for him, too.

Like most places in this town, the Rise and Shine bakery had a nostalgic feel to it. A bicycle had been repurposed as décor in front of the large store window. It had been painted dove gray, and colorful flowers spilled out of the wicker basket attached to the handlebars. The swirly hand-painted gold-leaf logo on the window said the bakery had been established in 1948, and Scout could well believe it.

A bell chimed as Emery marched through the door with Scout in his wake. The warm, delicious smell of fresh bread and sweet pastries hit them like a wave, and Scout couldn't help but inhale deeply.

He and his mom had often baked when his dad had been out of town. It had been their special time together without Scout's old man around to call him a sissy for liking anything remotely 'girly.' His mom might not have been able to stand up for them, but she'd shielded Scout as best she could in little ways like that.

The end of the bakery was entirely taken up by a glass-fronted display case filled with frosted cupcakes, glistening iced buns and slabs of homemade granola bars. Counters ran along both walls, leading to the display case with tall stools for customers to perch and eat their tasty food. High shelves were decorated with watering cans filled with more bright flower arrangements, hessian bags of flour and grains, and jars of different shaped and colored pastas. Menus handwritten on chalkboards hung from the walls, informing patrons of the types of sandwich fillings available, as well as quiches, salads and soups.

Several people were either sitting enjoying their purchases or waiting in line to take away what they'd ordered. But the guy serving behind the counter broke into a big smile at the sight of Emery walking toward him, like there was no one else in the room.

Scout worked very hard to push down the flare of jealousy that threatened to rear its ugly head. Emery was allowed to flirt with whoever he wanted, and if Scout was being honest, if Emery was breathing, he was probably flirting. Scout couldn't exactly blame this baker guy for taking a shine to the same guy Scout was trying to suppress his own crush for.

"Ben!" Emery cried, wiggling his fingers in a regal wave. "Darling, how are you? Looking gorgeous, as per usual."

The young guy, Ben, blushed as Emery reached over and squeezed his hands above the display case. He looked to be early twenties, petite, with soft honey-blond curls neatly cut short.

"I'm good, I'm good," Ben assured Emery. "Busy, but that's good."

"Of course," Emery agreed, looking around the store with warm affection.

He had his phone held against his chest. It was very rarely out of his hand. Unlike Scout, who could only just manage to make calls on his old brick, Emery's whole life seemed to be conducted on his state-of-the-art phone. At first, Scout had wrongly assumed Emery was a Facebook addict. But from what he'd gleaned, a closer description would be workaholic. His job just happened to revolve heavily around social media sites.

Gone were the sweatpants and plain T-shirt from yesterday. It felt like Emery had put his armor back on. He wasn't exactly sporting the booty shorts from Aquarium, but he'd paired skin-tight jeans with a satin tank and a shirt with sparkly details, finished off with chunky, glittery military boots and an expensive-looking choker around his neck.

Wherever he walked, people looked. It wasn't surprising someone like Ben lit up when Emery entered the room. He was fucking gorgeous. Scout should consider himself lucky Emery had ever looked his way. Better to have shared a moment together, however brief, than nothing at all.

At least, that was what Scout would keep telling himself.

Ben lightly touched Emery's arm, then pressed his hand to his chest. "I absolutely loved your last video about toxic masculinity in the gay community. I'd never thought about body shaming like that, but it does really tie in with fem-phobia."

"Aww." Emery reached back and also gave Ben a light touch. "That's wonderful, thank you, baby. That one was very close to my heart."

Scout observed the brief interaction with interest. Ben appeared genuinely moved. In the apartment earlier, Scout hadn't been trying to impress Emery or endear himself with his knowledge about Emery's life. He'd done his research and was sincerely interested and surprised by his client's work. Unlike the impression Christopher had given, Emery wasn't just some vapid influencer. He had a great deal to say about a variety of LGBT issues and was making a real difference by broadening his audience's minds. But it was different to see it actually happen in real life.

Scout was strangely proud of Emery.

"Do you want your usual?" Ben asked. Scout could tell he was the kind of person with a natural happy demeanor, suited to a role in customer service. He beamed easily and made whoever he was talking to feel important.

Emery nodded. "We'll take it to-go today, sweetie. We're busy little bees. And please get my friend whatever he wants. I'll pay for it all together."

"Oh, no-" Scout began.

Emery fixed him with a stare. "I'll be outside making a call. Pop everything on my tab, Ben, darling. Scout-" He flicked his eyebrows and gave Scout a wicked grin. "Sit. Wait. Good boy."

Scout gritted his teeth, watching Emery flounce out of the store. "Stay within eyesight," he barked, not caring what the bakery's other patrons thought. Emery waved his hand over his shoulder but didn't look back.

Scout counted to five in his head, then turned toward Ben again when he was more composed. He wasn't all that surprised to find Ben giving him a look of mild curiosity. He was probably wondering who the hell Scout was to Emery. But in less than a second, his genuine smile was back.

"What can I get you, sir?"

Scout ordered a sandwich that would be easy to eat on the move. He was so engrossed in scowling at Emery as he talked on the phone, Ben had to call his name more than once to get his attention to hand over their lunches. Emery was so captivating when he wasn't deliberately aggravating Scout, though. His smile was dazzling, and his body was so animated it was almost as if he was dancing. He waved and twirled his free hand, sashaying his hips and shoulders to a beat only he could hear.

Scout's heart ached.

It was as if Emery was behind glass that Scout would never be allowed to reach over and touch again. He was always going to hold Scout – his mere bodyguard – at arm's length. To Emery, Scout was just a plaything to be toyed with.

He stalked out of the bakery. "Come on," he said gruffly.

Emery rolled his eyes, still talking on his cell, but falling into step with Scout. Scout realized he hadn't asked where they were going next. However, Emery pointed toward the direction in which Scout had parked his rental car. He didn't have any bags with him, having organized with the various stores to either deliver them to the motel or to be ready for a courier to collect them later. It really was a different kind of life the other half lived.

On the one hand, Scout would be happy to finish the shopping trip. On the other, he was immediately wary of thinking about what Emery had in mind for the rest of the day.

This was ridiculous. Scout didn't worry this much usually about his client's itineraries. Whatever Emery needed to get on with, Scout would work around. Maybe he'd chase up the police department for any leads regarding the break-in. That wasn't his business, though – not really. He'd just be disturbing Detective Padilla when she could be getting on with her job. If anything came up, the department would let Scout or Christopher know.

But Scout needed to be honest. As much as Emery was testing him, Scout didn't want to leave his side. He felt electric in his presence, like he was fully alive. Not to mention he was mouth-wateringly gorgeous. Scout couldn't help being mildly turned on, no matter how hard he tried to be professional.

Of course nothing would happen. Emery was his client and clearly not interested. But Scout was weak, and he couldn't quite trample the flicker of hope in his chest that Emery might still like him, despite everything.

Emery had been quiet for a few moments, but then perked up again as if the person on the other end of the line had returned. "Oh, really?" he said, beaming and sounding delighted. "Yes, an upgrade would be wonderful. For my VA as well? Oh, sweetie, you're too kind!"

Scout resisted the urge to hum in disapproval. This really wasn't the best time to be gallivanting off on a trip, even though Emery had arguably taken as many precautions as he could. Scout knew he was just nervous letting him out of his sight, professionally as well as personally. But even for a client he didn't have an intimate past relationship with, he'd be wary.

"I just feel I need to double-check-" he began once Emery was off the phone.

"No," Emery snapped. "I'm not being scared away from work. I am not canceling at the last minute like some rank amateur when there is nothing to cancel for. These reviews are organized in good faith, and my currency is reliable word of mouth. You said I could go, so Dejohn and I are going."

Dejohn was the VA, Scout knew. He may be organized and good with maintaining Emery's privacy, but there was a difference between that and real security. What if the stalker used this vacation as a prime opportunity to pounce? The mere thought of it made Scout antsy.

"I understand you can't avoid traveling," Scout said sympathetically as they continued to walk. This time, he'd had to leave his car down one of the side alleys away from Main Street as the usual parking spaces were all taken. "I'm just uneasy about the security that will be available to you. I think it might be worth considering-"

"Nooo," Emery said, wagging his finger toward Scout's face. "You are not coming. I agreed to this little shadowing to keep Ava happy. If you need someone to fuss over, go make sure she's safe. You can check out her and Robin's family place if you like, too. And his twin brother Jay's apartment. I'm sure that will keep you occupied for a while."

"Mr. Klein, they aren't the ones-"

"Emery!" Emery snapped, stomping his foot and coming to a halt. He glared at Scout in the deserted alleyway. "My name is Emery. How is this so hard for you to understand?"

Scout could have kicked himself. "I'm very sorry," he said sincerely. "It's simply protocol. We're instructed-"

"I don't care what you've been told to do. If I have to put up with you, you will respect my choice of name!" He spun and began stalking toward the car, which was parked waiting for them by the dumpsters behind a Chinese restaurant. Scout immediately began walking after Emery, close enough to hear him mutter, "Fucking straight people."

"Actually-" Scout began, about to snap and tell Emery exactly how straight he was.

Then he froze, the words dying in his throat.

Was that a reflection under the car?

The locking mechanism worked on proximity, so because Scout had stepped within five feet, the doors had unlocked. Emery knew that and was walking to the door on the passenger side.

That wasn't a reflection under the chassis.

It was a blinking light.

"I just don't see-" Emery said, turning to face Scout as he placed his hand on the door handle and clicked it open.

"NO!"

It all happened so fast. Scout didn't second guess his instinct. He just lunged, throwing his arms around Emery's waist. He only saw a flash of Emery's horrified expression as he yanked him away from the car, slamming them both to the ground and rolling them toward the dumpster.

"What the *hell* do you think you're doing?" Emery

bellowed, trying to scramble away from Scout's hold on him. "What the fuck, Duffy? Get off-"

The explosion tore through the car, blasting hot air and fire in a several foot radius as the lid of the trunk banged up, the windscreen shattered and two of the four tires shot off the axle. Scout automatically flung himself on top of Emery, shielding him with his body. He gasped, his ears ringing as one of the wayward tires rolled past, flames clinging to the inside. The car hadn't been totally destroyed, but the blast had been enough to wreck it.

If anyone had been sitting inside or standing close by, they would have been seriously hurt.

Or worse.

As Scout's brain registered that neither of them had been seriously injured and the danger had passed, he realized he still had his arms around Emery. Emery was shaking uncontrollably, his head buried against Scout's chest, crying into his hoodie while a high-pitched whine escaped his throat.

Protocol dictated that Scout patted him down for any injuries he wasn't yet aware of. He needed to call the police and then Christopher. He needed to get Emery away from the smoldering wreck of the car to somewhere he was definitely safe.

Instead, Scout cradled Emery's trembling form to him, rubbing his hands over his back and resting his cheek against the top of his head. "It's okay, Emery," he whispered. "I've got you. You're safe. You're safe. I've got you."

No harm would come to Emery while Scout was around. So there was no way now he was letting him out of his sight.

"I've got you," Scout croaked again.

Emery nodded. His voice was small and muffled against Scout's sweater, but there was a hint of steel about it.

"I know," was all he said.

8

EMERY

"No, no, I totally understand, babe." Emery pinched the bridge of his nose, glad Dejohn couldn't see his face. He was processing several emotions at once, but Emery really didn't blame his VA for his reaction and pulling out of the trip. "It's not a problem at all. I'll go alone."

There was a moment's hesitation before Dejohn spoke again. "Are you sure *you* should be going? Whoever this guy is, he obviously did not come to play, hon."

Emery grimaced. No, he really didn't want to put himself in harm's way. He wanted to hide all the way under the motel comforter and make it all go away. Instead, he snuggled further down on the pillows and hugged the blankets to his chest, pressing the phone to his ear.

Dejohn lived in Portland and had been due to meet Emery when he'd touched down in Honolulu tomorrow. But after the near miss with the car bomb, Emery knew he couldn't ask anyone to travel anywhere with him.

What he should do was inform the hotel that there had been an emergency and he needed to reschedule. But Emery had scheduled the trip to specifically coincide with the massive marketing campaign the resort had running next week. He would be letting them down if he didn't make it this weekend, especially after they had given him so much amazing stuff, all for free. Aside from the flights, this entire trip was all on them.

"I'll be *fine*," Emery said down the line, pouring every ounce of confidence and bravado he had into those few words. "If I have to rearrange, that's what I'll do. Don't worry."

"Just let me know," said Dejohn earnestly. "I'll book anything you need. I'm happy to draft a statement for the hotel if you don't want to let them know the details but don't want to go either."

Emery bit his lip. It was so tempting to consider running away. His situation had changed from death threats to actual attempts on his life. The intruder the other night might have just been trying to escape when he threw that ceramic mug at Emery's head. But if you put an explosive under someone's car, you at least wanted them badly hurt, if not dead.

To make everything worse, 'ekleinhater' had popped up once again, asking Emery if he'd had fun shopping. It was terrifying enough knowing that someone was getting this close to him. But to have to suffer through their gloating was even worse.

Detective Padilla seemed pretty confident they were the stalker, but any attempts to trace the location of their dummy accounts was useless. They may have been evil, homophobic shits, but they knew a thing or two about computers and were bouncing their IP address all around the globe. So they were no closer to finding them.

They had to be close to Pine Cove to be carrying out these attacks. But would they follow Emery out of town?

If he admitted what had been happening to the hotel, what damage could it do to Emery's brand and reputation?

They might want nothing to do with him if they thought he was bringing danger into their establishment. Quite rightly so. Was it fair for Emery to potentially endanger vacation goers with his presence?

He really didn't believe his stalker could know where he was traveling or that he was going away at all. They weren't the only ones who knew how to bounce an IP address. Besides, if word got out that Emery Klein was bad news, how many other opportunities would he miss out on as more and more companies and brands withdrew their endorsements and sponsorships?

If Emery truly believed he'd be putting innocent people at risk, he would shut everything down. But until that point, he wasn't going to let some maniac trash everything he had spent so many years tirelessly working toward.

"I'll let you know," Emery promised Dejohn as he closed the call. Suddenly, he was beyond exhausted, and when he'd hung up, he hugged his phone to his chest and hid almost all the way under his covers. Only his eyes and hair were left peeking out, and even then he closed his eyes.

He wasn't sure how long he had lain on the sidewalk earlier, bundled up in Duffy's big strong arms. Emery couldn't ever remember being that terrified in his entire life. Not when his high school bullies had locked him in an old boathouse or threatened to strip him naked and throw him onto the turf during a Kraken football game. Somehow, as awful as those experiences had been, Emery had clung to the hope that it would all somehow turn out okay.

When that bomb had detonated, he truly had believed he was going to die.

But Duffy had saved him. He had pulled Emery away from the car and used his own body to shield him from the worst of the blast. Then afterward, when he'd been speaking to the cops and fire department, he'd acted like nothing extraordinary had even happened. It had just been another day in the office for him.

He'd even stopped some irate business owner from yelling at Emery about his loss of customers. Duffy had remained calm as he asked the man to step away when all Emery would have done was punch him in his ruddy face. He honestly hadn't cared that a bomb had just gone off, just that people had to walk around the police cordon to get to his camping shop for half an hour. Duffy had gotten him to leave, though, saving Emery once again.

Emery had been grateful for that, absolutely. But it had been in those few moments, when Duffy had simply held Emery, stroking his back and murmuring that it was going to be okay, that he was there for him, Emery had felt something entirely unexpected.

Emery had believed him. He had wanted to cling to the way Duffy had made him feel and bottle it for his darkest moments down the line. Emery hated relying on anyone else and refused to put himself at anyone's mercy. But fucking hell, it had felt good allowing Duffy to take charge and protect him, even just for a few minutes.

A knock on his door pulled him from his reverie. He knew he needed to tell his friends what had happened this afternoon before they heard it from someone else. It was a small town, after all. But they would undoubtedly try and talk him out of his work trip, too, and he wanted to make his mind up independently first. So, unless housekeeping was paying him an unexpected visit, there was only one person it could really be.

It was surprising that Emery found he didn't actually mind if it was who he thought it was.

Sure enough, Duffy's voice filtered through the wooden door. "It's only me."

Emery knew he should get out of bed and make himself

look presentable. Like he was tough and coping just fine with everything. But he honestly didn't have the energy, and he felt like Duffy had already seen him at his lowest earlier, crying in his arms like a scared little child. So instead he just called back that Duffy could let himself in. He had his own key to Emery's room, after all.

If he was surprised by the sight of just the top of Emery's head poking out from under the comforter, he didn't show it. Instead, Duffy held up the paper bag in his hand and closed Emery's door after he'd come inside. He'd changed from the jeans and hoodie he'd been wearing before. Presumably they had gotten dirty from some combination of the explosion and the ground like Emery's own clothes had. But he was in a similar getup, just slightly different colors. Unfortunately, he still managed to make such simple clothes look equally hot.

Goddamn it. Emery needed to stop those kinds of ideas from creeping into his mind. He did *not* need to add inappropriate thoughts about his straight employee to his long list of other problems.

"Hey." There was a kindness to Duffy's voice that couldn't help but soothe some of Emery's frayed nerves. "I got you some tacos. We lost our lunches in the kerfuffle earlier, and I thought you might need to eat."

Emery was glad his mouth was hidden by the comforter, because he didn't stop himself from biting his lip in time. Holy *shit* that was thoughtful. He hadn't even noticed they'd lost their food in the aftermath of the explosion, but he'd only had coffee for breakfast, and after the second surge of adrenaline on his system in a matter of days, he realized just how lightheaded he was feeling. Plus, he loved tacos, like any spicy foods.

He remembered Duffy had stayed with them for curry the night before. Had he specifically chosen spicy tacos, or was it simply a lucky guess?

Either way, Emery was too tired to ignore the warm sense of happiness that filled his chest.

"Thank you," he said genuinely as he sat up in bed. He was back in some of his comfiest pajamas, snuggled in bed, as Mexican food was placed in his lap. Suddenly, the world didn't seem like quite a terrible place anymore.

"I got a few options," Duffy said, taking the armchair by the bed. "I'll eat whichever ones you don't want."

Emery swallowed around the lump in his throat, attempting to chastise himself for getting worked up over some damn tacos. But why fight it? He'd had some of the worst days of his life. He was allowed to take comfort wherever it came.

He opened up a few of the packages, making a little picnic around him on the bed. He knew which of the items he'd prefer, but then he looked over at Duffy. He really hadn't needed to fetch him dinner. He probably hadn't needed to hold him the way he had after the explosion, either. He may come across like some big bad macho dude, but actually Emery couldn't help but feel there was some underlying tenderness to him.

"I'd like the beef one. Do you want to pick a favorite? Then we can share the rest."

Duffy's mouth quirked into a half-smile. "I'd like the chicken, actually. Thank you."

Emery gave him a small smile as he handed over the taco he'd requested. It felt nice to share with him, surprisingly.

"So…" Emery said after he'd taken a few mouthfuls and licked his fingers. He risked looking at Duffy, whose large form was almost too big for the armchair he was nestled in.

Duffy arched an eyebrow. "So?"

Emery fiddled with his taco wrapper. "Dejohn has pulled out of Hawaii. He says it's too dangerous and that I shouldn't go either."

"But you're going to anyway." There was surprisingly little accusation to Duffy's words. Emery was amazed at how much he had been anticipating his disapproval and how good it felt not to get it.

"I'd like to," he replied honestly. "It's a resort that is specifically launching their LGBT-friendly promo. They risk losing a lot of business by aligning themselves with the community, so it's really important people like me give them a boost. Just posting a few photos with a couple of carefully chosen hashtags could be the difference between their business going under or not. That's hundreds of jobs at stake."

He didn't care if he sounded dramatic. He knew it was true. He wasn't the only influencer who would be visiting over the next few weeks, but he was the first and arguably the biggest. He was by no means a household name, far from it. But in certain circles, he was fucking famous. People paid attention to what he had to say.

Yes, he wanted to help the resort succeed. But integral to that success was offering another safe space for queer people to go on vacation.

The LGBT community was always in need of more safe spaces. Until the world at large was their friend, Emery would never stop fighting for that.

"But I'm not an idiot," he continued to Duffy. "I want to be safe. But I don't want to let anybody down or ruin my reputation by canceling. I can't help but feel that's what this stalker person wants."

Duffy nodded. "They could well have meant you serious harm earlier today. But honestly? That device was far too easy for a trained professional to spot. I think they're taunting you."

Fucking hell. Abhorrence washed through Emery. What the shit was *wrong* with some people?

"So…" he said again. He was fully aware of how awful he had been to Duffy right before the bomb had gone off and couldn't help but feel sheepish. However, there was honor and dignity in admitting you were wrong, and it took strength to ask for help.

Duffy didn't gloat. He didn't look smug or laugh at Emery. He simply licked his lips and offered Emery a sympathetic glance. "If you need the company to have someone accompany you to Hawaii, that can be arranged," he said.

Bless him. He was giving Emery an out if he still didn't want Duffy himself to come specifically. But the idea of some unknown faceless goon rocking up in Honolulu gave him the creeps. He might as well go and cancel the whole damn trip.

No. He wasn't going to do that.

He knew what he wanted, and as he'd pointed out earlier, that was what he usually got.

"Can you come?" he asked simply.

Duffy regarded him thoughtfully, then nodded. "Of course, Emery. I appreciate you taking the situation seriously. I promise I won't let anything happen to you."

Emery looked down at the food in his lap. This was slightly too much. He hated being vulnerable, but it was even scarier how safe Duffy's assurances made him feel.

How much he was coming to need Duffy, desperately.

"I know," he said.

For a moment, they held each other's gazes. Jesus. There was just *something* about this guy that was getting under Emery's skin.

This was something else he was unwilling to think about right now. He and Duffy had come to an understanding and seemed to have tempered their earlier hostility, for now. Emery didn't need to linger on this vulnerability. Time to restore some normality.

"Well, dinner is all very well and good," he said, mustering up as much petulance and diva-ness as he could in his pajamas with taco sauce on his fingers. "But after yet another shitstorm, I am in need of some hard liquor. I'm pretty sure it falls under your job description that if I want vodka, you have to get it for me."

His mouth twitched as he fluttered his eyelashes over at Duffy, who quirked an eyebrow back at him.

"I don't know what kind of service you're used to, Emery Klein, but you'll find that in my room next door you have a choice of standard and raspberry vodkas, as well as several mixers."

That wasn't hot, Emery told himself. That wasn't hot. It *wasn't*.

He preened. "Well, off you go, then. Be sure you come back with some ice, too."

Duffy placed his half-eaten taco on the small table by the window and stood up. "Of course."

Emery watched him walk out of the room, his eyes lingering a little too long on his bodyguard's ass than was perhaps strictly necessary.

All right. Maybe this trip wasn't going to be a total disaster after all.

9

———————

SCOUT

"I'M SORRY. YOU WANT ME TO DO WHAT?"

Emery looked at Scout, arching an eyebrow over his French toast sprinkled with sugar and warm coconut. Scout himself had some kind of cheesy bacon and pineapple bake. So far, the food in Oahu had been incredible, but Scout was especially enjoying breakfast.

Or he had been until Emery had pounced on him with his request.

Scout was getting whiplash from Emery's wild moods. Since their truce on Thursday night where Emery had graciously granted Scout permission to accompany him on his trip to, you know, make sure no one else tried to *kill or maim* him, they'd been pretty civil. They'd almost had fun while they'd eaten tacos and Emery had drunk vodka.

But after that, other to confirm that he'd bought Scout his plane ticket, Emery had been quiet to the point of sullenness. He hadn't exactly been rude, but it was as if all through the drive to Sea-Tac airport, the wait in the first-class lounge, the six-hour flight itself, and the transfer to the hotel from

Honolulu, he was switched off, entirely absorbed with his phone and barely grunting at Scout.

Having worked with dozens of clients over the years, Scout felt like he could tell the difference between an asshole and someone who was stressed. He guessed Emery fell into the second category despite his attempts to make Scout believe he was troublesome.

But he couldn't help but wonder if he was struggling with depression as well. Scout had seen his own mother go through varying stages of mental illness, and he felt like he could detect several familiar signs with Emery.

Not that he would confide something like that in Scout, he was sure.

At least at dinner, he had opened up again, if only to talk about the weekend plans. He hadn't eaten a bite of his food, and their waiter had been quite rude about it. Emery had looked ready to ask for a manager, quite rightly so. What did this guy care if Emery ate the food or not? Their food was all-inclusive. Scout could have cursed the man for choosing that moment to be an asshole. Up until then, all the staff had been absolutely flawless, bending over backward for all their guests that Scout had seen, not just Emery. But this guy had taken it as a personal affront that Emery hadn't done anything more than poke his meal around.

Scout had done his best to placate the man, though, and he had to admit the gratitude he'd seen on Emery's face once the waiter had left had made it almost worth the hassle. Scout tried to convince himself he didn't care if Emery liked him or not, but by this point it was hopeless.

The spat with the waiter seemed to align Scout and Emery again as being on the same team. So Emery perked up a little and ran through his plans for the next couple of days with more warmth than he'd shown all day, allowing Scout a rare chance to plan ahead.

But Emery had missed a few details.

The resort was a little ways away from the city of Honolulu, in a blissful, paradise-like cove of turquoise waters, surrounded by lush green grass and swaying palm trees. The hotel was all-inclusive, and Emery was trying to get the most out of his stay as he could for his blog post encouraging other LGBT travelers to visit here.

So far, Emery had explored the spa almost immediately after their arrival, receiving several treatments while Scout waited outside. Then they had been spoiled by staff in one of the resort's three on-site restaurants for a dinner that even if Emery hadn't eaten any of, Scout had enjoyed very much. Emery had seemed content with the numerous cocktails that Scout had unfortunately had to decline while he was on duty.

He'd wondered if people in the restaurant had assumed they were a couple. It wouldn't be a huge leap to suppose they were, especially as Emery was so evidently queer. Maybe that had been the waiter's problem despite the resort claiming to be LGBT friendly? At least the incident had pulled Emery from his funk.

It felt to Scout like every step forward they made, Emery remembered to put his walls up again and take them two steps back. It was a shame. Scout was trying to accept that whatever spark had been between them at Aquarium was a onetime thing. However, it would be nice to feel like he and Emery were becoming friendly rather than bouncing back and forth like this.

But Emery had sashayed down to breakfast in the best of moods, chatting to Scout like they were BFFs on vacation together.

Then he had let slip that the bar he needed Scout to come with him to that evening was the island's premier gay venue, and the simple 'swim in the pool' scheduled right after breakfast was, in fact, a photo shoot.

And Emery didn't have his usual cameraman with him.

Scout perhaps shouldn't have been as surprised as he was. After all, last night he had been a good 'Instagram boyfriend,' dutifully capturing images of Emery walking along the beach during sunset, photographing him from behind like the pictures had just happened by magic and weren't at all staged. But the swimming pool scenario sounded very much staged.

And involved both of them in the water, in just their swimwear, while Emery posed for as many photos as Scout could take.

"Sorry," Emery said, not sounding sorry at all. In fact, his eyes twinkled and his mouth quirked with a wicked grin as he sipped his coffee. "I forgot to mention it. But an essential element of Dejohn's duties while we're away is to capture everything for my followers. That's sort of the whole point."

Scout shook his head. "I can cope with snapping some shots while you walk in front of me. That's pretty difficult to fuck up. But…this sounds like some sort of swimwear shoot. I wouldn't know where to begin."

Emery narrowed his eyes at him. "I'll teach you some of the basics and review all the photos as we go along. Unless it's all too homoerotic for you?"

There he went again. By this point, Scout was pretty certain Emery thought he was straight and enjoyed trying to make him squirm by testing his limits on how much gayness he was willing to tolerate.

If only he had any fucking clue.

Scout wiped his mouth with his napkin. They were sitting out on one of the other restaurant's outdoor terraces with a spectacular view of the ocean. The wind was light and breezy, and the soothing sound of the waves lapping against the shore would normally have been enough to give Scout the calm start to the day he needed. But he felt like he was being goaded. Taunted.

"Emery," he said firmly.

He was determined not to slip up and call him Mr. Klein again, because it really seemed to irk him. But Scout did find it lowered their professional boundaries, which was dangerous, given their history that only he seemed to know.

"Duffy," Emery said, mimicking his tone of voice. Scout sighed. It was especially difficult if Emery insisted on using his surname. The whole relationship felt very unbalanced.

Scout tried to remind himself that was how it should be. He was in Emery's employment. But it wasn't so simple to switch his thoughts or his feelings off.

"I am here as your bodyguard," Scout reiterated. There wasn't anyone sitting close enough to hear them, he was certain, but he still kept his voice soft as well as firm. "I haven't even brought swimming shorts with me. I need to be keeping an eye on your surroundings, not having fun in the pool."

Emery flicked an eyebrow. "You're right. You *are* my bodyguard. I'm paying you. So you have to do what I say."

"No," Scout growled.

"No?" Emery repeated playfully. "'No' means 'yes.'"

"No. I am *not* here to do what you say. In fact, it's the opposite. If I'm going to keep you safe, you need to be doing what *I* say, without question. If I say 'duck,' you duck. If I say 'shut up,' you shut the fuck up."

"Exactly," Emery said cheerfully. "And when you say 'strike a pose,' I'll give you my very best Gay Asian on Vacation Realness. You just need to be pointing my phone in the right direction."

"This isn't a joke, Emery."

"I know, Duffy." Emery leaned on his elbows, placing his fingernails under his chin in a picture of innocence as he batted his eyelashes. "It's very serious work in a tasteful one piece. That one piece just happens to be a thong."

The image of Emery's delicious red thong from the night in the club flashed unbidden in Scout's mind, and he gritted his teeth. "I don't care what you do, but I am here to ensure your safety. If you need someone to idolize you through a lens, I'm sure there are plenty of guys here who would be more than happy to help."

The resort might not have started its big LGBT media push, but it was already a queer hotspot from the looks of it. Scout had noticed several same-sex couples, particularly men.

Particularly men who had paid obvious attention to the painfully gorgeous Emery as he had strutted through various parts of the resort.

Scout kept telling himself it didn't make him jealous, picturing any of those guys asking Emery to come back to his room. Hell, there were plenty of couples who might want him to come back with both of them for a bit of spicy vacation fun.

Would Scout use security as an issue to dissuade anything like a hookup? There was an element of truth to his reluctance to letting Emery go off alone with a stranger, as well as indulging his own envious intentions. But here he was, suggesting any of those guys could photograph Emery as he frolicked through the resort's stunning pools. In that moment, it seemed like a preferable option to subjecting Scout's cock to the sight of a nearly naked, dripping wet Emery.

Who knew what might happen?

Emery stared at him. "I'm being targeted by a maniac, and you want to ask a stranger to get up close and personal with me?" he asked, somewhat scathingly.

Ah. Shit. Scout almost blushed. Yeah, that was a very valid point.

"You should have brought a third person with you if this was your plan. I can't do it. It's jeopardizing my ability to monitor you in a public place."

"And if I had brought anyone like Dejohn, *they* would have been the one in jeopardy after what happened in town on Thursday." Scout was impressed Emery didn't use the word 'bomb' just in case anyone could hear them. He also kind of had a point, again, and Scout knew it. "Stop being a baby," Emery continued. "How better to keep a watch on me than to literally not take your eyes off me? And before you ask, yes. This is necessary. These photo shoots are part of my brand. When I work with a company, it's with the understanding that I will show their facilities off in their very best light."

Scout ground his teeth, then took a sip of his now lukewarm coffee. Goddamn it.

"Half an hour, no more. Understood?"

Emery beamed triumphantly. "Yes, I promise. I also promise it'll be fun! You'll see."

Scout highly doubted that. With good reason.

The whole escapade turned into the torture he knew it would be.

First of all, Emery wouldn't let Scout buy the cheap swim shorts he'd wanted from the resort shop. In fact, he'd acted quite scandalized, shooing Scout back to the rack the second he'd seen the simple yellow shorts.

"Oh, dear *lord,* no!" Emery had shrieked, causing the sales assistant to look over in alarm. Emery didn't notice, however, as he was too busy snatching Scout's choice away from his hand. "You want me to be seen with you in those? Do you have such little self-respect? No. Awful. Come here."

"They're just shorts!" Scout complained.

"Exactly. A man of your physique should be in trunks and in a color far more complementary to your Gaelic skin tone. See, here. These are *much* better."

He thrust a new pair at him. Scout had to admit they were a beautiful forest green that would probably complement his eyes, and tried not to be too proud that Emery had bothered to notice that. But at a glance, they looked tighter than any of the briefs he owned, and they were definitely shorter.

And four times the price of the yellow baggy shorts. "I–"

Emery held up his finger, then plucked the trunks back. "Not a word. I'll pay, and then you'll see."

Of course Scout looked incredible in them. They showed off his body perfectly and were cut in a flattering way he'd never seen before. But there was no arguing that when he stepped out of the locker room, he felt extremely exposed. Not as exposed as Emery in his thong, but as Scout followed him out to the pool, he determinedly covered his junk with a towel.

It only got worse from there.

Emery didn't just want a million photos of himself in various positions around the pool. He wanted videos and something called a Boomerang, which was a kind of three-second video that rewound itself, then played again on a loop. Scout had been entrusted with his phone in a waterproof case, capturing every moment of Emery as he strutted around in the smallest bathing suit imaginable.

Scout was in hell.

So much for his half an hour rule. Emery seemed to have no concept of time, just a never-ending shot list and a perfectionist streak a mile long. But everything seemed to have been building up to this one particular video that he was determined had to be nothing less than spectacular.

The resort's swimming pool was actually several different pools made to look like beaches. Flawless artificial white sand lined the bottom and the edges by the deck chairs, connecting the pools on various levels with little gullies.

Emery had positioned himself by a small waterfall in a little nook surrounded by rustling palm trees. It was such a secluded spot. Scout could only surmise it had been designed for couples to canoodle in.

Thoughts like that were less than helpful when what Emery had been doing for the past ten minutes was continuously emerging from the water, flicking his lithe, muscular body up like some siren from the deep, then running his hands through his dripping wet hair and gasping as if he'd just come.

Scout was getting increasingly uncomfortable in his trunks. His sexuality wasn't going to remain private for much longer if Emery kept subjecting him to this soft-core porn shoot. Scout was dying a little with every take, his heart breaking with how much he wanted to hold Emery again and not being allowed to.

So far, Emery seemed totally oblivious to how much of a menace he was being. He was totally focused on watching each take back, critiquing every tiny thing, and correcting himself with each new attempt. But every time he came to stand beside Scout to watch the playback on his phone, it was as if his body was radiating heat, calling Scout to him. Scout tried not to look at him, lest his mouth watered too much.

This was completely and totally unprofessional. He should in no way be having thoughts about his client like this. As soon as he was able, he needed to remove himself from the situation. Preferably with the least mortification possible.

What made it worse was that Emery was applying some kind of filter or app to the videos now. So they started at normal speed, then switched to slow motion at the moment he flicked his hair, sending a spray of water droplets through the air, catching the midday sun. Purely by accident, they had managed to get the angle just right on this last take so the slightest hint of a rainbow could be seen in the water.

"Oh em gee, Duffy. You're a genius! Look at how pretty I am! This is going to get a million views. I can just tell!"

He wasn't wrong. He looked absolutely fucking stunning in the video as he re-watched it over and over again, absorbing every tiny detail of it, making sure it was perfect. No wonder he had tens of thousands of followers. Scout hoped it would do as well for the resort's publicity as Emery intended it to.

He couldn't help but feel a small amount of pride that he'd managed to capture the video. Obviously, Emery had done most of the work, figuring out the best angles and giving an outstanding performance in it. But Scout couldn't deny that hearing Emery praise him didn't feel incredible.

However, he was at real risk of exposing himself not only as gay but for also having inappropriate thoughts about his client. His pride was misplaced. He needed to put an end to this, now. Never mind his cock. His heart couldn't take much more of being so close to the one person he couldn't have.

"So, are we done?" he asked a little more gruffly than he would have liked. Hopefully, Emery would assume he was bored and impatient rather than so turned on he could barely think straight.

Even though it was what he wanted, Scout couldn't help but feel sad when Emery rolled his eyes and huffed. "Yes, all right. We're done. I'm sorry this was so incredibly hard for you."

If only he knew just how hard it was. Would he be pleased? Or disgusted? Scout still couldn't tell if Emery even liked him or not.

"I didn't have a problem being your cameraman," he

assured Emery softly, not quite able to meet his eye. "I just want to make sure this relationship remains professional and that I always have your safety as my number one concern."

He bit his lip. Damn, that might have been more telling than he meant it to be. But try as he might, he couldn't leave the pool with Emery thinking he was some kind of homophobe.

"Why wouldn't it remain professional?" Emery stared at him. The sound of the waterfall rushing behind him blended in with the sound of Scout's blood rushing through his ears. Yeah, Emery wasn't dumb. Far from it. Scout had said too much.

Now it was just a case of how Emery was going to take it.

At least the humiliation crawling through Scout's veins was wilting his hard-on. It would be safer for him to step out of the water now without revealing just how much Emery had affected him.

"Shall we hit the showers?" he suggested.

Because getting naked in close proximity wasn't going to make this situation any worse?

Fuck my life, Scout thought bitterly as he began wading over to the artificial shore. He didn't look back to see Emery's expression.

He wasn't sure he could take the rejection or teasing he was sure was coming.

His heart was in Emery Klein's hands. Scout just prayed he would be gentle with it.

EMERY

Holy shit.

Holy *fucking* shit.

Was Duffy turned on?

Emery looked between him and the phone as he walked out of the pool, water running down his spectacular body. The sunshine glistened on every sculpted muscle, the water clinging to the soft dark hairs on Duffy's arms and legs and particularly the light carpet dusted over his pecs, trailing down toward his navel. Duffy had his back to Emery now, wearing nothing but the trunks Emery had bought him and flip-flops. But Emery had been admiring his fur ever since he'd stepped out from the towel that had been wrapped around his waist.

Emery had assumed the towel he'd been using like a shield was to hide his uncomfortableness at being mostly undressed in a gay man's presence. Emery had to admit there was a small bit of him that had pushed to do this photo shoot because for some reason, as much as he was starting to like Duffy, he got a kick out of seeing him flustered and out of his depth.

But now he was wondering if he'd read the whole situation backward.

Were Duffy's protests against filming Emery *not* because he didn't like what he was seeing?

But because he *did?*

Duffy was toweling himself off on the bank, brushing artificial sand from his feet as he slipped his sandals back on. He was almost ready to leave, so Emery suddenly pushed himself through the water so he wouldn't be left behind.

He needed to know more.

Was Duffy not as straight as he seemed? Was this old news, or was he questioning himself for the first time? Either way, Emery was surprised at how excited this development was making him.

It hadn't just been the way he'd felt being held in Duffy's strong, steely arms after the explosion. It was the dumb tacos and vodka he'd thought to get because he knew Emery would like them. It was those stunning, smoldering green eyes and the way they turned intently on Emery. It was that firm, commanding voice and how it made Emery's knees turn to Jell-O.

Fuck professional boundaries. If Duffy turned around now and said he was interested, Emery would climb him like a tree.

He wasn't sure how to approach this potential new situation, though. So he merely observed Duffy as he toweled himself dry beside him. Duffy was determinedly not looking at him, but that could mean a number of things.

Emery knew he was out of line, but he couldn't stop himself from taking the quickest of glances toward Duffy's crotch, hoping it might give him a clue as to what was going on in his mind. But the tight trunks were keeping his cock supported and protecting his modesty, as it should. Emery needed to behave and not be so vulgar and invasive.

Still, it made him wonder…what kind of cock did Duffy have? The outline wasn't small in his current swimwear, that was for sure.

Without meaning to, Emery's mind flashed back to his tryst earlier in the week. God, that had been a spectacular fuck. More than that, though. The encounter with the stranger at Aquarium might have been relatively brief, but there had been an element of care from Emery's lover. Almost tenderness.

What would Duffy be like in the sack?

It was ridiculous, but for a second Emery felt a pang for that one-night stand. Thanks to the traumatic break-in right afterward, it had been easier than usual to block out any memory of the details. That guy could walk right by Emery and he probably wouldn't know.

Anyway, why was he dwelling on that when he had a fascinating development from Duffy right there on his hands? Perhaps he was scared of what it might mean and was lingering on thoughts of a past fuck that he was safe from any consequences of.

Emery had never been afraid of sex, and he wasn't about to start now. He fucking *loved* fucking. But it had been a while since he'd truly been surprised.

Duffy could surprise him, though, he was sure. If he was experiencing some sort of queer curiosity for the first time, Emery could show him how man-on-man loving could really blow your mind. Or maybe he was closeted? That tugged at Emery's heartstrings. In which case, perhaps Emery could share something beautiful with him and try and prove to him he had absolutely nothing to be ashamed of.

Or maybe big tough Scout Duffy usually liked his men all buff and macho, like him. Perhaps he was resisting any kind of attraction toward anyone so aggressively fem.

If it was that option, Emery would delight in nothing

more than proving him so wrong and fucking his brains out for the rest of the goddamn day and night.

Of course, he could be entirely wrong. Duffy could simply be a heterosexual guy, made confused and uncomfortable by what Emery had put him through in the pool. If that was true, Emery would feel thoroughly ashamed of himself and would spend the rest of the trip being nothing but wholly respectful.

But in his gut, he knew. *This* was why he'd been so keen to push Duffy and subject him to a shameless, provocative display.

God, Emery hoped he was right. Because forget checking out Duffy's trunks. His own thong was starting to feel very tight.

They walked back toward the changing facility in silence, the sounds of people at the pool, the rustling trees, and the not too distant ocean filling in the void between them. Emery kept sneaking glances at Duffy, studying his profile while he determinedly stared at the path they were walking on.

"I feel I've made you uncomfortable," Emery said, testing the waters as they entered the executive changing rooms. These were reserved for VIP guests and felt more like a luxury spa than a public pool. The walls were wood paneled and there were all kinds of exotic plants in pots, giving the place a tropical feel. If it wasn't for the tiled floors, Emery might really believe he and Duffy had wandered from a secluded lagoon to their own private forest. The steam that filled the air in the shower area even gave it that misty morning illusion.

There were worse people Emery could be stranded on a desert island with, he was sure.

"No, you haven't." Duffy stepped into one of the wooden shower stalls. They were only chest height, offering Emery a perfect view as Duffy twisted the faucet, sending fresh water cascading over his beautiful body. "I'm sorry if I was abrupt. I should have chosen my words better."

Each cubicle was already stocked with luxury products, so there was no need to rummage around looking for Emery's own shampoo or body wash. He just simply slipped into the cubicle next to Duffy's and started his own water going. There were beautiful pink flowers trailing on the trellises that linked all the stalls together, and the lighting was low. As if they were outside in the evening sunset, letting the nighttime wash over them, inviting them to come play.

"Your words were fine. I had fun."

Emery stepped under the water, running his fingers through his hair. Duffy still wasn't looking at him. Instead he was studiously scrubbing shampoo over his scalp, watching the suds circle the drain. Emery's chest ached. He needed Duffy to give him some answers. This wasn't just Emery trying to get some attention. He *cared* what Duffy thought about him, but he was too scared to come out and ask. It was safer to fall back on his flirty persona.

"I think you had fun, too."

Duffy clenched his jaw, blinking droplets from his eyelashes as he shook water from his hair and face. "Mr. – Emery." Good, Emery was glad he corrected himself. He would have hated that to dampen the mood.

He was just getting going.

"Come on," he practically purred, leaning on the wooden partition between them. "You can be honest with me. No one else is here."

"What does that have to do with anything?"

Duffy flashed him a look that – for a second – sent a chill down Emery's spine. But there was a sadness to it as well. For a second, he thought Duffy went to step forward or to reach for him. But then he pulled back. Emery was beginning to lean toward a kinder, gentler approach, sensing that maybe Duffy needed helping rather than teasing.

But then he spoke again.

"I don't owe you anything other than my diligence in your employment. Your personal life is no concern of mine."

Hurt and disappointment flared through Emery. He stepped back from the partition wall. "Are you suggesting there's something *wrong* with my personal life?"

Perhaps he had read this entirely wrong after all.

"Emery, I don't know what you want from me," Duffy pleaded. He turned to face Emery, his body hulking as he breathed heavily through his nose. In that moment, Emery was glad neither of them had decided to remove their swimwear. It would have left them too vulnerable.

"I want you to be straight with me," Emery snapped back. But then he arched an eyebrow, feeling devilish. There was a chance Duffy needed some pushing to stop dancing around the issue. Watching Emery in the pool had affected him, and they both knew it. So he smirked, putting on his usual act. "Or not. I think 'straight' is up for debate right now. Or are you too chicken shit?"

"To do what?" Duffy cried.

Holy fuck. He definitely slid his gaze up and down Emery's mostly naked body and bit his lip. Then Duffy took a deep breath, apparently composing himself.

"Emery, I am *not* your plaything! I took this assignment because your life is being threatened. Or have you forgotten that?"

Emery hadn't, actually. He'd had another message from 'ekleinhater' that very morning. But seeing as it had been fishing around asking where Emery had gone, he'd felt relatively relaxed for the first time in weeks here in Hawaii.

"No-" Emery began.

"Because I haven't," Duffy snapped. "If you want to push

my buttons, I can't really do anything about that. But if you want my respect, you can *stop* ignoring the reality of the situation by trying to torment me and see how far I'll go!"

Emery felt a lump of crushing disappointment rise in his throat, and he slapped his hands on the top of the wooden partition. "Ah, here we go. The truth comes out. I knew you didn't respect me. I'm just a fucking fairy to guys like you. If you were less afraid of a bit of cock, you'd be less miserable, you know?"

Duffy grimaced and threw his hands out. "Can you even listen to yourself? If you didn't assume everybody hates you-"

"Everyone *does* hate me!" Emery could either cry or laugh, so he laughed. "I'm a freak, that person society either wants to parody or wishes would just disappear. So I *don't* need asshole straight boys like you taking your frustrations out on me! I may be a freak, but I'm free!"

"You know *nothing* about me." Duffy jabbed his finger toward Emery. He was probably trying to intimidate him, but Emery stepped closer, goading him. "Obviously you don't," Duffy continued. "But if you stopped for one second, you'd realize you're *just* as guilty about making assumptions and judging people before you know what the hell you're talking about."

"Oh, please," Emery said. He was closer to crying now. He just wanted Duffy to be different from the other assholes Emery had fallen victim to in the past. "Do tell me what assumptions I've made. It's clear you're just like all those angry straight boys, taking out your toxic masculinity on the ridiculous fem boy."

"I'm GAY!" Duffy exploded, his fists clenched, breathing like a bull through his nose as he stared Emery down. "Not that I should have to divulge that to you, *sir*. But if it will stop you calling me homophobic and straight, so be it."

Angrily, Duffy smacked the faucet off and marched out of the cubicle, snatching a fluffy white towel from the pile in the open cabinet attached to the wall, heading for the locker room where they had left their bags of dry clothes.

Emery remembered how to breathe again, turning off his own water and dashing after Duffy, grabbing another towel to throw around his waist. "Okay. Wow. Wait, Duffy. I'm sorry. I didn't mean to be a dick-"

"Yes, you did," Duffy grumbled. But it wasn't entirely angry. Was that a twitch of a smile?

"Okay, but I think you kind of like me being a terrible brat." Emery waggled his eyebrows and danced around Duffy. "Don't you want to teach me a lesson now? I *swear* I can be good."

Duffy paused briefly in drying himself, groaning and licking his lips before quickly rubbing his hair and covering his face. *Yes!* Emery was almost shocked at how much he wanted Duffy to be interested in him. Not just another faceless hookup, but someone Emery was actually starting to like.

And it didn't hurt that he was hot as all sin.

Oh, god, Emery *loved* an angry fuck. Would Duffy give it to him if he pushed him hard enough? They'd been bickering for days, after all.

But more than that, there had been moments of tenderness as well. The thoughtful tacos. The way he'd held Emery after the explosion.

Emery wanted to explore it all.

He skipped around him like an excited puppy, splashing water all over the tiles. "Come on, it's okay. I think you're hot. Don't you want to have a little fun if you're stuck out here in paradise with me?" He bit his lip seductively. "I know I'm trouble, but don't you just want to give me a spanking to shut me up? Maybe gag me?"

"Emery, stop it," Duffy said tiredly, pulling the towel back down. "You're pushing too far."

For a second Emery paused, considering if he really was. But Duffy took a step forward, his cheeks flushed and his fingers twitching like he was desperate to reach out for Emery.

God, Emery wanted to feel his touch.

"Is that a 'no,' then? Because you know that 'no' means 'yes,' right? You're going to have to try harder if you want me to go away."

Duffy pulled his bag from the locker and squeezed his eyes shut. "Emery-"

That wasn't a no.

The thing was, Emery knew he should back off. But he was scared now. He'd put himself out there, which he wouldn't have done if he didn't believe he and Duffy didn't have wild chemistry. It had been building for days, ever since they'd met, despite Emery's childish behavior. If Duffy was willing to put up with that, Emery wanted to give him a chance to allow himself to give in to temptation now.

He probably had all sorts of rules about not fucking clients. It was most likely that was why he hadn't been open with his own sexuality before.

So Emery decided to try a different technique.

"What is it?" he whispered, slinking his way over to Duffy, touching a single finger to his chest. "Tell me 'no' properly, and I'll stop." He hadn't given Duffy a safe word, but he felt like he would know if he really wanted Emery to stop. His body language was telling him 'yes!' Sure enough, he just glowered at him but didn't speak. Emery grinned. "I bet I'm not your usual type. I bet you like 'em big and mean, huh? But I've done things that would turn your hair white. I can be just as good as any of those masc guys you've fucked. Better. I can be your kinky little baby, and I promise you'll love it."

"Emery," Duffy growled, not quite looking him in the eyes as he swallowed.

Emery hummed. "It's okay, I promise. You don't have to hold back. I think you'd like a bit of kink, wouldn't you? Shall I tell about the husbands I went home with recently? How one fucked my mouth while the other fucked my hole, and I loved every second of it?"

Duffy closed his eyes. "Oh god," he whispered. Emery was torn. He didn't sound like he wanted Emery to actually stop, and Emery had told him his 'no means yes' rules. He wanted to give Duffy a chance to give in, to succumb to temptation and not hold back just because of their business arrangement. But he might need a real out.

"That's not really 'no,' is it? You can say 'Speedos' if you really mean 'no.'"

He met Duffy's eyes to make sure he got it. They were wide, and he was panting, but he frowned and gave him a nod.

Excellent.

"How about I tell you about my friend I see every now and again who knows all kinds of ways to tie me up?" Emery touched his own throat and gave a little moan. "Sometimes he doesn't let me come for hours. He makes me cry. It's divine."

"Is any of this true?" Duffy asked, looking pained. Emery hoped it was from lust.

He grinned back, bobbing and weaving in front of him like they were in a dance off. "Does it matter? Come on. I'll let you do whatever you want. I wasn't kidding about the spanking. I've been so naughty. You know I have. Duffy, look at me. Don't you want to know what I taste like? Why I have a hundred thousand followers and most of them want to bed me?"

"You're my client-" Duffy began.

"Bullshit. You're fired."

Emery could feel tears pricking behind his eyes again. He couldn't bear it if Duffy rejected him because of some work crap, not when it felt like neither of them could hardly keep their twitching hands from reaching for the other in that moment.

"Come on. I always get what I want, and I really, *really* want you to want me right now."

"No."

"Do you mean 'Speedo'? Or do you mean 'yes'?"

"Emery-"

"We're all alone. You can fuck me here."

"Stop it." Duffy's breaths were ragged, his eyes wild and desperate.

"No." Emery placed his hands on Duffy's chest, trying to soothe him. "Please. *Please* tell me you want me."

"Emery-"

"Duffy-"

"*Guppy.*"

They both froze, eyes locked together. Why did that set alarm bells off in Emery's mind? How did he know he'd just crossed Duffy's hard limit, and why did he immediately feel so fucking devastated? What had he done? He thought he'd read the signs right. That they'd just been playing.

Carefully, Duffy took hold of Emery's wrists and pulled his hands away from his chest. Then he picked up his duffle bag full of clothes, walking out of the changing rooms in his towel, leaving Emery all alone.

His breathing was shallow. He'd only been teasing. He was sure Duffy was attracted to him. He'd honestly never meant to take it so far. Consent was incredibly important to him, but he couldn't help but feel like he'd cocked something up badly.

Guppy. *Guppy.* Why did that-?

Oh no.

It couldn't be – could it? There was no way…

Emery hadn't been that drunk. Sure, he'd been drinking, but he'd made it enthusiastically clear he'd been up for fucking on Tuesday night with the handsome stranger who had gone along so beautifully with Emery's whole scene.

Emery had given him a safe word in case he got out of his depth.

Guppy.

Duffy couldn't be the guy from the bar. He would have said something. The universe wasn't that small. But then again…Emery had experienced a flash of recognition when they'd first met, hadn't he?

Holy shit. Holy *fucking* shit. This was a disaster. It *was* him, wasn't it? Emery had gotten so good at blanking his fuck buddies he really had spent the last few days with one of them, hadn't he? The guy out of all of them he'd actually considered seeing again, thinking it would never be possible.

Then his horror redoubled, and Emery grabbed his hair. He'd been so busy winding Scout up all morning he'd looked past the many tattoos on his arms and chest. They'd all blended together in a general hot aesthetic. But now Emery could see the one on his bicep so clearly in his mind's eye. *The wolf.*

There was no doubt. Duffy was his bathroom hookup from Aquarium.

Emery hadn't recognized him. Instead, he'd played several damn games. He'd teased and flirted and probably made Duffy feel awful. Emery certainly would if a guy he was interested in completely forgot all about him.

He felt guilty and stupid. Normal people didn't forget faces as easily as Emery did. He should have known one day it would bite him in the ass. But why hadn't *Duffy* said anything! He'd played Emery for a fool!

It didn't matter now. Duffy was gone, fuck only knew where. Had he been annoyed, genuinely pissed off, or both?

One thing was certain. Emery had to find him, now. He had to set this right.

Because this wasn't just a game. There was something between him and Duffy, and Emery wasn't going to sabotage it before they'd even had a chance to see what it was.

At least, any more than he already had.

SCOUT

THERE WAS ONLY THE FEEL OF SCOUT'S FISTS AS THEY HIT THE punching bag again and again.

The resort's gym was underground, like an air-conditioned, timeless bunker. The perfect place for him to get lost and try and forget everything that had just happened.

What a fucking mess.

Of all the stupid, irresponsible things. *Fuck.* He was going to be lucky to still have a job at the end of this, he was sure. But that was by far the least of his worries.

Oh god. Emery.

Scout sighed and jabbed his gloved knuckles against the cracked and peeling leather of the heavy bag. *Smack. Smack. Smack.* His heart was thumping like a racehorse, and sweat was pouring down his chest. He'd disposed of his T-shirt after he'd finished lifting weights. Now he was just in sweatpants that clung to his hips and his old beat-up sneakers.

He felt raw, ripped open. He'd never meant to come out to Emery like that.

But he'd certainly *never* meant to admit to their one-night stand.

For the past few days, he'd operated in a sort of limbo, where he wasn't entirely sure if Emery had blocked him from his memory or simply had an astonishingly good poker face. It was like that cat, the one in the box. While the box was closed, the cat could be both alive and dead.

But Scout had opened that box with his confession, and it had been clear that Emery was confused, horrified, speechless…all reactions that suggested he really hadn't known that it had been Scout fucking him against the wall not even a week ago.

Scout should have said something the moment he'd met Emery again, or he should never have said anything at all. He shouldn't have taken this job. He should have been honest with Christopher from the second he'd seen the file on Emmerich Klein.

But no. Scout had been a selfish asshole, so desperate to see his crush again he'd thrown his morality out the window. He was pathetic. Worse, he was a predator.

He now saw as clear as day the terrible position he had put Emery in. There was a power imbalance. Emery had never had all of the facts. It was Scout's job to protect Emery from threats, but he'd never stopped to consider the threat Scout himself was posing.

Emery must have worked it out by now. It had been hours. At first, Scout had felt sure it wouldn't be long before his client discovered him in the gym. It was quite heavily populated, after all. But as the Saturday afternoon turned into evening and most people prepared to head out for the night, Scout found himself more alone as he moved from the treadmill to the rowing machine to the free weights until finally, he had asked a member of staff if they had any punching bags.

Scout had been expecting to be told 'no,' but when the member of staff had beamed and said they did, he'd thought he was going to be taken to an old room tucked away with maybe a single old bag and a naked light bulb hanging overhead. But the only glimmer of happiness in the whole miserable day so far had come when the staff member had proudly unlocked a room that was tucked away but had by no means been neglected.

It was beautiful. A slice of time, perfectly preserved. Apparently, before the resort had gotten all fancy, it had been something of a sports venue, hosting small boxing matches back in the fifties and sixties. Since then, someone had obviously loved this room very much. It was clean and tidy, and although the gear had been well used, it was all maintained wonderfully. Old gloves hung from the wall beneath signed photos of acclaimed competitors. There were new gloves and jump ropes that guests could use. The member of staff had even said Scout could go in the ring if he wanted.

He'd thanked her, but all he'd needed was the punching bag. God, it was like being back in Chicago as a kid, when training had been the only way to escape his old man's filthy temper before his mom had finally been able to divorce him. Just like then, Scout now felt more at peace with the rest of the world shut out beyond the closed door. It was just him and his body and the bag he was bending to his will.

Emery hadn't come. Scout didn't have his phone on him, as he'd left it back in his room to go to the pool, so he didn't even know if Emery had tried to call. He was just grateful he'd packed workout clothes to change into after the photo shoot, allowing him to escape quickly and efficiently from the shitshow he'd created.

But the longer the hours dragged on, the more awkward it was going to be when they finally did run into each other.

And…fucking hell…Scout was supposed to be watching Emery around the clock!

Fuck.

In his own turmoil, he had totally abandoned his post, not ever realizing the implications until this very moment.

He stopped punching, resting his fists on either side of the bag and his forehead on the cool, scratchy leather. He was a disgrace. Forget being fired. He needed to resign.

The only sounds cutting through the room were his ragged breaths over the hum of the air conditioning. Despite its efforts, after he'd worked out for so long, the air was still thick with the scent of Scout's sweat and musk. He squeezed his eyes shut as perspiration ran down his face, and tuned in to the loud thump of his heartbeat.

He needed to grow the fuck up, go find Emery, and do his damn job. He needed to apologize and give Emery the opportunity to switch to someone else. A bodyguard who would behave like a fucking professional, for a start.

Scout had been so outraged at the idea of his mildly bigoted colleagues not being up to par when it came to looking after someone gay, and here he was acting like a goddamned train wreck. He needed to get it together. The disgrace and humiliation were bad enough. But he couldn't help but feel like he was contending with a broken heart as well.

Which was insane. He'd only met Emery five days ago, and half that time had been spent fighting. But he couldn't help it. Something like a sob mingled in with his panting breaths. Jesus Christ. If he could do it all over again, he was pretty sure he'd change absolutely everything.

The touch to his wrists startled him back to reality with a lurch. His training kicked in immediately as he snapped his eyes open and snatched his hands away. Except it wasn't an intruder standing on the other side of the bag.

It was Emery.

Oh, god. He was *devastatingly* beautiful. He was simply wearing a rainbow tank, jeans and flip-flops. No makeup, no glitter, no sequins.

He might as well have been naked.

The look he gave Scout was pure sadness. All things considered, Scout was pretty sure that was worse than rage.

"I've been searching for you." Emery's voice was small and raspy. His dark eyes were wide. He rested his hands where Scout's had been, stopping the heavy bag from swinging. When the squeaking chain stopped, the room felt far too quiet.

Scout gritted his teeth, then bit at the strap of one glove, yanking the Velcro apart so he could jam his fist between his arm and ribs to pull the glove off. He repeated the process with his other hand, then snatched up his water bottle from where he'd left it by the shelves full of towels, drinking deep. He must have looked disgusting, but he couldn't really care about that in this moment.

"I should *never* have left you alone," he croaked. He hadn't realized his voice had gotten so hoarse. He glanced at Emery, who was watching him like he was a wild animal pacing its cage. "I understand if you want to file a complaint and have me replaced. We can have someone out here by tomorrow morning or to meet you when we land at Sea-Tac-"

"I don't give a fuck about that!" Emery spluttered, finally looking mad. "Duffy – Scout. What the actual *shit?* You're the guy I met at Aquarium on Tuesday night?"

"Yes," Scout grunted.

"Right before the break-in?"

Scout closed his eyes and grimaced. "Yes. And then you were my client. And I probably should have said something. Anything. But you didn't recognize me. At all."

"I block all my hookups out," Emery said matter-of-factly.

"It's nothing personal. I naturally have a terrible memory for faces. That's before going through a trauma and a head injury. But what the hell possessed *you* not to confront *me*? You clearly remembered!"

Scout scoffed. "If I was that forgettable, why the fuck would I make a big deal out of it?"

"Because it's creepy!" Emery barked. "You lied to me!"

There was no arguing with him there. It didn't matter that Scout had done it for the right reasons. He was in the wrong. "I'm an asshole," he said quietly. "I'm sorry. I just wanted to protect you. I told myself the one-night stand didn't matter, no matter what I wanted, especially if you didn't even remember me. But…"

Oh, god. This was it. He was finally going to ask the question he had been too terrified to even think about until now.

Emery stepped around the bag. "But what?"

Scout swallowed, then took a steadying breath. "But…but if you didn't remember me, if you were that drunk…did you know what you were doing? Did you really consent?"

Scout's throat was thick, and his eyes burned. He waited for the answer with dread, but he would hear it, whatever it was. He had to take responsibility here.

Emery hugged the side of the punching bag to him, resting his temple against the leather as he and Scout looked at each other. "Yes, your face was a blank," he said evenly. Scout's heart cracked a little more. Then Emery licked his lips, glancing down and up Scout's body. "But the rest? The rest is crystal clear. Seared into my brain. If I hadn't been attacked so many times between then and now, I know I would have been thinking about what we shared every waking moment. Yes, I consented. Yes, I loved it. And yes, I'm happy it turned out it was you." He glowered. "But I'm not okay with the lying afterward part. Okay?"

Relief made Scout briefly dizzy. "Yes, yes, of course. I should have never kept our history secret. I just…I guess I don't normally feel the need to see hookups again either. But you?" Scout shook his head. "I didn't want you to leave. Then your photo was in my hand, and I *couldn't* let you go twice."

Emery plucked at his tank top with his fingertips. "Well," he said, a hint of petulance ringing through the word. "I *am* exquisite."

Scout couldn't help it. His nerves were frayed, and all the anguish he'd been putting himself through was ebbing away. He let out a laugh, covering his eyes as another one escaped his throat. "Oh, Emery," he choked out, his eyes still covered. "I'm *so* sorry. I'm sorry for lying over and over. I'm sorry for not checking you really consented sooner. I'm sorry for abandoning you for hours when that's literally my only purpose here-"

The palms sliding over his bare abs stopped his apology mid-flow. He gasped and dropped his hand, looking down at Emery and his hands on Scout's chest. "That's not your only purpose here," Emery said, shaking his head. He bit his lip, dragging it slowly through his teeth.

No. Oh, no. Scout couldn't do this. He *shouldn't.* His moral compass had been nonexistent ever since he'd met Emery Klein on that dance floor. He needed to remove his hands right the hell now and take this relationship firmly back to professional while they sorted through this mess. Scout was still Emery's bodyguard, after all.

But Emery made Scout weak. He made the world less dull, if only for a moment. He made it less lonely. Scout felt like he'd been in one fight or another since the day he'd been born.

He didn't want to fight now.

"It's not my only purpose?"

Emery shook his head. "You're here to make me happy, to do what I want, remember?"

Even in the midst of such a tense moment, Scout couldn't help but arch an eyebrow. "I *distinctly* recall telling you that *I* was in charge here, and it's *you* who needs to do what I-"

Emery seized hold of either side of Scout's face and dragged him down into a filthy, passionate kiss. "I think," Emery said breathlessly, still holding Scout's face and staring deep into his eyes, "that we can both agree on what we want here. And I'd like there to be absolutely *no* doubt in your mind. This time, I am definitely giving you my consent."

1 2

———————

EMERY

ALL THE CURSING AND CRYING HAD BEEN WORTH IT. THERE was a good half an hour when Emery had convinced himself that Scout had left the island altogether.

But then he'd thought of the gym.

Emery worked out because he had to. He liked looking good, but he found it boring as hell. Duffy, though…Emery was sure he'd be the kind of guy who'd run himself ragged for stress release. You didn't get a body like that if you didn't enjoy pumping iron just a little bit.

At first, Emery had been bitterly disappointed as he'd practically run down into the resort's gym and there had been no sign of Duffy. He felt like he'd walked the rest of the damn hotel three times over already, so to assume at first that his hunch had been wrong had made him want to punch something. But then the idea of punching had helped him remember that Duffy was a former boxer.

Emery had asked around when he hadn't seen anything hanging up in the main body of the gym, not expecting to find much. His plan had been to start Googling for nearby boxing rings. But to his surprise, the member of staff had

113

shown him to the door leading to the nostalgic room filled with former glories.

As well as a very sad-looking Duffy.

He'd been hugging the punching bag with his eyes closed, the picture of remorse. Emery's heart had ached as he'd quietly closed the door behind him and approached.

And now here they were.

Duffy looked fucking delicious in nothing but damp gray sweatpants and some battered old sneakers. Sweat was dripping down the divots of his abs, running down the cum gutters inside his hipbones, pointing Emery to the particularly gorgeous cock he now knew was nestled in his pants, hiding, waiting for Emery to discover it again.

Yes, he was still fucking pissed about a number of things. But they could talk about that later. Right now, he wanted Duffy's hands back on him in a carnal way.

Emery ran his fingers down Duffy's neck, then through the soft dark hairs on his chest. He smelled so fucking manly it was driving him wild.

But of course, Duffy was going to resist him. Emery was kind of banking on that, though.

"We shouldn't," Duffy said gruffly in a weak protest. He wasn't touching Emery yet, but he hadn't removed Emery's hands, either. He was watching as Emery caressed little circles over his rock-hard chest, playing with the light smattering of dark fur he liked so much. Christ, how could Emery *not* have recognized this body? Especially the wolf tattoo. Well, he could continue to kick himself, or he could get over it and enjoy the moment now.

He figured he'd pick the latter.

Emery smirked. "I locked the door on my way in," he said as casually as he could muster. Which, when his cock was starting to throb in his jeans, wasn't that casual at all.

"Obviously you can unlock it if you want to leave. But no one's going to disturb us."

Duffy was breathing hard. "I don't want to leave."

"Good." Emery looked up into his forest-green eyes. "What do you want, my barbarian? My brute."

Something seemed to shatter in Duffy. His shoulders slumped, and he let out a gasp of despair. "I want *you.*"

Emery cupped his face again, placing urgent kissing on his cheeks, his eyelids, his nose. "You can have me. I want you to take me. I'll do anything you want. I'm *yours.*"

"It's not right-"

"What wasn't right was lying to me," Emery snapped, cranking the sass up to a ten. "So now you're going to make it up to me, aren't you, Scout?"

Scout opened his eyes. "Scout?"

Emery flicked an eyebrow. "That is your name, isn't it?" Emery had decided if he was going to be screaming this guy's name in a minute, it would be nicer to use his given one. Besides, it felt like a fresh start after the confusion of the last few days.

Scout gave him a light chuckle. Some of those nurturing feelings from earlier crept back into Emery's chest. There was something telling him that Scout might need a little tenderness still.

After Emery was done punishing him for his poor behavior.

"Duffy is also my name," said Scout.

"'Duffy' is my pissy bodyguard, who's going to have some explaining to do in the morning."

Emery ran his hands down Scout's neck and squeezed his shoulders, digging his fingernails in and scratching down his arms. Scout hissed but didn't otherwise flinch. Good.

"'Scout' is the guy who's going to throw me to the floor and fuck me, isn't he? Because I've been a very, *very* bad boy."

Scout suddenly moved, seizing Emery behind his back. Their lips hovered millimeters apart. "You're such a fucking brat, you know that?" Scout rasped.

Emery grinned, sensing victory was in his grasp. "I know," he said remorsefully with a pout. "But I'm also so *damn* pretty."

Scout launched for him, crashing them together as his tongue plunged into Emery's mouth. He lifted as Emery jumped, and suddenly Emery's legs were wrapped around Scout's thick waist as they stumbled against the wall. Emery grunted as his back hit the brick, pushing the air from his lungs. Then he grinned against Scout's lips.

"You *beast*, you," he hissed. "You remember that safe word, right?"

"Guppy," Scout said as he kissed and bit and licked down Emery's throat.

Emery pushed at Scout's shoulders, testing him. "Stop it, you monster. I'm still mad at you!"

Scout spun them around, taking Emery's breath as he dropped them to the floor. Emery's back hit the padded mats with a thud, but Scout was cradling him, taking most of the impact. "Oh, baby," he growled, making Emery's toes curl and his cock ache. "You think you're mad? I've had to suffer your little tantrums and follow your demands all week. You're a menace. *Someone* needs to teach you a lesson."

"Oh god, oh fuck." Emery scrambled to get purchase on the floor, now slippery with their sweat. He clawed at Scout's arms and thrust his straining dick up to rub against Scout's bulge in his cotton sweatpants. He was pinning Emery down, dominating him just the way he loved. "What are you going to do to me, Scout? Please. I promise I'll be good."

"Oh, I know you will." Scout kissed his mouth mercilessly. "So good, so pretty for me, baby."

"Are you going to fuck me?" Emery asked.

He cursed himself for not thinking to pocket any supplies earlier, but honestly, he wasn't sure if he'd even packed condoms for the trip. Besides, he didn't want to spend time messing around stretching out, even if it wouldn't take that long. He'd needed to come about three hours ago when his anger with Scout was at its peak.

Luckily, Scout appeared to be on his wavelength. He knelt and began aggressively undoing Emery's jeans. "Shirt off," he commanded.

Emery's tank was flung across the floor in less than two seconds.

He'd purposefully changed into another snug thong, like the one he'd worn to Aquarium. He may not have been subconsciously thinking of fucking again, but he'd almost certainly wanted to mess with Scout and tease him for his bad behavior.

Sure enough, Scout groaned, running his hand firmly over Emery's bulge. He gasped at the rough touch on his sensitive length. "Baby," Emery groaned.

Scout took his time skimming his hands over Emery's chest, scratching his sides, and tweaking his nipples. Emery bit his lip even though he was grinning like the Cheshire cat. He knew he was slim, but he was still pretty ripped. He'd worked his ass off to get his own modest muscle definition. But in that moment, with Scout staring down like a starving man who'd found a buffet, he had to say all those mindless hours in the gym and the boring diet days were one hundred percent worth it.

Scout grinned at him, sending shivers all over Emery's body as he yanked his jeans down and off his legs, discarding them along with the flip-flops. Then he ran his hand over the leopard print thong, cupping Emery's straining cock and squeezing it almost painfully.

"I'm going to hold you down and suck your cock for a

while. But you're absolutely not allowed to come, do you hear me? You need to learn some manners."

Emery was pretty proud of himself for not coming that very second. Holy *fuck*, Scout was good at this. For someone who gave the impression he hadn't really dominated that much, he was playing along with the scene perfectly, driving Emery crazy.

"Scout," he whined like he was protesting. "But I'm good, I'm *so good.*"

Scout moved so fast Emery almost blinked and missed it. In less than a second, Emery's heels were over Scout's shoulders. His large hands were roaming over Emery's thighs, his bare ass cheeks, his ticklish stomach, then finally his cock through the shiny, silky material of his underwear. Emery's hands were thrown on either side of him, his fingers digging into the soft mats as if anchoring him there.

"I want to see you squirm," Scout whispered.

If Emery was with a regular sub/Dom hookup, he would have pleaded no, he didn't want that. He would have told his lover he was a good boy who deserved to be freed.

Instead, he looked Scout dead in the eye. *"Yes,"* he hissed like an angry snake.

Scout caressed his fingertips over the edge of Emery's thong. He was dripping sweat and stank of man. Emery was in heaven. He cried out as Scout suddenly hooked his fingers under the waistband and yanked the underwear, hard, pulling it over Emery's cock and out of his ass crack, up his legs and over his feet. His heels dropped back on either side of Scout's neck.

He was completely naked and at Scout's mercy.

It was *sensational.*

His cock bobbed against his stomach, rock solid and leaking droplets of precum that ran down his shaft. Scout squeezed his hips *hard.*

"I could make you come so many ways," he rasped, staring at Emery's cock, lost in his lust. "I could be cruel and not let you come, period. You have been bad, after all."

"No-oh," Emery whined, stretching out the word as long as he could. "I want it, Scout. I *need* it."

Scout smacked the insides of Emery's calves, knocking his legs down. Emery was hella flexible, so he dropped his knees practically in line with his hips, splaying himself out in all his glory for Scout's pleasure.

Apparently, Scout liked that very much.

He moaned, running his hands along the sensitive insides of Emery's thighs. His cock was reaching for him from his neatly trimmed thatch of dark curls. Emery liked to have some hair down there. He liked the texture and felt it didn't distract too much from giving head. But everywhere else was waxed and bleached and perfect, ready to go at a moment's notice.

Scout stroked the curls, apparently approving, to Emery's delight. Then he wrapped his fingers around Emery's shaft and began to tug.

"I could fuck you a hundred different ways and not get bored," he growled. "But right now, I want to suck you, and you're going to lie there and take it."

Emery half-moaned, half-squealed in wild insatiable pleasure. Scout let go of his cock, bending down and swallowing the whole length.

Oh, yeah. He was gay all right. No straight boy knew how to deep throat like that on their first attempt.

Emery wailed and smacked the mats, but he didn't resist or touch Scout in any way. He'd been told to lie there and take it, so that was what he was going to do.

Scout sucked and swallowed, rolling Emery's balls in his hand and rubbing his taint. "Scout, Scout," Emery whispered, feeling mildly delirious. He wasn't allowed to come until

Scout said he could, so he focused on his breathing, letting his eyes flutter closed. "Hold on, hold on," he told himself.

Scout popped off his cock, perhaps mercifully, and maneuvered himself so he was looming over Emery, claiming him in a dirty open-mouthed kiss. Emery tasted himself on Scout's lips, and he fucking loved it.

"Hold still," Scout growled. He kept himself level, using just one arm (while Emery *died* over that core body strength) and used his other hand to shove his sweatpants down to his thighs.

Of course he wasn't wearing any underwear.

Emery still had his legs wide open, waiting for his lover to satisfy him. Scout positioned himself on top, roughly grabbing both their cocks and began to jerk them off.

"Scout," Emery begged, hearing the sob in his voice as his length felt so unbelievably good rubbing against Scout's. "Can I touch you? Please, baby. *Please.*" He had to. He needed to feel him under his skin. He needed to know it was *real.*

"Yes," Scout uttered, nodding frantically before kissing Emery's mouth again messily.

Emery didn't wait for a second invitation. He flung his legs back around Scout's waist and grabbed his hair so hard he was surprised he didn't pull any out. They kissed and panted into each other's mouths as Scout jerked them off, and Emery thrust his hips in time with his.

"Yes, yes, yes," he moaned, tears leaking from his eyes. He couldn't keep them open, succumbing to Scout's control. "Can I come?" he begged, almost weeping. "Please, Scout. You're so gorgeous. Let me come. I love it. *I love it.*"

"Come, baby," Scout rasped, speeding up his hand. "Make it pretty for me."

Emery wasn't sure about pretty, but he certainly achieved enthusiastic without any trouble. He wailed, thrashing and gasping as his orgasm overwhelmed him, taking him over and blacking everything else out. The next thing he felt was Scout nuzzling his cheek with his stubble, shuddering and grunting as he spurted over Emery's stomach.

Emery tried to catch his breath, but it was like he couldn't quite inhale all the way. He blinked in confusion, his fingers clawing against the mat. He was too overwhelmed, his body reacting to the stress and emotional fallout of the past week.

Then Scout held the back of his head, kissing his jaw gently. "Shh," he whispered. "It's okay. You were perfect. I'm here."

And just like that, Emery could breathe properly again, and he knew everything was going to be okay.

13

SCOUT

Scout rolled onto his back as his senses returned to him. He stared at the ceiling so long the light fittings left an impression on his retinas when he blinked and looked away. His breathing was slowly starting to calm again.

Ah shit. What had he done?

He was dripping in sweat, but Emery had taken the brunt of the cum splatter. He was lying totally naked with his eyes closed, his hands dropped by his head, and a sleepy grin on his face. He hummed. "Oh, Scout. You really outdid yourself there."

Scout pulled his sweatpants back up to his hips, then sat up, looking for the T-shirt he'd discarded earlier. It was hanging over one of the sets of ropes around the ring, so he stood and yanked it off. He rubbed his face down with it, then he held it over Emery.

"Here," he grunted.

Emery opened his eyes and blinked. "Oh, thank you." He sounded kind of sweet, and he gave Scout a shy smile as he sat up and took the proffered shirt, wiping away the mess from his chest. Then he dropped the screwed-up material into his lap, covering his modesty, looking warmly up at Scout.

Fuck. Scout needed to manage this situation ASAP. Never in his whole career had he crossed a professional line like this.

"Emery-"

Emery cocked an eyebrow. "Now, I know you're not going to try and tell me some bullshit about how this was a mistake, are you?"

Scout huffed. "You're my client-"

"Which is ideal," Emery interrupted. Apparently, he was determined not to let Scout get a sensible word in edgewise. "This way, you can keep an even closer eye on me, can't you?"

Scout rubbed the back of his neck and knelt down to Emery's level. "All I'm saying is that this complicates things."

Emery gave him a withering look. "You're not going to tell me you didn't enjoy that."

Scout's laugh was hollow. "No," he admitted ruefully. "No, that's the problem. I like you, Emery. A lot."

He preened. "So there's no problem, is there? We're in paradise. No one needs to know what we're doing, if that's what you're worried about." He waggled his eyebrows. "It's not like I'm going to run off and tell your boss."

Scout shook his head. "He'd have a good reason to disapprove. If we become intimate, that compromises my objectivity."

"I hate to break it to you, sweetheart," Emery said coolly. "But that ship has sailed. I'm *not* blanking you out this time."

Scout wasn't sure he could make Emery understand without upsetting him. He reached forward, cupping his hands between his own larger ones. "I'm trying to find a solution here. But we're both adults. We might have to put this on hold for a while. That's all I'm saying."

"No." Emery snatched his hands back and stood, looking

around until he found his jeans and put them back on. "No, Scout. Why should we have to do that?"

He sighed and also stood. "If it wasn't very clear to you already, you kind of mess with my head, Emery."

"That's not my fault," he said with a sniff, trying to untangle his rainbow tank top.

Scout rubbed his mouth, his lips still tingling from all the kissing. Then he walked over to place his hands gently on Emery's shoulders. "In a good way. You're captivating. I've honestly never met anyone like you." Emery gave up on the tank and huffed. "But you're my work. I can't be worrying about making decisions if they're going to hurt your feelings or get in the way of…whatever *this* is between us. Your safety – your *life* – has to be my only priority."

"So – what?" Emery snapped his big brown eyes up to glare at Scout. Scout wasn't dumb, though. He could detect the pain and fear there. "I'm just supposed to wait around for you?"

Scout shrugged, rubbing his thumbs against Emery's warm skin. "I – I don't know what to say. I live in Chicago and travel a lot for work. This might all seem exciting now, but when this case is over, when the danger has passed, do you really see this going anywhere?"

"Oh for *fuck's* sake," Emery exploded, flinging Scout's arms off him. "I have to decide that right now? I don't see why we can't just hang out while you're going to be around me anyway. That way, we can see if we can stand each other. I don't…" He clicked his teeth and shoved himself back into his tank top, then crossed his arms. "I don't fuck people twice, okay? Not for a long time. You should be a lot more honored than you are that I'm interested, in case *that* wasn't very clear."

Scout scrubbed his face. "I'm just trying to be responsible-"

"Well, stop it! It's no fun at all! Be reckless. Life is too short!" Emery jammed his hands on his hips as he breathed heavily in and out. His thick hair was all tousled from the sex, and his body glimmered in the artificial light. "In case you'd forgotten, someone might very well be trying to *kill* me. So no, I don't particularly feel like dicking around, smelling the roses while we weigh up the pros and cons, when we could just be getting on with some damn good fucking!"

Oh, god. Scout wanted to be reckless, he really did.

"All right," he conceded, opening out his hands. "What if – what if I did contact my boss and say there's been a complication and you need a new man to watch over you? Then I could take some personal leave and stay at the motel another week."

Emery gave him a scathing look. "Why? We won't be able to do anything together if there's some third wheel monitoring my every move. I'm serious – what's the problem here? Surely it's the ideal solution. You can keep your eye on me day *and* night." He gave Scout a sultry look. "I'll give you *very* intimate access to me, baby."

Despite having only spent itself several minutes ago, Scout's cock threatened to perk up again. Damn the thing. "I need to be thinking with my brain, not my cock," he insisted.

Emery scoffed. "You're a clever boy. You can do both. *And-*" he batted his eyelashes, slinking dangerously closer "- I'm very good at taking orders. If you tell me there are only certain times we can have fun, I'll listen. I swear."

"Really?" Scout said skeptically.

Emery nodded. "Cross my heart and hope to die."

Scout sighed. "That's just the thing. The next attack could actually be deadly. We still have no idea who is doing this to you, or why."

"Oh, come on!" Emery cried. "It *has* to be that

'ekleinhater' person, and judging from all the messages over the last day demanding to know where I am after those other taunting DMs, they have to be in Pine Cove! Detective Padilla will catch them soon enough, and for now, we're out here in paradise." Emery hugged himself. "And as for the 'why'? Because I'm a dirty queer, don't you know?" he said bitterly. "People like me shouldn't make it good, especially on their own. People don't like that."

Scout stepped closer. He knew he should stay away when he was fighting so hard to drag this relationship back to a level of professionalism. But in that moment, he just *had* to hold Emery in his arms. Thankfully, Emery let him hug him to his chest.

"I'd never forgive myself if something happened to you," Scout murmured, meaning it with all his aching heart. "Let me do this for you. Let me keep you safe. Then, when it's all over and done with, maybe I'll take that personal leave after all. I'm overdue a vacation. We can see how we feel then."

Emery sighed and shook his head against him. "And then what? You said you live in Illinois and take jobs all over the country. I don't want to be your summer fling, Duffy."

Scout closed his eyes, pained. "Don't call me that again," he begged.

Emery sniffed and pushed himself away from Scout's embrace. "Why not? I'm making it very clear I want you, here and now. I'm not anybody's afterthought. I'm not dancing for you like a puppet on a string. If you just want to be my bodyguard, nothing more, then I'll call you Duffy. That's *professional,* right?"

Scout huffed in exasperation. "That's not it at all," he complained. "You can't ignore the facts. I'm here because you've received death threats. If I indulge these feelings for you, I might hesitate. I might second-guess myself. That split second could be the difference between life and death, and I *won't* put you in danger like that. Why can't we just wait a little while? I don't have all the answers. The logistics may be fuzzy right now, but god damn it, Emery. I like you. A *lot.* Despite all the shit you pull." His mouth tugged in a smile. "Actually, I think that might be one of my favorite things about you."

But Emery wasn't laughing. In fact, he clenched his jaw and shook his head. "I'm glad I amuse you. But I don't ever offer the chance for a guy to get with me on the regular. Like, *never.* So that's it, done. I'm taking it back off the table. I'm an all-or-nothing girl. I'm *nobody's* back up."

"Emery, please!" Scout lifted his eyebrows in disbelief. "You're being ridiculous."

"Oh, *am* I?" Emery snatched his leopard print thong off the floor and jammed his feet back into his flip-flops. "If that's so, it should be easy enough for you to do your job and forget this ever happened, then, right?" He flipped the thong over his shoulder, then sashayed toward the door. "If you want to lurk around and do your *job,* I'll be in my room for the rest of the evening, ordering food up."

"Emery!" Scout barked. "You're being completely absurd."

He looked over his shoulder and fluttered his eyelashes at Scout, but his mouth was in a grim line. "Then it's lucky you only fucked me twice, then, isn't it? Goodnight, Duffy. See you around, I guess."

And with that, he slammed the door shut behind him, leaving Scout all alone, feeling like he'd lost everything all over again.

14

EMERY

"You still love me, baby, don't you?"

"I hope you're not talking to me."

Emery looked up at Ava from where he was lying on the sofa, gently rubbing Sonic's nose. The little hedgehog had obviously missed his daddy and was currently scampering over Emery's chest, where he'd laid a towel to stop himself from getting pricked. Emery was hand feeding him broken up dry food pellets, the ones he loved the most.

Ava had brought him over when Scout – no, Duffy – had dropped him back to his apartment. It was now the cleanest it had been in months, thanks to Lola bringing a team in while Emery had been away. A new, state-of-the-art lock system had also been added to his door. Emery was impressed that the building superintendent had also organized new keypads for the front door as well as on each level, already issuing new fobs to all the tenants.

He should have felt safe and homely. But the knowledge that Duffy was sitting outside on the street in his replacement rental car was not doing his mood any favors. And while he logically appreciated his home looking the most pristine it probably had since he moved in, that also kind of meant it was currently feeling pretty alien to him. He wanted the familiar comfort of his mess, not to feel like his apartment had become a hotel room.

He'd had enough of hotel rooms.

He had done his best to shoot enough footage to make a couple of dozen different posts and stories that he would upload throughout the week now he was back in Pine Cove. However, it had been a struggle to go out and do anything at the resort after he and Duffy had fought.

After they'd had sex.

God, Emery felt fucking used. He bit his lip and swallowed until the lump in his throat faded. He knew he'd been the one to put his foot down and walk away, but that was because he knew he was better than hanging around and waiting to see if Duffy wanted him after all. The *one* time Emery had stuck his neck out and said he'd want to keep seeing someone, they reacted like that.

Asshole.

He blinked as he realized Ava had knelt down next to where he was lying. Before Emery could say anything, she had slipped her arms around his chest and buried her face against his neck. Her bushy black hair tickled his face, but he didn't protest.

"He's not worth it," Ava said firmly. "Just say the word. I'll slash his tires."

Emery sighed and laughed. He knew she probably meant that, but violence wasn't going to make him feel better. "It's okay," he grumbled. "I guess Duffy does sort of maybe have the teeniest tiniest point. But I still feel shitty about it."

Ava knelt back on her heels and narrowed her eyes at him. "I think it's vodka o'clock. Let's get shitfaced and post cute photos of Sonic. They always get a bazillion likes. That'll make you feel better and forget all about Mr. Poopy Face."

Emery snorted, and Ava's mouth twitched in a hint of a smile. "Okay, yeah, sure."

Except they had only just poured the drinks when a knock came at the door.

Emery froze.

"Hey, it's okay," Ava said, immediately serious. Emery's heart had jumped into his throat, and he realized he was shaking. Ava put her drink down and placed her hands on his shoulders. "The only people who could get in have keys, and your stalker isn't going to knock, is he?"

Emery took a few breaths and looked between her and the door. God, he wished Duffy was here. But she was probably right unless 'ekleinhater' had gotten really brazen. So he nodded. "Shall we answer it instead of making whoever it is stand out there like a dick?"

Ava gave him half a smile. "Let me look though the peephole, okay?"

She squeezed Emery's arms, then crossed the apartment to check through the door. Then she turned, folded her arms and arched an eyebrow. "It's *him*." She didn't bother to keep her voice down.

Emery blinked. "What – *Duffy?*" he whispered. She nodded.

If stubbornness was an Olympic sport, Emery reckoned he could compete for Team USA. So once he had walked out of that gymnasium in Oahu, he hadn't spoken a word to Duffy unless it had been absolutely essential for his safety or their trip arrangements. Determined to play everything by the book, Emery had run his every move through his bodyguard, and they'd agreed he would keep watch outside. So Emery had said a clipped goodbye to him several hours ago after he'd driven them back from the airport, ending another several hours of tense, exhausting silence.

Emery's initial reaction as he clenched his jaw and

screwed up his fists was to open the door only to scream at Duffy to fuck off, then slam it back in his face. But if he had come up to Emery's floor, it might be something important. Even urgent. So he sighed, shaking his head, and walked over to the door to open it with Ava by his side.

Duffy didn't look surprised by Ava's presence, which was a good thing. He was paying attention to who was coming and going from Emery's building, after all. He nodded at her, then turned to Emery. "I was hoping we could talk?"

Fuck, he looked good, if only in a damn hoodie and jeans again. It was like they clung to his body in all the right ways. Emery sipped his drink and swirled the ice cubes so they clinked against the glass. "About what?" he asked icily.

Duffy licked his lips and gave Ava a considered look. Ava squared her shoulders and raised her eyebrows. To his credit, Duffy didn't back down. He just looked back at Emery. "This arrangement isn't working."

"Well, who's fault is that?"

"Mine." Duffy didn't flinch away from Emery's stare. *Damn it.* Emery didn't really want to respect that, but there was a tug on his heartstrings nonetheless.

"Yes, it is," Emery said, resisting adding the 'duh' he sorely wanted to tack on the end. "I don't really see what there is to discuss any further, though."

"Please?"

Duffy's green eyes were sincere and intense. Emery cursed his stomach for flipping and his knees for trembling. But mostly he could have killed his dick for aching.

"Fine."

Emery spun on his heels, swishing the silk kimono he was wearing over his soft shorts and T-shirt. The strut back to his couch might have been more impressive if his big, fluffy socks weren't slipping slightly on the recently polished wooden floor. But Emery flounced his heart out anyway, sipping on his vodka and raspberry lemonade as he flopped back down onto the sofa. Sonic was back in his cage and snuffled around some of the fresh wood shavings.

Duffy and Ava looked at one another. Ava's was more of a glare, though. "Do you want me to stay?" she asked.

Emery sighed. "No, it's okay, babe. I promise I'll be good. You won't need to referee. And Duffy's going to behave, *aren't* you?"

"Yes, ma'am." Duffy gave Ava a nod.

Ava looked him up and down. "Okay," she said gruffly to Emery. "If you want me to come back and get drunk, just call." Then she looked at Duffy. "Don't be an asshole, asshole."

Duffy's expression was contrite. "I'll do my best."

Ava harrumphed, then strode past him out into the corridor.

Emery looked ahead, only seeing from the corner of his eye as Duffy carefully closed the door and locked it again. "I know you're mad at me-" Duffy began.

Emery scoffed and sipped his drink. "Nope. I have no feelings on the matter. I was rejected. I'll get over it."

What he really meant was he wasn't going to embarrass himself by crying at Duffy to change his mind. But he was fucking pissed that the one and only time in years he'd opened himself up and invited a guy into his life, he'd been shut down. He crossed his legs and bobbed his foot, his focus on the blank TV screen mounted on the wall.

Duffy slid into his vision, sitting on the coffee table directly in front of Emery. He clasped his hands between his knees and looked at Emery like a puppy who knew he'd been a very bad boy.

"You weren't rejected. I promise you, sweetheart."

The pet name stung, mostly because Emery hated how much he loved it. He angrily sipped his drink and looked out the window instead. But Duffy placed a hand on his knee. Immediately, Emery stopped bouncing his leg.

"I hate that I hurt you. I'm only trying to do my job, I swear."

Emery swallowed and blinked tears back from his eyes. "I know," he whispered.

Because he did know. In the past twenty-four hours, he could see that. But the thing that had brought them together was the thing now keeping them apart. It was some kind of torture that he needed to have Duffy around him continuously until the threat was neutralized, but he was insisting that if they kept being intimate, it would compromise his ability to work.

Emery disagreed, but what did he know? He posted provocative pictures of himself online for attention. He could kid himself that the charity work made him noble, but that was only a small part of what he did.

Were his haters right?

Was he nothing more than a queer whore?

Duffy's touch was gentle as his finger and thumb tipped Emery's chin to look at him again. "But here's the thing," Duffy said. "I'm definitely not doing my job now. I'm distracted as all hell, and you've got me at arm's length. You're probably more at risk than you were before. So we either be civil. Or…"

Emery blinked and gave him his best sullen look. "Or?"

Duffy bowed his head, rubbing little circles against Emery's thighs with his thumbs. "Or…we try it your way. But you have to *promise* you'll listen to me. That you won't question me when I'm on duty. That you'll trust I know what's best for you."

Emery's traitorous heart skipped, but he gritted his teeth. "What if I don't want that anymore?"

Duffy looked up at him remorsefully. "Then I'll respect

that and do my job. I won't let any harm come to you, and you can hate me all you like. I'm sorry this whole thing between us has been such a mess. I wish it had been different."

Emery sniffed and sipped his drink. It was like the glass was acting as his shield, giving him a barrier between him and all the scary feelings Duffy was making him feel.

No, not Duffy. Scout. Scout, with the sadness in his eyes and the tenderness in his hands as he carefully held on to Emery's legs.

"Wishing doesn't do anything," Emery said stiffly. "You can't wring your hands and pretend things could have gone differently. You can only take charge of your destiny and move forward."

Scout nodded. "Okay. I'll never forgive myself if I let you go again without trying. You're one in a million, Emery Klein. A billion. I'm sure you hear that all the time-"

Emery couldn't help but laugh hollowly. Yeah, he got told that he was fuckable as much as he was told he should shut up and die in a fire. But no…not many men had told him he was special.

Made him feel lovable.

"But the ball is in your court," Scout continued. "I tried to do it my way, and it became very clear very fast all it was going to do was make us both bitter and angry, not to mention jeopardize your safety. If you've had enough of my bullshit, though, I'll walk away. I'll find someone else from the agency for you to work with. A guy that will be professional and not judgmental."

The tears were hot behind Emery's eyes, and he tried not to let them spill, but they were already flowing. "I don't *want* someone else," he bit out, scrubbing his cheeks. "I want *you.* But I don't want you making me feel cheap and disposable again, all right? *I* chose to not invest in guys. *I* hit it and quit it. *I* forget their faces. You don't get to rip my heart out like that again."

Scout reached up and cupped Emery's jaw, brushing another tear away with his thumb. "Not even if you're a real super brat?"

Emery laughed, then smacked Scout's knee, hard. "You love it when I'm difficult," he said thickly. He may have still been crying, but he was laughing too.

Scout reached up to hold Emery's jaw with his other hand as well. "Yes, I do," he murmured.

Emery bit his lip. He shouldn't forgive Scout this easily. He should fight back and make him beg. But honestly, Emery just wanted to be held.

He slammed his glass down on the table and crawled into Scout's lap, clinging to his neck and burying his face against his chest. "You better fuck me *really* fucking good, barbarian."

In one fluid motion, Scout stood with Emery scooped in his arms, cradling him to his body. "I'm going to make love to you, you little brat, and you're going to enjoy it."

Emery was scared to admit it, but he kind of hoped he would.

15

SCOUT

SCOUT MUST HAVE CHANGED HIS MIND TWENTY TIMES BEFORE he had finally let himself into Emery's apartment building with the key fob he'd given him. He knew one hundred percent there was a damn good reason he shouldn't go up there and beg for forgiveness, but none of that seemed to hold up when Scout simply pictured Emery's heartbroken face in his mind.

And now he was back in his arms, and he smelled so sweet and fresh, and his skin was warm against Scout's neck as he walked them toward the bedroom.

There was no going back this time. For real. Emery wouldn't give him another chance if he chickened out again, but more to the point, Scout would be too angry and disappointed at himself anyway to try.

So he had to get this right. There was no need to rush. For once, they were in a private bedroom, and the doors were completely locked. No one listening or threatening to burst in. As hot as the previous encounters had been, Scout wanted this to be something else.

Emery's bedroom was beautiful. Dark wooden floors

with cream walls, large gilded mirrors and French doors leading out to a balcony beyond gauzy curtains. The bedsheets were all purple silk and cream cotton, the chandelier (yes, chandelier) was gold with very convincing fake candles, and there were swans everywhere; ceramic ornaments on the dresser, paintings on the wall, even carved into his wardrobe. His bed was an honest-to-god four-poster complete with drapes, and he probably had half a dozen throw pillows scattered at the top of the mattress.

There was a spicy yet vanilla scent in the air, probably from the incense sticks Scout noticed balanced in a glass jar. It took a second glance to realize the thing in the corner was a genuine sleek black record player, next to which was a dark wooden cabinet filled with LPs stacked vertically.

All Scout had known for most of the past decade were soulless hotel rooms or his empty apartment, which he'd never bothered to decorate. It was like he was in another world.

Scout suddenly noticed he was standing still by the foot of the bed, staring. Just as he did, Emery looked up and touched his face. "Do you like my room?" he asked shyly. "It's…uh…not usually this tidy."

"It would be beautiful, even if it was a mess," Scout assured him. "It's very you, but at the same time, it's surprising."

Emery blushed. Scout hadn't seen him like this before. So vulnerable. It was gorgeous. "I – god – I'm still that little boy that wants to be a prince." He laughed, but Scout knew he wasn't joking.

Carefully, he placed Emery down on the floor and led him toward the bed, his feet making little *pat pat pat* sounds in those ridiculously adorable fuzzy socks he had on. Scout had been an utter imbecile to think he could walk away from this precious guy. He'd just have to work extra hard and be hyper-vigilant. But if there was any luck in this world, why did he have to discard this time with Emery?

Scout really didn't know what would happen when he would have to go back home or, more pressingly, travel for his next assignment. But they could cross that bridge when they came to it. For now, Scout was done denying himself the first true connection he'd felt with a man in years. He was done talking himself out of tasting Emery again, of touching him and claiming every inch of him.

"Is it wrong if I say you're not a prince; you're a queen?" he asked as he sat down on the edge of the bed, tugging Emery to him by his hips.

Emery groaned and bit his lip. "It's a good job you're a smooth talker. I might punish you a little less."

Scout ran his hands up the silky material of Emery's robe, looking up into his beautiful brown eyes. "I'm so sorry." He shook his head. "I know I was trying to be sensible, but..." He sighed. "I think you scare me, sweetheart."

"Me?" Emery lifted his eyebrows. "Aren't you some championship-winning boxer?"

Scout laughed, loving how easily the pet name had been to say and how easily Emery had accepted it. He *was* a sweetheart.

"I came second, once. And I'm sure you'd be quite the spitfire if you ever had to defend yourself." He growled and pressed his nose to Emery's belly, inhaling his naturally sweet scent as well as all his fruity products. "It's more my heart that's scared of you."

It was easier to admit with his eyes closed and his cheek pressed against his stomach. But Emery gently placed his hands on either side of his face and encouraged him to look up. "Don't be afraid," he whispered.

Scout smiled, attempting to diffuse the serious

atmosphere that was threatening to surround them. "You're right. You're a little kitten. I've got nothing to worry about."

Emery grinned and licked his lips. "Kittens have claws too, baby."

"Can I undress you?" Scout asked. Emery had made it pretty clear he liked to have someone else take charge during sex. So far, that had been a little rough with a lot of smack talk between them. Scout wanted to try a different approach for their first time in Emery's gorgeous bedroom.

Emery moaned and nodded, not taking his eyes off Scout. He realized they hadn't kissed yet, but he was kind of glad for that. He wanted to take his time tonight. After almost cocking things up so spectacularly, he wanted to worship Emery as best he could.

He started by slipping off the silky kimono, watching it flutter to the ground. Emery giggled and bit his lip, closing his eyes.

"Nooo," Scout said, dragging out the word. "Look at me, Emery. I can talk all I want, but I'd rather you saw on my face how I feel about being here with you."

"You talk too much," Emery grumbled. But he blinked and looked down at Scout as he slid his hands underneath his T-shirt and brushed his tight, defined stomach. They smiled at each other. Scout had never put much stock in that saying about having butterflies in your chest, but in that moment… maybe he felt like he got it. Emery made him lightheaded.

And now they were finally doing this right, he couldn't help the spark of hope that flared inside him, either. They still had too many obstacles in their path and no way to predict what the future might hold. But right there and then, with all the bullshit pulled away, it was just two men in a beautiful bedroom, promising themselves to each other for the whole night.

At least, that was what Scout hoped.

Emery allowed him to gently peel off his T-shirt. It had a picture of a chubby unicorn on it that read *'I'm perfect.'* Scout couldn't really argue. Then he dragged his soft purple shorts over his hips, surprised to find regular black briefs underneath.

"Sorry," Emery mumbled, kicking the shorts away and holding his hands in front of his crotch. "I was having a comfy day. There was ice cream. I even made Ava watch Legally Blonde."

Scout shook his head and eased Emery's hands apart. "You don't ever need to hide from me, and you *definitely* don't need to apologize. You're stunning, no matter what clothes you wear or makeup you have on."

Emery rolled his eyes. "Most guys normally want one or the other. Hyper fem, like a doll, or they try and tell me I don't need that shit."

'That shit.' Fuck, that made Scout angry. Some men – gay or straight – just dismissed anything even vaguely feminine as being weak and without value. His old man was just like that.

Fuck them.

Scout frowned, tracing his fingers lightly up and down Emery's sides. "Doesn't all the shiny things and glitter make you happy?"

Emery nodded. "Some days, it's like I can't breathe if I don't sparkle. Others...well, every girl likes her jammies, doesn't she?"

"I think," Scout said as he tilted his head and slipped Emery's fingers through his, "that what makes you beautiful is when you're happy. Skimpy thong days or grandma panty days."

Emery snorted and pulled his hands free to cover his face while he hooted with laughter. Scout used that as a good opportunity to tug him down into his lap and wrap his arms around his waist.

Emery stopped laughing, although there was still a twinkle in his eyes as he touched his fingers to Scout's stubble. "Can we not think of my *oma* right now or her panties?"

Scout grinned. "Agreed. I only want to think about you."

Emery bit his lip and glanced down. *Uh-oh.* "Are you sure? Really, *really* sure? I – I don't think I could take it if you left right after again."

Scout carded his fingers through Emery's thick, dark hair. "I'm sure," he said with as much sincerity as he had in his bones. "Can I stay the night?"

Emery leaned forward, claiming his mouth for a kiss. In some ways, it felt like their first kiss. So sweet and tender. Like they were starting afresh.

"Yes," he whispered against Scout's lips. "I'd love that."

Scout kicked off his shoes and rolled back on the bed, pulling the nearly naked Emery down beside him. The purple silk cover on the comforter was slippery and cool, but the cream sheets were cotton and soft. Scout pushed several of the throw pillows off the bed so they could lie down. The evening sunshine spilled through the gauzy curtains, giving Scout plenty of light to see by as he ran his fingers over Emery's slim but muscular body.

Emery was lying almost naked on his back, looking up at Scout as he spooned beside him, still dressed in his jeans and hoodie. He got a thrill from the power imbalance their clothes implied, knowing that Emery was trusting Scout to take care of him while he was in charge.

Dominating – as in, being called a Dom – was something Scout had never thought of before. He would have been too wary of wielding his strength over anyone in the bedroom without being prompted. But now that Emery had asked for it, begged for it even, he found something oddly soothing about the role. It was less domineering and much more caregiving.

He was quickly becoming addicted to it.

That didn't mean he wasn't still learning the ropes, though. He figured it was okay to ask questions. That was probably the easiest way to make sure they were both happy and there were no misunderstandings.

He thought it best to keep it simple. "Is this okay?"

Emery nodded, beautifully placid, waiting for Scout to pleasure them both.

He almost double-checked what he wanted to do next was okay as well, but that wasn't what Emery wanted.

He wanted to be *told* what was going to happen. Any problems, they had their safe word so they could stop. Or Scout had read online that people used a traffic light system. Red for stop, yellow for unsure, and green for go. So he needed to just go for it and give Emery what he craved.

Because what Scout wanted was to hear Emery's praise again, like he had during the pool photo shoot. He wanted this incredible, unique, dazzling man to tell him he'd done good.

It was probably the most psychology Scout had ever considered with sex. But then – when was the last time he'd had sex with the same person three times?

Most of these thoughts had occurred to Scout while he'd been waiting out in the car. As he stared down at Emery now, it was more like the highlights flashed through his mind, reminding him of the steps that had brought him to this moment.

"All I want you to do is keep looking at me as much as you can, baby." Scout ran the palm of his hand over the gentle bumps of Emery's subtle abs. "Let me take care of you. Tell me if we need to stop – you know the word, right?" Emery nodded. "Otherwise, just let me make you feel good, okay? Eyes on me."

Emery's breathing got heavier – almost panicky – but he nodded and kept his gaze on Scout's. Scout hooked his fingers under his underwear and began to tug it down. Emery didn't protest, so Scout kept going, freeing his lover's hardening cock, the tip already a little shiny with precum. He pulled the briefs all the way down Emery's legs and discarded them on the floor with the rest of his clothes.

Emery was glorious. His skin was a rich tanned copper that almost seemed to shine as well as being warm to the touch. Scout was covered in little scars and odd tan lines, but Emery's body appeared without blemish. Scout could feel Emery watching him as he drank in the sight of him completely stripped bare, just like Scout had told him to do.

"Good boy," he murmured, glancing toward his face. Emery's gaze flinched away, but only for a fraction of a second. Then he bit his lip and looked back, holding Scout's stare. It must have been difficult for him to break the ingrained habit of not looking at who he was having sex with. Eye contact took a lot of trust, after all. Scout swelled with pride. *Very* good boy." Scout leaned down to capture Emery's plump lips in a kiss as he slipped his hand between Emery's closed thighs, stroking the soft skin he found there.

Emery moaned as Scout released his lips. They watched each other as Scout lifted up Emery's leg closest to him, hooking it over his hip, completely exposing his crotch at the hard cock bobbing between his open thighs. Emery's breathing was definitely shaky and his eyes wide, but he didn't look away. One arm was tucked under Scout's shoulder, the other was up, with his hand resting by his head.

"How are you feeling?" Scout asked.

Emery swallowed. "Like I want to hide." His eyes were shiny.

Scout experienced a moment of doubt whether he was doing the right thing. Was he pushing Emery too far?

"I want to see you, though," he said. "I want to know you see me. Can you do that?"

Emery nodded right away, easing the tension that had been crawling into Scout's chest. "Yes, Scout. Yes. I promise."

"Good boy."

Scout gently kissed his lips. To his surprise, Emery still didn't close his eyes, so Scout copied him. He'd never kissed someone with his eyes open like this, but looking at Emery through his eyelashes was extremely thrilling. Even though he was still dressed, he felt almost as vulnerable as Emery looked.

Then he pulled back, licked his palm, then wrapped his fingers around Emery's half-hard member. He gasped, but he behaved, still looking directly at Scout. Scout had to admit, it was slightly unnerving. Naturally, he wanted to break the tension and look away just for a second. But he needed to prove something to both Emery as well as himself. There would be no more hiding or forgetting, and the only pretending they would do would be in the rules of their games.

He, Scout Duffy, was here with Emery Klein. Making love. He needed them both to be wholly present in this moment, to acknowledge it.

They didn't speak as Scout began to tease and play with Emery's cock, feeling the shaft harden further under his touch as he jerked him off. Emery whimpered and gasped, Scout's lips only an inch away from his, their breaths mingling as they panted. Their bodies were already becoming slick with perspiration, and the delicious, raw scent of men fucking was starting to mingle with Emery's spicy incense.

"Can I come like this?" Emery asked. His thick hair was

all tousled over his head in a big wave, like a cartoon character.

He was so sweet and gentle, begging in little more than a whisper. Scout almost hated to disappoint him. But he was starting to learn that Emery needed pushing to be satisfied, in bed just as much as in life.

"No, baby, not yet. But I will jerk you off, okay?"

Emery nodded as Scout began to slow down the strokes on his weeping cock. Scout was painfully hard in his jeans, turned on by the erotic sight of Emery's stiff dick bouncing in his hand as he whacked him off. He was desperate to join in the fun.

With a kiss to Emery's temple, Scout relinquished his hold on him, slipping away to hastily divest himself of his hoodie and jeans. His cock sprung free as soon as he yanked his own briefs down, adding them to the growing pile of clothes thrown haphazardly on the wooden floor of Emery's bedroom.

Emery watched him throughout the process, smiling shyly as Scout glanced at the nightstand. "There's lube, if you like?" Emery jutted his chin at the top draw. "Different flavors. Also toys, cock rings..." He grinned as Scout swallowed, his heartbeat racing. "Cuffs too. The nice soft leather kind."

Scout opened the drawer. Unsurprisingly, it was a total mess, but everything looked clean, and there were lots of condoms in shiny foil packets. He pushed down a wave of insecurity that Emery was used to much wilder and kinkier sex than Scout. He wasn't there to compete with anyone else. He was there for Emery and himself, that was it.

"I got tested not long before we met," Emery said, unprompted. "All negative. I haven't fucked anyone else but you since. How about you?"

"Uh, yeah."

Scout trailed his fingers over the dildos in different shapes and sizes. Anal beads, butt plugs, little wheeled things with spikes on. He'd used cock rings before, but some of the more exotic things might require some internet research.

He cleared his throat, looking back at Emery, who was still watching him, but he also had his hand around his dick, slowly stroking it. "Sorry," Emery said genuinely, glancing down at himself. "I figured you'd want me to stay hard."

Scout chuckled, sitting back on the edge of the bed and kissing his lover. "Good boy," he praised.

He needed to stay focused and not get distracted by the candy store of playthings on offer. If they were going to keep seeing each other, Scout could go away and think of more imaginative ways to tease Emery before letting him come. But today wasn't for that. It was for intimacy, connection. Today, they'd just keep things simple.

"I got tested after the last guy I slept with wanted to go bareback."

Emery smirked. "Bad baby," he said, lightly smacking Scout's thigh.

Scout laughed sheepishly. "Yeah, yeah, I know. It came back negative too, though. But, uh, that's not what I want to do right now." He cleared his throat. "It's not what we're going to do."

"Okay, sweetie," Emery said, happily compliant. He angled his head, arching his back up, asking for another kiss. "Tell me what you're going to do to me."

Scout touched their lips together. "If you still want to come like how we were before – with me jerking you off – then I'm going to fuck you from behind, between those smooth, pretty thighs. You have to watch me, though, the whole time. And you can't come until I say. Can you hold it, or do you need a cock ring?"

Emery panted, beads of sweat on his forehead. "I might need a ring," he said, jerking himself a bit harder.

Scout batted his hand away. "Tough," he said. He hadn't intended to play games, but it seemed like Emery couldn't help but test him. He loved it, though. He grabbed Emery's cock and squeezed the base, making him gasp and pout. "Calm down. No cock ring, but I say when you come. If you really can't hold it, tell me. But if you come without warning, without asking permission, then you'll be punished."

That seemed the right sort of thing to say. Emery certainly responded well to it, moaning and biting his lower lip. Then he nodded, his breathing ragged and a smile twitching at his lips. "I'll be good. I'll be perfect. You'll see. Fuck me however you want, barbarian."

Scout felt the teasing moment was over, so he released Emery's cock and stroked the side of his face instead. "Scout," he said gently. As much as he wanted to test Emery's discipline – instinctively he knew he needed that in some way – he didn't want to play any games.

Emery's breathing began to calm. "Scout," he repeated.

Scout kissed his mouth softly. "Emery, baby," he murmured against his lips.

Scout's cock was stirring again. Emery turned, and they held each other, the skin of their naked bodies rubbing beautifully together. But Scout had made a plan, and he was going to stick to it. So he broke away, holding Emery's gaze as he reached in for one of the fruity lubes he'd seen. That seemed so very Emery, he didn't mind adding another scent to the bedroom aroma.

Obediently, Emery lay on his side, a pillow between his arm and his head so he could look over his shoulder more easily. Scout squirted the sweet berry gel onto his fingers, then luxuriated in spreading it all over his throbbing cock while Emery watched him hungrily. Scout dropped the tube, then propped himself up on his side and spooned up against Emery while he leaned on his elbow. Emery looked up adoringly at him as he slid his cock between the tops of his thighs, just below his dark and heavy balls.

The pressure on his cock was blissful. Not quite the same as fucking Emery's hole, but still good. Wonderful, even. Just different. Then Scout reached over with his wet hand, wrapping the fingers around Emery's cock again.

There was no need for a slow buildup. He just began jerking him off and thrusting between his thighs. Emery was holding his legs tightly together, clamping his leg muscles to make it all the sweeter for Scout.

Forget Emery holding on to his orgasm. Scout wasn't going to take long at all to come.

He felt so fucking good, though, he didn't care. He'd drag it out next time. Emery's expression was one of perfect torture anyway as he squealed and gasped, his eyes begging Scout for release but never once looking away.

Scout pounded into his thigh gap, the *slap slap slap* of their damp skin filling the elegant bedroom. Emery was holding his breath for several seconds before letting it go in ragged gasps, then inhaling again. His fists clenched the silky bedsheets.

He was beyond perfect.

Scout didn't bother trying to hold on to his climax. In fact, he chased it.

"I'm going to come," he rasped, nodding at Emery. "Do you want to come with me, baby?"

"Please!" Emery cried. "Scout, yes!"

Scout couldn't talk as he sped up, letting his body go as his balls contracted, and he suddenly shot his load between Emery's thighs. Emery thrust his pelvis into Scout's hand for the last few strokes on his cock. Then he followed suit and splattered cum all over the comforter. They both grunted and gnashed their teeth as they shuddered, chasing the last seconds of their highs.

Then Scout collapsed, gathering Emery in his arms, turning him so they were facing, and covering his face with fluttering kisses as they breathed heavily. Emery clung to him. "Thank you," Emery stammered in little more than a whisper. "Perfect, baby. So perfect."

Scout nodded, his chest filling with pride. After all the fighting and ups and downs, that had to be the best makeup sex he'd ever had. Emery was beautiful and difficult and complicated.

And, for now at least, all his.

16

EMERY

"You're trembling."

Emery blinked and looked up at Scout's concerned face. They were still lying on the bed, naked in the evening sunlight spilling through the window. The mess on the sheets and their damp bodies was beginning to cool, and Emery's heart rate had almost slowed down to normal again.

Swallowing, he realized Scout was right. He was shivering slightly. He smiled and tried to make light of it.

"Good sex," he said with a grin, tracing his fingers over Scout's solid pecs.

Scout was smart, though. Not the dumb thug he might have you believe. He stroked Emery's hair and tilted his head as he looked down at him. Emery was resting his temple on his shoulder, so the gaze was pretty intense. He looked away. The scene was over. He didn't have to obey Scout's rules anymore.

And Scout didn't make him. He allowed Emery to snuggle against him and half close his eyes. But because he was smart, he had probably worked out that there was more going on in Emery's head than he was letting on.

Wasn't there always?

"Are you okay?" Scout gently touched the back of Emery's neck, playing with the short hairs there. "I'm still learning how you like to do this. The sex. It's a little different to what I'm used to."

Emery bit his lip. "Do you like it?"

Scout scoffed and shook his head. "Loving it. It's a whole new world. I like that it's not just one way, either. I enjoyed the rougher stuff, but what we just did there…it's thrilling, but it's also kind of soothing." He paused, enough that Emery looked up. Scout studied his face. "Can I ask you a question?"

A dozen possible scenarios flitted through Emery's mind, and his defenses immediately threatened to flare. But he inhaled and tried to quash them. Scout didn't look tense, and he certainly didn't seem to be trying to run away. He'd asked to stay the night, after all.

Emery couldn't remember the last night he'd had sex with *anyone* in this room, let alone had allowed them to stay until morning. Even if his emotions were warring, he had to acknowledge there was something special about Scout.

"Sure. Ask away."

Scout licked his lips. He was still playing with Emery's hair. Then he shook his head. "Hang on. You're still shaky. Get under the covers with me?"

Emery did his best not to let his heart flutter as he allowed Scout to move them around and pull back the comforter. Most of their mess had spurted on top of it, so he felt quite comfortable as he slipped between the sheets. Scout spooned up behind him, cuddling him close. It was easier not to look at him directly if they were going to talk, but Emery could still glance over his shoulder at him if he wanted.

"That's better." Scout kissed that sweet, ticklish spot just behind Emery's earlobe.

"What did you want to ask?"

Scout trailed his fingers over Emery's tummy, and Emery wondered if he was choosing his words carefully. "Giving up control like that," he said after a few moments. "I kind of get the impression it makes you feel calm."

Something warm blossomed in Emery's chest. He was still wary of Scout, not entirely convinced he wasn't going to bolt again. Emery was also scared that his heart seemed to be running away with things. Yes, he liked Scout a lot. There was no denying the chemistry was wild between them. But he never got too involved. It was dangerous to get attached. If you let people in too close, it was inevitable one day they would eventually hurt you.

Which was probably why Scout had been asking if he was okay. Emery was debating with himself because he couldn't help the thrill he felt at hearing Scout's words. It was rare for anyone to figure out anything that was going on in Emery's head without him spelling it out. He smiled, pretty sure Scout couldn't see from where he was lying behind him.

"Yeah, it does make me feel calm. Is that weird?"

He felt Scout shake his head, rubbing his nose against Emery's neck. "No, actually. I get it. But – well – that must take a lot of trust in the other person."

Emery threaded his fingers between Scout's and kissed his knuckles. "Duh," he said, thinking if he teased him, it would lighten the gravitas of the moment. Because yes, it took a monumental amount of trust to properly scene with someone, and Emery usually only played around a little with inexperienced guys. Normally if he wanted to be fully dominated, he'd hook up with a professional or experienced Dom. But Scout…Emery had just known at first sight he'd have the knack. Jesus, he'd even offered to let the man cuff him up. They probably weren't quite there yet, but maybe it wouldn't be long before they were. It made Emery deeply content that his hunch had paid off.

Scout merely chuckled at Emery's flippant remark, most likely understanding what it really meant.

Yes, Emery trusted Scout. Probably more than he should.

But he couldn't help it. Scout made him feel safe, and not just because he was his damn bodyguard – someone trained to look out for others. It was the way he seemed to truly *see* Emery, and so far, he wasn't trying to change one thing about him. It was so refreshing it almost made Emery dizzy.

He kissed the back of Scout's hand again. Yeah, this man was trouble. Emery's heart was in real danger here. But he was pretty sure it was too late to back out now.

"How does it make *you* feel?" Emery asked, turning the tables. He wanted to see Scout's expression when he answered, so he shifted slightly to look over his shoulder rather than just glance. "Acting that way? You seem pretty natural for someone who says he hasn't done much kink before."

Scout raised his eyebrows. "Well, there's kink. Then there's…this. Dominating. Doming? How do I say it?"

Emery snickered and squeezed his hand. "You're such a dork."

"Shut up." Scout grinned and kissed him on the mouth. "Honestly, it makes me feel kind of calm, too. I mean, horny as hell. But…even when I'm being mean and bossing you around, it's really like I'm taking care of you."

Emery let go of his hand to touch the side of his face. "That's exactly what you're doing."

They shared another sweet kiss. "Good. I want to look after you and make sure you're happy. That makes me feel good, too. And, uh…"

He started to go red. Emery snorted and laughed. "Holy fuck! You're blushing! Scout Duffy, big macho man, all embarrassed! I love it."

Scout tickled his ribs, making Emery squeal in delight. In

his wriggling, he ended up facing Scout face-to-face, where he wrapped him back up in his arms. There was no escaping that intense gaze now, but Emery wasn't sure he wanted to.

"Fucking brat," Scout muttered affectionately. "Okay, I like it when you tell me I did good. It...kind of turns me on and makes me feel satisfied. That's so pathetic, I know-"

Emery cut him off with a kiss, his damn heart fluttering again. He *loved* it when people confessed their bedroom quirks, and quite frankly, there wasn't enough praise kink in the world. Why shouldn't people get a rush from being told that they made someone else happy, that they nailed something? It didn't matter if it was in the boardroom or the bedroom. Even though Emery loved teasing and fighting and sometimes even pretending he didn't want the sex his Dom was giving him, he was all for the sweeter side of things too and rewarding and acknowledging a job well done.

In life and in love.

It was a good thing he was still busy kissing Scout because otherwise he would have scoffed out loud. Love? That word needed to be tossed out the window, pronto. That was ridiculous. Emery *loved* his friends and his work and sometimes even his folks. He didn't love men. They were playthings. If he was lucky, sometimes they became friends once the sex went away, but...no. Emery Klein didn't love the men he fucked.

But he did like Scout a whole lot, and he figured that was okay for now. They broke apart and looked into each other's eyes. "You make me feel safe," Emery told him, figuring he deserved some more praise for a job well done. "You're amazing in bed and even vaguely tolerable when you talk." Scout tickled him again, but there was no missing the pleasure on his face as he kissed Emery between his yelps and squeals.

When they calmed down, Emery sighed while Scout played with his hair. "Thank you," he said softly.

Emery kissed the tip of his nose. "You're welcome."

"So…you're okay?" Scout asked again. Damn. Emery had kind of hoped he'd forgotten that he'd never really answered that question before.

Emery knew he was all over the place and wasn't really sure how to answer that. But when he thought about what really mattered…yes, in that moment, he was happy. He liked Scout and the sex was good. Normally Emery would run a mile from fucking the same guy regularly, but he wanted Scout in his bed as long as he could keep him there.

And on the sofa…atop the kitchen counter…in the shower…

But where would that end? When would they call it quits? Emery chewed his lip. This was why he usually hit it and quit it. He hated when things got messy. He liked to keep his walls up and stop anything complicated from getting too close. That was the only way to stay safe.

But Scout made him feel pretty damn safe.

He sighed. That was too many words to try and piece together. So instead he smiled. "I'm good."

Scout seemed to consider Emery carefully. "If we're going to do this thing, we need to make sure we communicate properly. I'm pretty bad at it, I have to say. With guys. But I've learned a lot through this job, and you gotta talk if you want to work well with someone."

A little spark of fear flared through Emery, but Scout wasn't asking him to go to couple's therapy, was he? He just probably meant like they'd done earlier. Saying they were sorry and stuff.

"I talk for a living, honey," he said smugly. But truthfully, he knew he was terrible at bottling up things that upset him, too. Sure enough, Scout looked patiently at him and rubbed his back.

"This is different," he murmured. "If I do something that upsets you or I could be doing something better, please tell me." He rolled his eyes. "I mean, if I haven't already realized I fucked up. You tried to tell me in Hawaii, but I was too pigheaded to listen."

Emery had to agree with him there. He chewed his lip. "All right. I'll try."

"Especially with the sex." Scout arched an eyebrow. "This is your game. I'd like to know more of the rules if we're going to keep playing."

That was totally fair. In fact, there *was* something Emery knew they needed to go over. "Do you know what aftercare is?"

"In a non-medical sense?" Scout shook his head.

"Well, it is kind of medicinal in a way. It's mental health." Emery gently rubbed Scout's arm. "I love being pushed and bossed around. I love saying 'no' when I mean 'yes' and being dominated anyway. I love being told I'm bad and naughty and a little slut who deserves it. But…afterward… sometimes it might not feel as good. Like maybe the Dom really meant those things or that I was disgusting or embarrassing."

"No, no-" Scout began earnestly, but Emery stopped him with a finger to the lips and a smile.

"I know, but that's why aftercare is important. If you're nice to me afterward, it balances out the fun we had before and makes sure it doesn't turn nasty."

Scout frowned and nodded. "Okay, that makes sense. Are there certain things you like?"

Emery smiled again. "This right here is great. Just cuddling, kissing, talking. Maybe we could have a bath or take a shower. Lots of touching is good. Sometimes I need a few glasses of water if it was a long session, maybe even food."

Scout was nodding and rubbing his back when a look of absolute horror dawned on his face. "Oh *fuck*," he rasped, his eyes searching Emery's. "After the gym, you were all alone!"

Emery didn't really want to rehash how he'd felt between the gym sex and Scout showing back up at his door tonight. It had been humiliating, assuming they had something, only to be told Scout didn't want that. But now they were here, together, so there was no sense dwelling on the black thoughts that had swirled in his mind for those thirty or so hours.

"Oh, it was fine," Emery tried to say flippantly, but Scout touched his finger and thumb to Emery's chin. He raised his eyebrows. Ah. This was one of those communication moments. "Okay," Emery admitted with a sigh. "There might have been some sub-drop there, too. But I was mostly mad at you for other reasons."

Scout held his gaze for a moment, then gently and carefully pulled him into a tender embrace. Emery tucked his face against Scout's neck and allowed himself to be petted while Scout placed soft kisses against his hair. *Fuck.* He could cry, it felt so good.

"I'm so sorry," Scout murmured in the quiet of the room. "I was only trying to protect you, and I hurt you in so many ways."

A treacherous lump rose in Emery's throat. No. *Nope.* He was not swooning. Scout was *hot.* That was why Emery liked him. Emotions needed to stay out of it. Like he'd only just reminded him, Scout's job meant he'd be off soon enough. Emery was a spoiled brat who wanted what he wanted whenever he wanted until he didn't want it anymore. *That* was why he'd gotten so mad at Scout trying to walk away.

If he let emotions in, that implied he was looking at this

as more than just sex and fun flirting. That wasn't possible.

"You're here now," he said evasively. Because he meant it. He didn't want to think about how furious and wounded he'd been before. He wanted to live in the moment, and right then, he was safe and warm and cherished. "And you know, we don't have to scene every time. It's been a while since, well, you know." But Scout raised his eyebrows, asking for more explanation. Emery sighed. He'd said this in Hawaii, but he supposed it wouldn't hurt too much to say it again. "Since I've been with the same guy more than once. But even so, I want different things from different guys at different times. It depends on how I'm feeling. I guess I'm just saying that you don't need to stress. Sometimes I like vanilla sex too."

Scout blinked slowly, a smile playing on his lips as he looked down at Emery. "That went from no words to a lot of words."

Emery rolled his eyes. "You're so difficult to please," he grumbled, not really meaning it.

Something was creeping over him, though. He found he almost wanted to keep talking. The unfortunate side effect of Scout making him feel safe was that his usual defenses were crumbling. And that was exactly what he wanted to explain. It seemed important in that moment as they cuddled in bed with the sun setting outside the windows.

"I don't like letting people in," he blurted. Scout raised his eyebrows in surprise. But as usual, if Emery was going to go for something, he wanted to jump in with both feet. "I'm fem and Asian. Have been since the moment I was born. But I'm also biracial. My dad's family is German, and my mom's is Chinese, and…none of them really knew what to do with me. Mom just wanted me to be *normal.* I know it's because she didn't want my life to be hard, but since I came into the world, all I knew was people telling me to stop, that I was too much. Too gay for the straights, too fem for the homos. Too loud, too angry, too provocative."

He paused, chewing his lip and looking at the ceiling of the four-poster bed.

"No fats, no fems, no Blacks, no Asians," Scout murmured, reciting the familiar Grindr tag. God, the gay dating scene was a toxic pile of shit sometimes.

Emery nodded. "Not long after I started having sex I worked out I liked – no, loved – being submissive. A guy pushed me onto the bed and told me to shut up, and I almost came on the spot. But…it took me a while to work out that not all guys who want to dominate are any good at it. So I figured I had to take charge, top from the bottom. And if I'm the beautiful Asian, the hilarious fem, the perfect sub…then people couldn't hurt me anymore. Then I'd be an ideal, a stereotype, not a person. And if I didn't let anyone in, I'd be safe." He fiddled with the bedsheets, not looking at Scout. His skin felt hot and prickly. "How's that for communication?"

Scout closed his eyes, looking pained. Then he opened them and gently capture Emery's mouth for a kiss. "Amazing," he said quietly. "But I'm sorry you feel like you can't let anyone in."

"I don't want you to be sorry," Emery said, trying to keep the irritation from his voice.

This was exactly why he kept people out. They loved him when they saw how happy and shiny and successful he was. No one would like him if they knew how lonely he was most of the time. Luckily he had Ava, who always seemed to know when to leave emotional stuff alone, and his baby, Sonic, who was the perfect pet. Neither of them asked too much, because he didn't have all that much to give anyone else.

That was what happened when you purposefully kept yourself empty.

Scout touched his thumb to Emery's chin. "My old man

liked the bottle," he began. "I don't remember a time when he didn't used to rough up me and my mom. That was just how life was. I wasn't like you. It wasn't very obvious I was gay. But I was never quite the son he'd wanted. I was a momma's boy." He laughed ruefully. "I took up boxing because he said it would stop me from becoming a sissy. Backfired on him when I used it to start hitting back."

Coldness was washing through Emery. How could he say his life had been hard when people like Scout faced real horror like that as a child? His parents didn't hate or hurt him, not on purpose, anyway. They just didn't understand him.

"Oh god, I'm so sorry," he said, echoing Scout from earlier. Emery shouldn't have jumped down Scout's throat when he'd told Emery he was sorry. He wasn't pitying Emery when he'd said that, just as Emery wasn't pitying him now. He cared about Scout, and his heart hurt to think Scout had been in pain. "That's awful."

Scout smiled ruefully. "I almost said it was fine. But it wasn't, you're right. I coped the best way I could as a kid. Mom and I went to church without Dad, and I found sanctuary at the boxing ring with the trainers and other kids there. It was the church that helped her get divorced when I was finishing high school." He laughed again and shook his head. "We both thought they'd try and make her stay, like a good Catholic should. But they were awesome. It gave me the strength to come out to her around the same time."

"And she was okay with it?" Emery couldn't help but ask. In his experience, religion and queerness didn't always mix well. But Scout smiled genuinely.

"Yeah, another surprise. But she was. I think by then, she knew I could take care of myself. She was kind of sad about grandbabies for all of one minute until I reminded her there was adoption and surrogacy. After that, no big deal."

Emery rubbed Scout's arm, sincerely happy for him. "That's wonderful. And…your dad?"

Scout's face darkened. "We talk on the phone sometimes. I think he likes to keep an eye on me, even though I'm in my thirties." He tutted and looked out the window. "He gets shitty and says it's just because he cares, but he's just trying to cling to some control."

"Asshole," Emery grumbled.

That got a little laugh out of Scout, and for a while, they just lay there and cuddled. Then Emery could feel Scout giving him a thoughtful look. He smiled and looked up at him.

"What?"

"The fem thing," Scout began. "Is that why you don't like being called 'Mr.' or 'Sir'?"

Emery chewed his lip. Normally, discussing this made him irritated, but that was because he could tell when people were judging him. Scout was just curious, though. He was sure.

He nodded. "Yeah. Pretty much. Just because I was born with certain things between my legs, people wanted to treat me accordingly. But it's bullshit. Women can wear trousers, and they don't have to wear makeup all the time. People may still get weird about it in certain situations, but it's a lot better these days. Why can't I be the same way? I'm just a man who likes lip gloss and, from time to time, dresses. So I guess the 'Mr.' and 'Sir' thing is just me giving the middle finger to gender binaries." He peeked up at Scout. "Is that okay?"

Scout looked genuinely confused. "Of course it is. It's pretty awesome, in fact."

"But…" Emery almost didn't want to ask, but he felt he had to, based on past experiences. "You don't feel it makes you any less gay or something?"

Scout actually scoffed, surprising Emery. "No. What the shit? If other guys have said that to you, no wonder you didn't fuck them twice. No, I know what I'm about. I like fem guys, and well, you're pretty remarkable."

Emery couldn't have contained the warmth blossoming in his chest if he tried. "Thank you."

Scout ran a lock of Emery's hair between his fingers. "How about you? You like macho guys with muscles?"

Emery could hear the hint of incredulity, and he couldn't say he blamed him, as gym bunnies could be as misogynistic as much as any gay guy, if not more so. But Emery was happy to set him right.

"Not particularly," he admitted. "I can appreciate a great body, but that doesn't always mean the biggest muscles. I'm attracted to authority, and you'd be amazed how many badass, toppy twinks there are out there."

Scout raised his eyebrows. "Really?"

Emery nodded. And if he was going to be honest, he might as well go the whole way. "I've been pegged by a few women, too. Well, most of them were nonbinary, I think, but, yeah. I don't really have a physical type." He grinned. "I'm not going to say you're *not* insanely hot, though. Nuh-uh."

He ran his hands over Scout's arm and down his chest. However, Scout tilted his head and seemed a little sad. "I do like the way I look, but…it was kind of born out of necessity. Working out meant Mom and I could be safe."

Fuck. Emery cupped the side of his face. "But now look at you. You keep other people safe. You save lives."

Scout smiled at him, resting their foreheads together. "And you raise money and awareness to help millions of kids like us feel accepted. You save lives too."

That lump threatened to rise in Emery's throat again. Most days, it felt like everyone in the world thought he was a vapid attention seeker. It didn't matter he had all those precious messages of thanks hidden under his bed, not when people told him he deserved to die painfully and that he was going to hell. When people invaded his real life and tried to hurt him and the ones he loved.

But Scout got it. He'd just explained in a dozen words why Emery devoted his life to glittering on social media, drinking too much at parties, and doing interviews on lifestyle channels. Because if people could see him, if he was out there in the world refusing to hide away, then god only knew how many other people would feel like they were looking at someone like them. That they weren't alone.

If him being a walking stereotype helped keep one child from committing suicide, helped one parent stop before they kicked their queer kid out onto the streets, then his time on Earth would have been worth it.

Emery blinked back tears and huffed. "You were supposed to come in here and fuck my brains out," he grumbled. "Not go all Dr. Phil on us."

Scout laughed and hugged Emery to him. "Okay, no more therapy. But you asked for aftercare, so technically, it's your fault."

"I liked it better when you were a brute," Emery said, poking at Scout's sides.

Scout grabbed Emery's wrists and held them just tight enough to send a thrill of excitement through Emery's cock. "Like this, brat?"

Emery licked his lips. "Get off me."

Scout grinned. "Not a chance," he growled. He rolled Emery onto his back and loomed over him. There was no way they could come again so quickly, but Emery was willing to spend some time trying anyway.

Then he was going to make Scout order them pizza, and Emery wasn't going to share any of his.

Well…maybe if Scout asked *very* nicely.

SCOUT

Scout had never been woken up by anyone sucking his cock before. He had to say, after he got over the initial shock, it was a hell of a rush.

He hadn't felt Emery pushing the covers off him, but he'd certainly stirred into consciousness when he'd wrapped his lips around Scout's morning wood and began to suck and swallow.

"Fuck. Yes," Scout rasped.

He lifted his head to look into Emery's devilish eyes, then dropped it back down on the pillow as he carded his fingers through Emery's thick bed hair. It was late morning, and sunshine was spilling around the curtains they'd pulled after dinner the night before, when Emery had dragged Scout back to bed to make out and jerk each other off.

Emery was insatiable, but Scout had to admit he made him feel the same way. He'd forgotten how incredible sex could be when you actually knew the person, let alone if that person was kinky.

Scout had been relieved when Emery had said last night that he didn't always want to scene when he fucked. But

Scout had to admit he was looking forward to getting his horizons broadened. Which was a good thing because Emery was about to challenge him in a way he hadn't been for years.

He came off Scout's cock with a pop and smirked with his shiny, plump lips. "I'm going to fuck you," he announced.

Scout arched an eyebrow back at him. "All right, then."

But Emery shook his head. "No, barbarian. I'm going to top, and you're going to bottom."

"Am I?" Scout blinked, unsure how he felt about this plan for a moment.

He had tried bottoming when he was a teenager. He'd fooled around with plenty of guys his age who were just as horny and inexperienced. But he'd naturally gravitated toward topping and couldn't remember the last time he'd let anyone fuck him up the ass. When he had, it had been another masc guy, he was sure. Scout generally preferred twinks, and none of them had expressed any interest in switching roles.

Until now.

Of course Emery wanted to shake things up. He looked positively sinful with excitement at the prospect. As if to prove it, he reached down and stroked his equally hardening cock, showing it off for Scout to see.

It was a nice size. Long and pretty thick, considering Emery's slim frame. Scout could probably get it inside him.

But did he want to?

For a second he almost told himself he didn't. But why not? He wanted to make Emery happy, and he was clearly very keen to fuck him. Considering the vast sexual experience he'd alluded to and the drawer of inventive toys, he was going to be leagues better than any of the teenage boys Scout had messed around with in his youth.

"Yes, you are going to let me top," Emery continued,

sounding confident. "And you're going to love it. Hold your knees and show me that ass."

Scout hadn't showered since yesterday morning, and they'd had sex twice since then. But unlike so many of Scout's recent hookups, Emery didn't seem fazed by a bit of man musk. In fact, he dove right in, pulling Scout's ass cheeks apart, then licking and kissing his hole with vigor, probing with his strong tongue and moaning.

Scout gnashed his teeth and dug his fingers into his knees. "Fuck, baby. You can wake me up anytime you like."

Emery chuckled, taking his time as he licked and fingered Scout's entrance. Scout groaned, lying back and relaxing into the moment. He'd forgotten how good rimming felt.

Fuck. He'd promised himself he'd at least do a sweep of the building and check in with Christopher as soon as he woke up, but he hadn't set an alarm. Emery was already making his job more difficult. But, *hell*, if he was here in bed with him, then he wasn't in danger.

Scout needed to shut his mind down. He recognized when his brain was trying to disassociate in a situation that troubled him. But he wasn't backing out. He'd agreed to bottom for Emery, and he was going to go through with it. He wanted to. Nerves were only natural, but if he was going to do this, he wanted to be fully present. In the moment.

So he banished any thoughts of work and responsibility from his mind, trusting that Emery's building security and locked front door would be enough to protect them for the next half an hour. Instead, he focused on the exquisite way Emery played with his hole, helping him relax for the penetration to come.

But then Emery grinned. "I'm going to torment you for a while, barbarian," he announced. He wiped his mouth with the back of his hand before scampering naked off the bed and opening the drawer of toys that Scout had rummaged around in briefly the night before. Emery retrieved the lube they'd used for intercrural as well as one of the many dildos. This one didn't look like a cock. It looked like the length of anal beads Scout had noticed, except the spheres started small and got bigger toward the base, and the silicone wasn't as flexible.

It was also pink and sparkly.

Scout snorted. Emery crooked his eyebrow in an unamused fashion as he drizzled a healthy amount of lube onto the thing. "Oh, you want a bigger one?"

"No, no." Scout shook his head and waved his hands as he laughed. "It's just – I've never seen a sex toy look so much like its owner. Fabulous and a little unusual."

Emery snorted. "Oh, honey. If you think this is 'unusual,' I've got some shocks in store for you. Be thankful I'm starting off gentle."

Scout swallowed, his nerves fluttering again. He wanted to say he appreciated that or thank you or something, but the words got lost in his throat. His expression must have given him away, though, because Emery abandoned his smirk. He sat back down on the bed with the dildo and lube in one hand. With the other, he caressed Scout's cheek.

"Is everything okay, Scout?"

He was giving Scout an opportunity to back out. It was just the thing he needed to make him relax again, and the tension that he hadn't even appreciated was tight in his chest evaporated in a second. He grinned and nuzzled his stubble against Emery's palm.

"I will be if you get on with your twinky little butt toy. I haven't got all day."

Emery responded to their return to a playful tone immediately, bouncing back down the bed and smacking Scout's thigh with enough force to make it sting.

Scout's cock liked that.

"Leg's up, then, you caveman. I'm not doing all the work here."

"You're not doing any work, princess," Scout shot back as he gripped his knees once more. Emery already had more lube on his fingers, and he wasted no time rubbing it onto and inside Scout's hole. He snickered and licked his lips.

"You're right," he said with a sigh. "But I *am* going to make you work. So behave if you want me to play nice."

And with that, he didn't waste any time pushing the dildo through Scout's entrance.

"Oof!" Scout cried before digging his fingers into his knees and taking several deep breaths. Emery was still grinning as he forced the beads inside, each one increasing in size. But it wasn't a particularly big toy, and once Scout relaxed, he found it fit with relative ease. He still grumbled "Brat" at Emery, though, perspiration beading on his forehead.

Emery hummed and watched hungrily as he began to pulse the toy in and out of Scout's ass. The ridges felt all right, but Emery scoffed.

"I told you I'd make you work. Clench harder, Scout. Fight me."

Scout swallowed and made use of the ring of muscles currently wrapped around the dildo. *Oh, fuck.* Yeah, clenching made a big difference, and he groaned in response. Emery looked smug as he forced the sparkly toy back inside.

"That's better. Christ, you look hot, barbarian. I bet you want to touch your cock."

Scout nodded. His prick was rock hard and leaking, bouncing above his stomach as he twitched and writhed. "Can I?"

He wasn't sure if this was what Emery considered vanilla sex or if he felt like this was still subbing or if he'd just decided to change the rules of the game entirely and become the Dom. But Scout got an answer as Emery scoffed again.

"You don't need my permission, sweetheart," he said with an eye roll. "You do whatever makes you happy."

Still subbing, then. Although Scout had to admit he was a bit surprised by the turn of events, he was still enjoying it. Having not had anything up his ass for years, he had to say the ribbed dildo was doing it for him. The intrusion felt good, welcomed.

But if he remained the Dom, that meant his job was still to look after Emery. "I want whatever's going to make you hard the quickest," Scout said, curling his lip for effect. "Don't think you're getting out of this. You promised to fuck me, Emery Klein, and I'm not coming until you're balls deep in my ass."

That did the trick.

Emery's jaw dropped open, and he took a couple of panting breaths, his hand stilling momentarily. Then he blinked. "Stroke yourself – slowly. Show me how much you're enjoying it."

Scout smirked, taking himself in hand. He'd leaked enough precum that he could rub it down his length for lubrication, allowing his curled fingers to glide up and down his throbbing cock for Emery's pleasure.

Emery moaned, pulsing the toy again and squeezing his own cock. "Fuck, yeah, Scout. You look gorgeous. So perfect. I want you."

Scout's skin prickled deliciously at the praise. "You can have me," he rasped.

Emery pulled the toy out so fast it made Scout jerk and cry out. But the discomfort was like the initial intrusion or the slap Emery had given him. The shock and burning only made his cock harder, and the sensation quickly turned into pleasure. Particularly as Emery eagerly doused his own cock with lube and lined the tip up to Scout's aching hole.

As he pushed, Scout exhaled and consciously relaxed the ring of muscle, welcoming Emery's hot, hard cock inside him. Releasing his knees, he wrapped his legs around Emery's waist and grabbed either side of his ribcage. As soon as Emery was inserted enough, he released his dick and seized Scout's shoulders, rocking into him. He was covered in sweat, which ran down his skin, dripping onto Scout's chest.

God, he was turned on.

This was absolutely nothing like the clumsy attempts his teenage hookups had made to fuck him. Naturally, as none of them had known what the hell they'd been doing. But holy crap, Emery knew how to work his dick as he slid into Scout's ass, filling him up, driving him wild. He dug his fingernails into Scout's shoulders and grunted as he began to thrust, the sound of skin slapping filling the bedroom.

Then he found Scout's prostate, and Scout bellowed, some remote part of his brain wondering why he'd ever stopped bottoming in the first place.

Jesus *fucking* Christ that felt amazing. Emery managed to laugh between pants as he continued to pound at the same angle. "Oh, you like that, huh? You brute. You like the little twink fucking your hot, tight ass?"

"Yes, Emery, for fuck's sake. Shut the fuck up and *fuck* me!"

He was probably leaving bruises on Emery's rib cage, but Emery was definitely scratching his shoulders. They were marking each other, claiming the other as their own. It was primal and messy, and Scout was loving every second. He began jerking himself off again, his gaze narrowed at Emery.

"I'm going to come," he growled in warning. "So you better hurry up if you want to come, too."

Emery whimpered and bit his lip, thrusting faster. "Please let me come, Scout. *Please.* I want my cum in you."

"Hurry up," Scout rasped.

He knew he was going to hold it until he saw Emery orgasm, but he enjoyed making him pick up the pace. He got a kick knowing Emery was desperately trying to do as he was told because Scout had told him to do it. The power was heady. But what was better was knowing how much they were both getting off on what was really such a simple little game. Really, all they both wanted was to please the other, and wasn't that what sex should be about? Mutual satisfaction and connection with another human being.

Emery moaned and dropped his head back, snatching little breaths as he chased his climax. "Scout, I'm going to…I need to…"

"Do it," Scout commanded.

He released his cock, allowing Emery to ride him until he arched his back and gnashed his teeth, groaning as he emptied his balls deep inside Scout. Scout bit his tongue, holding on to the climax he was so close to. When Emery fell forward again, placing his palms on Scout's chest, Scout grabbed his wrists and shoved him just enough to push him backward and out of his ass. Emery was shaky, but just as Scout had thought, he was still with it enough to rock back on his heels.

"Suck my dick," Scout hissed, using his mean voice. "I want to come in your pretty mouth and stop you talking for a few fucking seconds."

Emery scrambled down, desperate to comply as he swallowed Scout's cock all the way down to the root. Scout gasped and cried out, gripping roughly onto Emery's hair, yanking him and pushing him, fucking his face as hard as he dared. Emery dug his fingernails into Scout's ass cheeks, scratching him there, too. His throat muscles contracted all around Scout's cock, tipping him over the edge.

He bellowed as he came, and Emery swallowed every drop of cum beautifully, whimpering in pleasure. He moved his mouth once Scout was done, sucking on the tip of his cock as he softened and stroked his balls. Then he popped off, kissing his way between Scout's legs until he was lapping and kissing at Scout's sensitive hole, eating his own cum.

Scout rubbed his forehead as he watched him, trembling all over in his post-orgasm bliss. "Fuck, baby. That's so hot." It was almost too much on the tender skin, but Scout relaxed until he almost felt numb, his body zinging from so much stimulation.

Eventually, Emery seemed satisfied and sat back on his haunches, wiping his mouth and panting. He blinked, disheveled and glistening with sweat.

Fuck, he was perfect.

Scout reached over and snagged his fingers with his own, tugging him to come closer and drop beside him so Scout could envelop him with his arms. He gently kissed Emery's temple and stroked his damp hair.

"I'm going to have to make a complaint," he said breathily.

Emery's brown eyes went wide with concern as he looked up at Scout. Scout knew he shouldn't tease, but he couldn't help it. "Oh?" said Emery, his voice small.

Scout cupped either side of his face and kissed his lips tenderly. "If every time we have sex it's this incredible, you're going to spoil me for life."

Emery's face broke into a relieved smile, and he rolled his eyes. "Honey, she can't help being a sensation."

Scout hugged him tightly again, nuzzling his nose into his hair, inhaling the delicious scent of sex and musk and the last lingering whiff of Emery's shampoo. "No, she can't," he agreed.

His heartbeat began to slowly calm down as he gently stroked Emery's back and placed lazy kisses on his cheeks, his hair, his nose, even his eyelids.

But he couldn't stay away from Emery's gorgeous mouth for too long. He captured his pretty lips, kissing them reverently as they met again and again. It was sleepy and sloppy and totally wonderful.

Who was Scout kidding?

He closed his eyes as they eventually tired and simply held each other, dozing in their post-orgasm glow.

This was no ordinary fucking. This wasn't just hooking up.

Scout's heart was aching with longing and desire and sheer contentment. Emery felt *so right* nestled here in his arms. He never wanted to let him go.

But how long could he realistically keep him there when there was so much working against them? This wasn't a long-term thing. It couldn't be. There was no way.

But for now, Emery was all his. His to protect and cherish. So Scout was going to do his damnedest to make sure that was what he did, for as long as he could.

1 8

EMERY

"I can go to the gym by myself," Emery tried protesting as he and Scout exited his new car. Apparently, the rental company had been furious that the previous one had been written off with a homemade incendiary device, but Scout had pointed out it was technically covered in their terms and conditions. It wasn't his and Emery's fault they'd never had to deal with it before, so they'd provided a new vehicle within the hour.

Emery wasn't so impressed with that – he had a lot of experience asking to speak to managers, after all. But he was moved that Scout had referred to the car as 'theirs,' not 'his.'

Except...then Emery had been forced to wrestle with himself again. He shouldn't care about that. He and Scout weren't a couple. They were just banging for a while. And not banging anyone else. But that didn't make them a couple.

It *didn't*.

So instead of analyzing those feelings like an adult might, Emery fell back into teasing Scout. That was much safer.

"Honestly," he wheedled as they walked toward Aspire

Health and Fitness. "I'm getting a *self-defense* lesson. What's safer than that?"

Scout arched his eyebrow in a way that made Emery's stomach tighten and his balls clench. Bastard. He probably knew exactly how hot that was.

"Me watching you get a self-defense lesson from a treadmill," Scout replied. "That's what's safer. You promised not to make my job difficult, Emery. If you play up, I'll have to punish you."

It was almost tempting to mess Scout around just to see if he knew how to administer a proper reprimand. But Emery *had* promised to behave for the sake of his safety. They still didn't know any more about his stalkers since this whole mess had started. As much as Emery was trying not to look, he knew he was still getting the usual disgusting threats from 'ekleinhater' that he'd sadly gotten used to.

So he scoffed and rolled his eyes, but he didn't put up any more of a protest. He could save that until all this mess was over and done with. Then he could have some fun testing Scout's limits, teaching him how to punish him properly.

Except…would there be an 'after'? No, he couldn't think about that. Otherwise it would spoil the little arrangement they had now. But try as he might, Emery couldn't quite stop the way his heart panged as he considered the very real possibility that finding and stopping his stalker would mean losing Scout.

For good.

He clenched his teeth together and jogged up the steps to the gym. He could deal with that when it happened, not before. Until then, he was putting up his walls and not thinking about it. He was good at that, after all.

Aspire looked more like a hunting lodge at first glance. The outside resembled a big log cabin, much like many of the buildings here in Pine Cove. But inside, it was all sleek white walls and air conditioning and electronic key cards to get beyond reception. Another reason he felt safe coming here, but he wasn't going to tell Scout that. Secretly, he quite liked the idea of Scout watching him work up a sweat.

"Hey, babe!" Mindy at reception beamed as Emery approached, waving and making her many beaded bracelets clack.

She was Asian American with long black hair framing her perpetually excited face with bangs across her eyebrows. She always made Emery feel at ease, like she'd been waiting all day for him to step through the door. He hoped she made everyone feel like that, and got the feeling she did.

"We haven't seen you in a while! I've been watching your Insta stories, though." She wagged her sparkly pink manicured finger. "That one of Sonic with the little surfboard and beach towel. Oh my god, so cute! How was Hawaii?"

Emery plastered on his work smile and preened. "It was decadent, darling." He pretended to fan himself. "Such breath-taking scenery, you don't even *know*."

She got his innuendo and giggled, probably imagining all the oiled-up guys Emery might have had fun with on his vacation.

But beside him, he felt Scout bristle.

Damn. Emery would need to smooth that over when they were alone in a second. But this was part of his brand. He had to act it up and give his viewers the fantasy they wanted.

He chatted with Mindy a little longer while he signed Scout in as his guest. She looked Scout up and down curiously but didn't make any comment or ask who he was. That was why Emery liked coming here. Mindy and several other members of the staff were openly fans of his, but when it came down to it, they never tried to push too far or invade his privacy.

Which was a good thing because Emery wanted a moment alone before they went into the main body of the gym.

Scout pushed the door of the men's changing room open, checking the coast was clear before they entered. It was mercifully deserted for the moment. Emery wasted no time in taking hold of Scout's hand and pulling him into a private cubicle and shutting the door. It was a pretty tight squeeze with Scout's stocky frame, but Emery didn't intend on staying in there long. He had a lesson in ten minutes, and he wasn't going to be late, even to trade blow jobs with this hunk of a man. As much as he was tempted to.

For once, he had something more pressing on his mind than sex. And that was making sure Scout was okay.

"I'm sorry," Emery whispered. "I have to pretend things like that. Most people follow my account for the tease. They like imagining I'm getting fucked by a different hot guy every night. I know that sounds whorish," he added bitterly. He personally was passionate about supporting sex workers, but balancing the line between teasing and actually selling his body always made him uncomfortable.

Except Scout took hold of his shoulders and made him pause. "Hon," he whispered back. "I know that. I don't mind at all. It's another game you have to play, right?"

Emery relaxed slightly. "Yeah," he said, breathy with relief. "It's just an act. For show."

Scout looked down at him and rubbed his thumbs against Emery's T-shirt. Emery realized what he was doing in that moment was trying to tell Scout that the image he projected wasn't real…because he didn't want Scout to think there was anyone else in his life right now.

Well, shit. That definitely fell into the emotions category. If Emery was just fucking his bodyguard, he wouldn't care if he got jealous. But he did.

It made Emery feel itchy and restless. He hated being vulnerable like this.

Scout gave him a sad smile. "I got pissed off because I was reminding myself what a prick I'd been in Hawaii. But that's behind us now, and I need to let it go. So long as you're all right?"

Emery lifted his hands to play with the material of Scout's tank top. God fucking damn it. Why did he have to be so cute and thoughtful? He really wasn't making Emery's life any easier.

"I'm fine," he promised. He stood on his tiptoes and pressed his lips to Scout's. "Look at us, being all grown up and communicating."

Scout grinned. "Go us," he murmured.

Emery couldn't help but shiver. The sex that morning had been nothing short of spectacular. He couldn't remember the last time he'd been so desperate to top a guy. Most of the time, it wasn't something that interested him at all. Perhaps it was the looming yet unknown deadline they had, the ticking clock that told Emery that before he knew it, Scout would be whisked away from him. But he'd been desperate to feel what it was like inside him.

And the bastard had still managed to dominate him beautifully. It scared Emery how right he'd been with what he'd said right after they'd come. They were both going to be spoiled for sex with other people if they carried on this streak.

He wasn't exactly going to turn down spectacular fucking, though, just because he was worried about what he might feel in the future. So Emery licked his lips, then sucked on Scout's earlobe.

"I'll show you what other grownup things I can do later, if you like."

Scout groaned. "Jesus Christ. Don't you have work to do

at some point?"

Emery grinned. "You'll be amazed how quickly I can get through my to-do list with the proper motivation." He walked his fingers up Scout's chest. "Especially when you're right at the top of that list."

Scout crooked his eyebrow again. Yep, he knew *exactly* what effect that had on Emery's cock. "I think I've let you do enough of the *doing* today, you little brat. It's my turn to do you thoroughly."

For a second, Emery considered abandoning his lesson altogether and dragging Scout straight back to his apartment. Hell, they could fuck right there and then if they were quiet. Sometimes Emery loved the rush from trying to be silent during public sex. But Emery was never late, and he didn't let people down. So instead he huffed and rearranged his tingling cock before opening the changing room door.

"Down, boy," he growled.

Scout smirked. "Just for now," he hissed back. "No promises for later."

Emery smacked the back of his thigh, then spun around to march toward the water fountain. They'd showered at home – there was no way they could have left the apartment unless they did. They'd stunk. But he was getting all flustered again, and he hadn't even begun his warmup.

So he took a long drink of cold water, then filled up his metal canteen for the session ahead.

It was an important one, after all.

Usually, he had a varied routine of cardio and weight resistance that he liked to hammer out with his earphones in, alone with his racing heart and labored breaths. But when all this trouble had really amped up, although he'd been resistant to Ava's suggestion he hire protection, he had been quite easily talked into booking a private self-defense session with her big brother.

Swift was the oldest of the Coal kids, always there when Emery had hung out with Ava and the twins during their high school years. He was sweet and quiet, but Emery liked him all the same. He was the only straight one of the five Coals, but he'd been nothing but supportive by all accounts, even going so far as to defend any of them when trouble broke out in the school corridors. It hadn't taken Emery long to find himself included in that arrangement.

Swift was exactly who Emery wanted to learn some self-defense from because he knew from experience that although Swift was large and athletic, he had never once used his size to intimidate anyone without proper cause. The youngest Coal, Kestrel, often joked Swift was the biggest Hufflepuff out there, so sweet and kind-hearted. Emery wasn't even sure he'd ever hit anyone. He just let people think he could if it was needed.

Emery didn't want to learn how to hit people. Otherwise, he could probably have asked Scout for some moves. No. What Emery wanted was some 'just in case' options. If anyone tried to come for him again, he needed to know how to defuse the situation and, if necessary, how to get away.

Blond and handsome, Swift smiled and waved as Emery pushed open the glass door into the small studio they'd booked for an hour. The wall was glass too, so as promised, Scout could keep an eye on Emery while they trained. Emery did his best to smile back, but nerves did their best to make him falter.

Getting self-defense lessons made this real. Of course, it had been real when his apartment was being ransacked, and he'd been chased onto the street. It had been real when Scout's car had exploded in a ball of flames. But by admitting that Emery needed to prepare for a future scenario was somehow worse. It was admitting that this situation was totally out of his control until the police caught whoever was harassing him.

Suddenly, Emery was taking Scout's concerns very seriously indeed. This wasn't an idle threat. This could get really bad – worse than it had already.

Emery looked over his shoulder and gave Scout a small smile as he stepped up to his treadmill. Scout's expression was serious but also somehow warm as he saluted back at him. Emery felt like he was telling him not to worry. That he was going to keep him safe.

Emery believed it. He exhaled and turned back to Swift with a beaming smile. "Hey, babe," he said, sashaying over to kiss his cheeks. "You're looking gorgeous as usual. I'm excited to learn a thing or two today."

For a moment, Swift looked between him and Scout as he began to run. Damn. He didn't want anyone reading anything into him and Scout when Emery himself didn't even know what was going on. So he didn't respond. He just kept smiling until Swift's focus was back on him.

"I'm good," Swift said. "Happy to teach self-defense for once rather than PT. Most people in this town just want to work on their summer bodies rather than learn anything like this."

Emery gasped and clutched his chest. "Yes, how tragic the people of Pine Cove have such a low crime rate to contend with and feel safe on the boardwalk at night." Swift looked mortified for a second, so Emery laughed and squeezed his impressive bicep. "Honey, I'm teasing. I know you like making people feel safe, and you want everyone to learn these things. Just be grateful they don't have to."

Swift smiled bashfully. "I'd just feel better if more people did. You never know when you might find yourself in trouble. It would be great to teach a regular class. I'd just rather be safe than sorry."

"Ava said that Kes is a little too good at it," Emery said, hoping to break the tension by mentioning Swift's kid sister. Sure enough, he scoffed.

"She beat my *ass* when I gave her lessons. So if tiny little her can grasp this, anyone can."

Emery preened. "Excellent. Where shall we begin?"

Swift took him through a standard warmup that got the blood flowing, then they stretched for a while. "Okay," he said once they had a light perspiration going. "We're going to start with the basics. If someone approaches you, the best way to try and deal with it initially is simply to shout. Don't swear. Just tell them to get away or back off. If that doesn't work – if they keep advancing – shove them hard on the chest. Ideally, you want to just run. But you might need to push them away to give yourself time to do that. Make sense?"

Emery nodded. "Sure."

"I'll come at you now," Swift continued. "Try shouting at me as angrily as you can, then give me a push. I'll keep coming, so just keep going." He waved his hand in the direction of the gym floor where several people were on the machines. "Don't worry about anyone else. They're used to me doing private sessions in here."

Emery took a sip of water, then nodded again. "Sounds good to me, hon. Ready when you are."

He jumped up and down a few times, shaking his hands. Then Swift marched toward him looking the most menacing Emery had ever seen him in his entire life.

For a second his mind went blank. Panic flooded his system, and in the blink of an eye, he was back in the corridor of his apartment, running for his life from the intruder who had tried to hurt him.

Swift pulled up a foot or so away from Emery, his eyebrows rising in concern. "Everything okay, buddy?"

Emery could feel himself trembling and tried to shake it off again. "S-sorry," he stammered. "I choked."

Swift shook his head. "Perfectly natural. That's why we're drilling this now. It's all well and good to read about what to do if someone comes at you, but that's not good enough. You need your body to act automatically on its own, without your brain. You feel up for trying again?"

Emery swallowed and wiped his forehead. "Shout, then push," he repeated. "Okay, yes. Let's try again."

Swift put some space between them, then began storming toward Emery once more.

This time he was ready.

"BACK OFF," he yelled clearly. *"GET AWAY FROM ME!"*

As Swift reached him, Emery shoved him above his pecs, like Swift had shown him. But a clattering noise distracted him, and his attention was drawn out into the gym. Scout was no longer on his treadmill. He was halfway between it and the private studio, his water bottle and phone scattered on the floor, his fists clenched and fury on his face.

Emery threw up his hands and shook his head. "It's okay," he mouthed, surprised at the ferocity with which Scout had responded to his cries. Damn. Emery probably should have warned him.

Scout stopped, looking between Emery and the bemused-looking Swift. He took a breath, nodded, then went back to his treadmill, ignoring the stares he was getting from the people around him as he picked up the things he'd knocked down in his haste to get to Emery.

Emery chuckled, a nervous sound that escaped his throat before he'd even realized it. Wow. Scout had been ready to murder someone.

"Who's that?" Swift asked evenly, causing Emery to look back at him.

Emery shifted. He really didn't want to go into it with

Ava's older brother. It was complicated, after all. Swift knew about the threats…but how did Emery explain Scout?

"He's a friend," he said lightly, hoping to diffuse the situation. "He's looking out for me right now, you know, with all this silliness."

Swift considered Scout, who was running again and looking purposefully forward, not directly at Emery or Swift or anyone else. But Emery knew he was still in his peripheral vision, in case anything should genuinely happen.

"*That's* your bodyguard?" Swift's tone was interesting. Was he accusing Emery of something? Ava had obviously explained that she'd hired Oakley security. Had she also mentioned how resistant Emery had been?

Or possibly that he'd recklessly fucked the man who was supposed to be protecting him, because they'd accidentally hooked up before, then acted like a heartbroken teenager when he'd rejected him?

Was Swift judging Emery for his behavior? Or…was he glaring at Scout like the protective big brother he was, wondering if he needed to step in like he had with so many school bullies?

Yeah, Emery was pretty sure he knew where his friend's brother's intentions were at. Bless his heart.

"Yeah, that's Scout," Emery said gently, touching Swift's arm. "But everything's fine. We're working well together, and he knows his stuff."

Swift switched his gaze to Emery, eyeing him up and down. "Yeah?"

"Pinky promise," Emery said. "We had a little… misunderstanding. But things are fine now."

Swift grunted and didn't look all that convinced, but after a moment, he nodded and resumed the lesson. Emery had a feeling Scout was on his shit list, though, and had better tread lightly.

It was kind of nice, in a way. Emery purposefully kept things vague when he talked with his folks every few weeks, and certainly never mentioned dating. Not that Emery had tried dating since his early twenties, but any hint of his love life was generally met with confusion and pursed lips.

He was aware that his mom in particular just wanted what was best for him. But 'best' to her was 'normal' – i.e., married (to a woman) with at least two children and a nine-to-five job. No matter how hard Emery tried, he couldn't seem to get through to her that a life like that was so out of his realm of happiness he couldn't even entertain it. He knew who he was. But it was like his parents were still waiting for him to 'calm down' and 'be sensible.'

So for Emery, it had been a long time since anyone had fussed over whether or not a man was good enough for him. Having Swift – the closest thing Emery would probably ever have to an older brother – take an active interest in who Emery was possibly seeing warmed his heart. It made him feel valued.

Except – there he was again, acting like he and Scout were a couple. Damn it. For once he'd rather be thinking with his dick, but it was as if his heart had finally taken control of the wheel and wasn't letting go.

He liked Scout. He knew he did. But he couldn't have him, so why was he tormenting himself?

At least right then he was distracted by physical activity. It was hard to pine over Scout when Swift was coming at him like a steam train.

"The trick to getting free of someone's hold usually comes down to twisting away," Swift said as he lunged and grabbed Emery's right wrist with his left hand. "If they use the hand on the same side, like this, twist your hand as if you're looking in a hand mirror."

"Oh, I can do that," Emery joked.

Swift arched an eyebrow, obviously not willing to let Emery joke around to diffuse his nerves. But, *shit*, Swift was a lot bigger than him. How was he going to get away from him?

As if hearing Emery's thoughts, Swift nodded. "Try pulling away. Like you're playing tug-o-war." Emery did, grunting and straining, but he got nowhere. "All right," Swift continued, indicating they could stop. "Now try looking in the hand mirror, then use your other hand to push mine away – after you've twisted. Go."

Slowly, Emery turned his arm so his palm was in front of his face. Then he pushed at Scout's arm.

He came off Emery immediately.

"Whoa." Emery blinked and looked between their two arms. Swift beamed.

"It's just physics. Leverage. Try it again, but faster."

They ran the drill several more times, each one moving quicker than the last. Then Swift had Emery make a kicking motion at the same time – not quite slamming his foot into Swift's shin but close enough that Emery could imagine how it would feel to do that for real to an attacker.

"Good, good," Swift said, nodding. "Now I'll use my opposite hand. You need to twist my arm like a doorknob, then pull me off balance so you can then push me away. Like this." He gently demonstrated a couple of times on Emery. "Now you try, but harder, and with the kick again when you feel ready."

Emery was sweating a fair bit now and feeling a little dizzy. Wild sex followed by a workout with only several cups of coffee and half a bagel in his stomach maybe wasn't the best idea. Scout had tried to make Emery eat more, but Emery had insisted he was fine. Luckily, he had some protein bars in his bag he could eat later. For now, he just needed to suck it up and nail this move.

Swift wasn't going easy on him, resisting like a real attacker would. But like the previous move, it all came down to technique. Once Emery had that down, Swift spent the last ten minutes of their lesson showing Emery what to do if he was grabbed from behind. Namely, drop his weight by bending his knees and then elbow the assailant in the gut.

"There's a lot more we can go through," Swift said as he drank from his water bottle and wiped his face with a towel. "But that should give you a good start for now. Maybe you can practice with your buddy out there?"

They both looked at Scout, who was still running at the exact same pace he had been before, like a machine.

Something flipped in Emery's gut.

He had enjoyed playing with Scout, but did he want him to pretend to attack him? The idea repulsed him so strongly he was shocked to feel a wave of nausea. No, for all their teasing, Emery trusted Scout to keep him safe. He didn't even want to pretend like he might actually hurt him.

Emery smiled at Swift, though. "Maybe," he said lightly. "Until then, can we say the same time next week?"

Logically, Emery knew it would be a good idea to practice his new self-defense moves. What was the point of learning them if he couldn't use them in a moment of crisis? But an irrational part of him wanted to keep a bubble around this thing he and Scout had.

It scared him how much he wanted to protect that bubble.

Emery chewed his lip, and he signaled to Scout that they were done. Right away, Scout pressed a couple of buttons on his treadmill and began to cool down his run.

Emery wasn't a child. He needed to stop flip-flopping about what he wanted. He either needed to make it clear that he was all in with Scout, or they should call the whole thing off. Because as much as he kept trying to convince himself they were just fooling around, he knew in his heart that wasn't true.

He cared for Scout. He wanted Scout to care for him. But could they do that with the pressure of these death threats looming over them, not to mention the time limit they were under? Once the stalker was caught, who knew where Scout would be assigned or when he could come back to Pine Cove.

Like it or not, Emery had let his walls down, and now his feelings were a total fucking mess. He didn't want to get hurt, but he didn't want to let Scout go, either.

Maybe he just needed some space. The last twenty-four hours had been pretty intense, what with their makeup, several in-depth conversations, three separate mind-blowing fucks, and then the self-defense lesson just now. Emery probably needed some time alone. That was usually how he recharged his batteries despite coming across as a massive extrovert. He more than likely just needed some time with his feelings so he could separate himself from the heady rush Scout was giving him.

Just because they were amazing together in bed didn't mean they'd make a good couple. Just because Scout made Emery feel safe and special didn't mean they actually had anything in common.

With a heavy heart, Emery headed to the changing rooms. He didn't know if he could make this decision now, but he wasn't sure he could keep pretending it was only fucking going on between them. His instinct told him to run. That was what he usually did when he got too close to dangerous emotions. Far better to smile and drink and act like everything was fine.

He wasn't sure he could do that right then, though. He was pretty sure that whatever way he looked at it, he was already on the route to heartbreak.

19

SCOUT

For a second there, all logic had flown out the window.

Scout had *known* Emery was in a self-defense lesson. He'd *known* it was just the teacher in the studio with him. And yet at Emery's cry, Scout had been halfway across the room, ready to smash the door down, before he'd even known what he was doing.

He'd had a lot to think about during the rest of his run. Primarily, just how far was he prepared to go for his client?

And when was he going to let go of that last insistence that Emery was really just his client?

Sure, Scout was still doing everything he could to protect him, but he'd never in all his years at Oakley felt like this on a job.

He'd felt like this with his mom, though.

There was no calm objective here. Scout was doing his best to do everything by the book, but a Neanderthal part of him wanted to drag Emery back to his cave and keep him safe from the whole world.

The reasonable side of his brain knew that wasn't what he

wanted at all. Emery was too bright, too special to be kept hidden away. The whole planet deserved to share in his light. But Scout also knew he'd do anything to protect him, whether by the book or not.

Emery seemed preoccupied as he walked ahead of Scout back into the men's locker room, like he'd done on the way to Hawaii. Scout was starting to appreciate that he had mood crashes, and he felt the best way he could help Emery was to give him some space. It made sense, in a sort of way that someone so loud and exuberant needed to balance that out by powering down every now and again.

So Scout didn't bother Emery as they showered. He even let Emery finish up first and head back into the main body of the changing room alone. From where he was showering, Scout could see the entrance and the end of the bench where Emery was toweling off perfectly. Scout's attention snapped over to him when the noise of something hitting the tiled floor rang out, but it just looked like Emery had dropped some papers or photos or something from his bag.

Nothing to worry about.

Scout had plenty on his mind anyway, whether he wanted to or not. Because despite what he'd said about not caring when Emery had insinuated he'd been fucking every guy in sight while in Hawaii, the thought was lodged in Scout's brain and would not budge.

It didn't help that Scout had just endured an hour watching another guy – an arguably very handsome one – putting his hands all over Emery. Again, his lizard brain was arguing with his rational one. The guy was just teaching Emery some self-defense. Emery had rightly pointed out that he didn't want any fighting moves. If Emery got in trouble, he needed to get out of there, not try and take on his attacker. So Scout understood why Emery had booked the lesson with this guy over asking Scout himself.

But if they were going to work on their feelings and communication skills, Scout had to acknowledge that seeing Emery with another guy ruffled his feathers.

So what was he going to do when he abandoned Pine Cove and Emery Klein for his next job?

The very idea made Scout feel sick. He was fully aware they had only spent a short amount of time together, but it had been intense. Could he really leave all this behind, knowing Emery would seek comfort in another man's arms?

Or would he? Emery had been very clear that he didn't date, that he hadn't for years. Somehow, the notion that he'd replace Scout with an endless line of faceless hookups was even worse than picturing him with a new boyfriend.

Not that Scout was his boyfriend.

He rubbed the last of the suds over his aching muscles. Emery was sitting on the bench in his towel, so Scout could afford to take a few more minutes under the water.

If Scout really didn't like the idea of letting Emery go… should he say something to him? But if he did, what could he possibly say?

Well, first, he probably needed to establish if Emery felt the same way. Then, if he knew Emery was interested in pursuing this relationship further, what was Scout prepared to do?

Being with Emery meant staying in Pine Cove, when Scout's job was based wherever the work took him. He could be in Florida this time next week. Back in Illinois. New Mexico.

Unless…

He had savings. Christopher was pretty flexible with his workforce. Could Scout take a sabbatical? If he and Emery never gave this thing between them a chance, they'd never know if it could really work or not. But if Scout found some work here in Pine Cove for a while, maybe they could try being together.

For real.

Was he crazy? Their relationship had been based on an insane and highly unlikely amount of drama so far. From the forgotten hookup to the death threats, it wasn't exactly normal. Would they still have the same spark they did now when they were faced with mundane, everyday life?

Scout blinked water from his eyes and looked at Emery as he sat on the bench, looking at whatever he'd dropped from his bag. If Scout wanted him, he needed to jump in with both feet. Not dither about, worrying whether he was making a mistake. He'd never know if he didn't try.

Not trying didn't seem like an option.

As he switched off the faucet and grabbed a towel, he mulled over the best way to approach this little revelation of his. Would Emery be flattered? Or would he think Scout was nuts after them only knowing each other for a week? But it hadn't just been any week. Scout felt like he knew Emery better than some people he'd known for years.

At least, he thought he did.

By the time Scout exited the shower, Emery was already dressed and back on his phone, his bits of paper back in his bag. With all the sex they'd been having, Scout had almost forgotten how alien it was to see him without it clamped in his hand. It was almost as if it was surgically attached. He was most likely catching up on the endless emails and messages he seemed to have to deal with, so once more Scout left him alone as he dried himself off and got dressed in his jeans and T-shirt.

But the back of his neck was starting to prickle.

Emery's body language was closed off – not especially unusual if he was concentrating on work. But there was something…else. Scout couldn't quite put his finger on it.

However, he'd learned from his years in the ring, as well as on the job, that when his intuition spiked like that, he shouldn't ignore it.

"Everything okay?" Scout raised his eyebrows and waited for Emery to look at him. His expression was pinched, and he regarded Scout for a moment before speaking.

"Yeah. I guess…I guess working on those moves with Swift really hit it home. This isn't a game. Someone's trying to kill me – or at least fuck me up."

Scout glanced around. There was someone else in the shower and another dude using a hairdryer, but no one was listening to them or looking that he could see. So he sat down next to Emery and placed his hand on the small of his back.

Emery shifted away, clutching the strap of his gym bag and staring at the floor.

Icy coldness washed through Scout as he retracted his hand. But he swallowed his fears and remained focused on the problem at hand. Because it was clear there was a problem.

"Yes," he said evenly. "But I'm here. I'm not going to let anything happen to you."

Emery bit his lip and rose to his feet. He didn't seem to know which way to turn, fidgeting on the spot. "That's – that's just it. I think you might have been right. How can you protect me if you're thinking with your dick?"

Scout blinked and leaned away. "Ouch," he said, hearing the coldness in the word but not able to hold it back. Yes, he had said that, but they'd come to an agreement. Did Emery think he'd been doing a bad job? "I'm capable of thinking with my brain when we're on the clock. Emery, has something spooked you?"

Emery flashed his dark eyes at him. "The-the lesson," he stammered. "I told you. Swift, he made it clear that anything could happen. I'm just not sure we should be messing around if someone's actively trying to hurt me."

Something wasn't right here. Scout narrowed his eyes. "When I suggested that, you lost your shit."

"Yes, I did!" Emery exploded. "Because I'm a selfish brat who doesn't think things through! I don't want to die, okay?"

Despite the hostility, Scout softened. "Of course not." He stood and faced Emery, who was acting a lot like a cornered animal. His eyes were darting back and forth, and he was rocking, his bag strap gripped in both hands. Scout touched his hand to his elbow. "I won't let that happen. I promise. Not on my watch. And…" This was it, time to bite the bullet. "And if it makes any difference, I don't feel like this is 'messing around' between us."

Emery scoffed and wrenched his arm away from Scout's touch, leaving Scout's fingers feeling as if they'd been burned. Emery curled his lip. "If you're just going to pack up and leave, what else could this be other than fuck buddies?"

Before Scout could formulate a response, Emery spun on his heels and stormed out of the changing room. Scout blinked, his chest tight and his mouth dry.

"What the fuck?" he said out loud. The guy who'd finished using the hairdryer arched an eyebrow at Scout, but he didn't care what he thought.

He only cared about Emery, and something was obviously and very seriously wrong with him.

By the time he'd collected his wits, Emery was already back through the gym and going through the security doors to reception. Scout had to jog to catch up with him.

"Emery, hold up," he cried, aware Mindy at reception was watching them. Scout couldn't be concerned with that, though.

Emery was scaring him.

"Come on! Hold up!"

Emery didn't stop walking, though, until he'd pushed his way through the front doors back out onto the main street where the gym was located. The warm evening August air enveloped him like a blanket, and the scent of coffee drifted from the gym's café, Bench Press. Emery held his phone to his chest like it was a shield.

"I need some space, okay?" Emery flashed an angry look at Scout. "This is too much. You…you *lied* to me about Aquarium, and then you fucked me around in Hawaii, and I just let you back into my apartment like a love-sick puppy. *I'm* the sub so that means *I'm* in charge, all right?"

Scout held up his hands. "Whoa, yes. Of course. I know that. Sweetheart, where's this coming from?"

"Don't…" Emery's face contorted with pain. "'Sweetheart' isn't helping anything right now. I need some space. You can meet me back at the apartment. But I think I need to keep my distance for a bit. This is too much."

Scout tried not to feel like a knife was twisting through his heart. He was so blindsided he didn't know what to do. *Fuck.* Was this how Emery had felt in Hawaii? Was he intentionally trying to get even by pushing Scout away like Scout had done to him? Or was this karma finding its way back to Scout?

His brain latched on to the first practical bit of information it could. "Meet you back at the apartment? But…I drove you here."

Emery shook his head and looked at the car approaching them on the street. "I ordered an Uber. I really need some space." His voice cracked, and a tear slid down his cheek as he looked at Scout. "Please," he whispered. "I just can't right now."

"No," Scout uttered, then again, firmer. "No. That's not safe. I'll give you your space. I won't say a word. I'll walk you to your door, then stand outside. But, Emery, be sensible, please-"

"Uber for Emery?" the driver called out of the silver Toyota Prius's open window. Emery nodded at him.

"It's fine," he said stiffly to Scout, reaching to open the door. "You can meet me back there. I just…this is too much."

Anger flared inside Scout. He knew he was panicking. If Emery was so worried about his safety, why the hell was he ditching Scout? It made no sense! He was just saying the same vague crap over and over again.

"Emery, get back here!" Scout barked. If pleading wasn't going to work, perhaps orders would. "That's not good enough. You're not giving me an actual explanation here, and you're being reckless!"

But Emery just gave Scout a pitiful look as he slid into the car's back seat, still clinging to his gym bag and his phone. "Let me know when you're outside the apartment. I promise I won't leave once I get there."

And with that, Emery closed the door of the car. Scout felt like it had been slammed in his face as he watched the Toyota drive off.

What the hell had just happened?

2 0

EMERY

SHIT.

Shit, shit, shit, shit, *SHIT!*

Emery tried to steady both his breathing and his heart rate as he huddled in the back seat of his Uber, but neither was complying.

What the hell had he just done?

What he'd had to.

He glanced at the driver, but he had his eyes on the road. Good. Emery needed a quiet ride right now.

His phone still clutched to his chest, he carefully eased the zipper of his gym bag open so he could see the several photos he'd shoved inside. The ones that had fallen out of his locker just now. The ones that showed all his friends, his parents, and Scout, and had obviously been taken with a long lens around town.

And they all had their eyes scratched out.

Every one.

Mom and Dad. Ava, Robin, Jay. Even their friend Peyton and Robin's boyfriend, Dair.

And then there were the shots of Scout. They were plentiful.

Emery thought his heart might stop altogether as he carefully leafed through the terrible photos. Each one had a message hastily scrawled on the back in black marker. *'How much do you care about them?'* *'We're watching.'* *'Guess who's next?'* *'Fucking homos, all of you.'* *'Oh, yes. We know all about lover boy.'*

That last message was on one of Scout's pictures. Caring, wonderful Scout, who had just tried to comfort Emery, even when he was being completely horrendous to him. But it had been the only way Emery could think of to get away. Distract Scout until the Uber arrived by talking utter shit. He hadn't meant any of it.

He couldn't stop the sob that escaped his throat, but he forced himself to blink back the tears. He had too much to do.

"You all right there?" the driver asked.

Emery nodded stiffly. "Fine, thank you. Just…I'm looking forward to getting home."

Not that he was going to stay there, no matter what he'd told Scout about meeting him. Emery would have to compose some kind of message to explain, but it wasn't safe anymore in Pine Cove.

He hadn't bothered to unpack his overnight bag from Hawaii, so all he had to do was throw a few more bits of clothing in there as well as the spare cash, passport, and laptop from the safe, and he could be back out the door within five minutes. Then he'd find the first ATM he could and empty one of his accounts. Then…

Then he'd rent a car or something and drive out of state. He'd get himself as far away from the people he loved. It was him the stalkers wanted, not them. So he'd run, lure these bastards away from Pine Cove. Keep his friends and family safe until the cops caught whoever was behind all this.

Who knew how long that might take?

He shuddered with fear. He didn't want to be alone. He wanted to shout at his driver to turn around and take him back to Scout's warm arms. But there was no way. Emery cared far too deeply about him, so much it ached like a physical pain in his chest. It was as if the further Emery got away from Scout, the worse it was getting. Like he was missing a limb and hemorrhaging blood.

Emery rubbed his chest as if that would help. God, he wanted to take it all back, all those wobbles. He was in no doubt now. He wanted Scout – no – he *needed* him. How could he have ever thought he'd be able to give him away like he was just another hookup? He wasn't.

He was the best, most authentic thing that had come into Emery's life for years, outside of his dear friendship circle. If Emery got through the shitshow, he was sprinting back to Scout and begging him for his forgiveness.

He might even beg him not to leave.

It was stupid to think Scout would stay in a tiny town like Pine Cove when he led such a jet-setting life. Before going into private security, he'd traveled with his boxing. It was entirely possible that he wasn't the kind of man who would ever want to be tied down.

But hope – even wild hope – was all that was keeping Emery sane right now. He clung to it like he was his bag and his phone, letting it anchor him and stop his thoughts from spinning out of control. He may have been panicking, but he'd heard Scout say he didn't feel like this was just messing around between them. In Emery's desperate state, it had sounded like Scout had even been hinting he might want more.

With everything falling away in his life, Emery allowed

himself just a moment to fantasize about a life of stability with Scout. Even if they were to just try dating. In his mind, Emery envisioned introducing Scout as his boyfriend to the people he loved in those photos he was clutching. It was enough to calm him just a little and clear his mind. He bit his thumbnail, then angrily rubbed another tear away. He could cry later. Now, he had to focus like he was planning the Met Gala.

Like his life depended on it.

These photos were serious, and his friends' lives were now in danger. As selfish as he knew he was, he'd rather die than see a single one harmed because of him. So he needed to vanish, allow the cops time to do their thing and...

Fuck. Emery hadn't even thought. He'd just picked up all the photos with his bare hands. The stalker had probably worn gloves, but still – Emery should have been more careful to preserve any fingerprints. He ground his teeth and tried to think smart. But he was so fucking tired and trembling from fright. He'd had too much caffeine, and his blood sugar was probably low after not eating anything. Where were those protein bars...?

After he'd thrust half of one down his throat, he finally looked out the window. "Um, excuse me," he said as he eyed up the scenery. They were on the wrong side of the lake. "I don't think this is the quickest way?"

The driver shook his head, speaking again with a Pacific Northwest accent, which suggested he could be local. "I'm so sorry, sir. There was an accident on Main Street. I should have said, but you appeared busy."

Emery felt his mouth twitch in half a smile as he met the driver's eyes in the rearview mirror. That was kind of him. "No problem at all. It still shouldn't take all that long from here, should it?"

The driver shook his head and smiled. "We'll have you there in no time, sir."

"Thank you." He'd let the 'sir' go for now. There were other more important things going on, and it wasn't as if he was likely to see the driver again after this.

Emery took a shaky breath and unlocked his phone once more. He posted almost every day to Instagram and managed his own Facebook and Twitter. Even when he had help from his VA, Emery always had the final say on anything he posted. He knew how to wield words like weapons, as a balm, for laughs.

But what the fuck did he say to Scout right now?

I'm so sorry. Please forgive me. I'll do anything.

But anything like that would alert him that Emery might not have meant what he'd said. He'd come after him, follow him, when what he needed to do was stay far away and in safety. No. Emery needed to compose something practical to explain that he was going to get out of town and take care of this himself.

Another hot tear leaked from underneath Emery's eyelashes, fat and fast as it ran down his cheek. God, he *loathed* feeling like this. He wanted to go back to his stone-cold fortress, where it was all glittery and fabulous and no one could touch him. Like Queen Elsa's ice palace.

Except…he'd watched Frozen a thousand times. Elsa couldn't stay alone in her icy exile. In the end, she had to return to the real world and save the people she loved.

Emery swallowed around the lump in his throat. *Scout,* he began to type. Jesus fucking Christ. What the hell was he supposed to say? Angrily, he scrubbed the word clear. Really, he shouldn't say anything yet. He needed to leave it be, no matter how much it hurt, and drop a message to Scout once he was out of Washington. Preferably by carrier pigeon or owl post, so no one could track the GPS on Emery's phone.

He chuckled to himself at the idea of Sonic trundling along to slowly deliver a letter. He couldn't help it. The whole situation was beyond ridiculous, but there was jack all he could do about it. So it was probably a good idea to laugh. Otherwise he would start sobbing again, and that would make things awkward between him and his Uber driver.

Damn. He'd have to ask Ava to take care of Sonic once more. It was too risky to take him out of town. That sobered Emery again.

He shoved his gym bag onto the backseat beside him and cradled his phone with two hands. This hunk of junk was his whole life. He'd become hysterical once because he'd dropped the previous model into some dishwater until Ava had thrust it into a bag of rice and returned it to him a day later, practically good as new.

But right now, it couldn't give Emery what he wanted, which was a way to mend the damage he'd created between him and Scout. Was it even reparable?

Still, Emery kept WhatsApp open, typing Scout's name and then deleting it in a sad little ritual. He hoped that if he kept typing, though, the right words of inspiration would strike. But in his heart of hearts, he had to acknowledge the best thing now was to close his damn phone and not open it again until he'd packed a bag, pulled his cash, and was halfway across the country. That was the safest thing for Scout right now. Emery had to do this alone.

Even if it killed him.

No, no. He couldn't think like that. This was ridiculous! Yes, someone had been over the top in fucking with him, most likely that 'ekleinhater,' but that didn't mean they were serious. As much as he hated to admit it, that was a big problem with his generation of millennials. They were really very good at picking fights from behind the safety of their keyboards, but they did shit all when it came to a face-to-face confrontation.

Emery sniffed and rubbed his nose, still looking at the empty WhatsApp message box he had waiting to send to Scout. There was nothing he could say, but his frazzled brain wasn't giving in. It was as if keeping the line of communication open was the only thing tethering him to Scout and the promises they'd made.

Scout might forgive him once he knew the circumstances. Once he knew Emery didn't mean any of what he'd said. He had to cling on to that idea. Otherwise, he might totally fall apart.

The car began to slow as it approached a street corner. Emery frowned, taking in the man standing on the sidewalk who waved at them. Did he know the driver?

But to Emery's surprise, the car stopped altogether. There wasn't a light or signal holding them there. Instead, the guy who had waved was now calmly and confidently walking up to Emery's Uber. He opened the door and dropped into the vacant seat beside him, Emery's gym bag between them.

Emery tried not to howl in frustration. He had neither the time nor the patience for this. "I'm so sorry," he said, trying to keep his voice steady, "but there must be some mistake. I didn't order a Pool share."

He *never* ordered an Uber Pool. He was sure it was better for the environment, but he couldn't fight every battle, and the times he hailed a cab, he generally used the ride to recharge his batteries. No more so than now.

The guy who had entered the car smiled and laughed. "Oh, don't worry," he said with a chuckle as the door closed. His eyes narrowed, and his smile became lopsided. "Neither did I."

Which was the moment he pulled out the handgun and pointed it directly at Emery.

That thing Swift had said earlier about training the body to react when the brain failed hadn't fully made sense to Emery at the time. But as he stared at the shiny barrel and the black hole of the chamber, his thumb moved of its own volition. Before he, or indeed the gunman, could register it, he'd tapped to drop his location as a pin on a map, sending it to Scout via WhatsApp.

It would only last fifteen minutes, moving with him if necessary, but in another tap, Emery locked his screen, protecting the map and the little blinking pin from anyone else seeing.

Then the gunman lunged forward, grabbed the phone, and sneered as he leveled the weapon at Emery's head.

2 1

SCOUT

SCOUT SHOULD HAVE LISTENED TO HIS MA.

'Find a nice boy,' she'd said with her Irish lilt. 'Get yourself a lad who'll understand you.' 'The drama's never worth it, to be sure.'

Yet here Scout was, standing on the sidewalk by Aspire like an absolute chump, feeling like his heart had been ripped out and he'd been left bleeding all over the damn street.

He ground his teeth and looked from left to right, as if somehow that might give him an answer to the utterly inexplicable behavior he'd just witnessed. There he'd been, about to change his entire life, and Emery had thrown it all back in his face. Scout knew he needed to cut him some slack for being scared…but that wasn't it. He knew that wasn't it. What had happened to turn Emery into such an asshole?

But the thing was…how well did Scout really know him, after all?

It had been just under a week since they'd met at Aquarium. Only Saturday that Emery had discovered the truth of that hookup, then just yesterday, Sunday, that they'd come together and made a pact to try and be together. Even then, that had been laced with 'buts' and 'only if' clauses.

Scout was being blinded by amazing sex. He and Emery didn't really have anything between them. Emery was a spoiled brat, and he was so prickly, even his damn pet had spikes. Scout didn't really want someone like that complicating his life.

So why was he feeling so devastated that Emery had slipped away from him in a stupid Uber?

He rubbed his forehead. This was totally against the rules. He was never meant to let Emery out of his sight, no matter how heartbroken he was. He was a professional. So he needed to get into his car and drive over to Emery's apartment right now before anything really did happen in his absence.

Chances were that nothing bad would happen. But letting Emery go made Scout feel like he was failing at his job, so he needed to make a move and do something before he went crazy.

He was about to turn around and head back into the parking lot to retrieve his car when he realized another vehicle had pulled up to the curb. A guy with copper skin and dark hair looked at his phone, then back up at Scout. "Hey," he said in a friendly tone with just a hint of an accent Scout couldn't place. "Uber for Emmerich?"

Scout blinked in confusion. "No," he said. "Why would you-"

Oh no.

Holy. Fucking. Shit.

Horror rinsed through Scout's entire body like he was under a cold shower. If Emery's Uber was here...

Who the *hell* had he just gotten into a car with?

Scout forgot all dignity and practically tripped over his feet in his haste to get to the new – the *actual* – Uber driver's door. "Wait, wait, are you here for Emery Klein? He just got in a car with someone else."

The driver rolled his eyes. He was about Scout's age, he'd guess. Late twenties or early thirties with a goatee and thick-rimmed glasses. "Some asshole poach my fare?" he drawled, shaking his head. "Typical."

But Scout was in full-alert mode, his system flooded with adrenaline. "No, no," he gasped, yanking his own phone from his pocket, just in case he had a message there. "Emery thought it was his Uber." How, Scout had no idea. This was a dark blue Ford Mustang. He'd gotten into a silver fucking Toyota Prius.

The driver sucked his teeth and ran his hand through his hair. "Well, that's shit," he said with a sigh. "But I guess no harm. I'll cancel the job-"

"No! Hang on!" Scout looked down at his phone, then back at the Uber.

He did indeed have a message from Emery, but it was a little map, showing a location nowhere near Emery's apartment building. What did it mean? Christ, Scout needed to get better at technology one of these days. What was Emery playing at? Had a friend picked him up?

No. No, he would have said. He'd told Scout he was getting an Uber to his apartment, then he'd said he was going to stay in. He'd implied he'd wanted Scout to sit outside all night like any other boring-as-fuck job, but he'd been clear he'd thought he'd been taking an Uber to his home.

Yet here his Uber was.

"Your client," Scout began, not sure how to explain his thought process as he held his phone out to show him the map on the screen. "He's also my client. I'm his security detail, or at least I'm supposed to be. If you're his Uber, who did he get into a car with?"

The Uber driver's eyebrows shot up, and he looked

between Scout and his crappy old phone. "Ah, fuck me, dude. Please, *please,* don't tell me you're protecting this guy from kidnappers?" The guy looked as if he'd been joking, but when Scout's expression told him that was *exactly* what he was supposed to have been doing, he spluttered in shock. "No *way?* Are you serious?"

Humiliation and shame warred within Scout, but they both came a distant second place to the terror that filled his heart. "I'm concerned whoever's car he got into...that they mean him harm. Hang on. Can you just...hang on, okay?"

Scout exited WhatsApp and tried dialing Emery's number. But the call rang out. He was about to ring again when the Uber driver waved his hands.

"Stop, stop," he all but shouted. "You're saying your buddy – your client – is in trouble, and he sent you that pin?"

Scout frowned at him as he listened to the call connect and ring on his end. But it was just going and going. Emery usually had his phone on silent, so it wasn't surprising he wasn't hearing it.

God damn him.

"What do you mean? What's a pin?" Scout asked as he hung up again. His mind was running wild. Was he exaggerating, or was there a real threat unfolding right before his eyes?

The driver clicked his fingers and pointed urgently at Scout's phone. "You said he just sent that, right? After he got into the not-Uber? And that you're his security and you're worried he might have been grabbed or some shit?" Scout nodded and the guy grabbed his hair. "Fuck! I can't believe this is happening. Well, that's a pin. A live location. And he sent it three, no" -he checked his own phone mounted on the dash- "four minutes ago. That means you only have eleven minutes left."

"*What?*"

Dread like he'd never known flooded through Scout. He was usually pretty good at staying on his toes, but this was all way too fast, probably because it wasn't a client he could calmly assess.

Some fuckers had got the man he loved and were taking him god knew where.

There was a small part of Scout's mind that expressed shock that he was admitting he loved Emery. The rest of his brain tore past that – quite frankly – obvious fact and sped right onto the rage that was consuming him. It paused briefly enough to let him gasp and look back at the Uber driver who had, so far, proved more helpful than the police department had been all week.

"What do you mean eleven minutes?"

The driver bit his lip and glanced back at his phone. "Might be ten now. Basically – a pin broadcasts the phone's location for a set time. Then it stops. If you think your friend is in danger, we haven't got long to find him."

Scout shot a glance down the road Emery had taken, then back to the driver practically leaning out of his window, looking up at Scout with raised eyebrows. "We?"

The driver scoffed. "Fucking hell, man. Yeah, 'we.' You have a car literally right here?"

It was in the lot out back. "No," Scout admitted.

The driver grinned and winked. "Then get in, my friend. And throw me that phone." When Scout didn't move, the driver banged the side of his door. "Come ON! The clock is ticking, man! Do you want to find your buddy, or do you want to end up a tragic tale on 60 Minutes?"

Fucking hell, no. Scout was trained for this, and he needed to get his shit together. His judgment was truly clouded, thanks to his heart-wrenching panic over Emery. "Yes, yes, god, yes. Let's drive!"

For a brief second, he considered that they should drive

back to his own rental car and retrieve his firearm locked in the glove compartment. But they were literally talking minutes here. Minutes Scout couldn't waste if he wanted to find Emery again. God only knew how he'd managed to drop that pin location if he'd gotten into a car with…

Well, was it his stalker? The one who had robbed his home and rigged Scout's car to blow? 'ekleinhater'?

What was he going to do now?

He threw himself into the front passenger seat and thrust his phone with the drop pin location at the driver, who grabbed it and nodded at Scout. "I'm Kamran. I'm good at driving."

"I'm Scout. How good at driving?"

Kamran wagged his finger with one hand as he yanked his own phone from the holder that was attached to the windscreen with a suction cup, chucking it on the back seat as he jammed Scout's phone into the cradle without pause.

"Scout, Uber is my part-time job." Kamran threw the Ford into reverse, then swung the car around before kicking it back into drive and slamming his foot on the accelerator. Scout almost gripped the seat in shock. "You know all those film and TV shoots that come through here?" He shot down the road, narrowly avoiding two hatchbacks and a delivery truck. "Well, I drive stunts for them. So do you really think your friend might be in danger?"

They bolted down the road, the wheels almost skimming off the asphalt. Scout gritted his teeth, looking at the little blinking pin that was still slowly moving, showing Emery's location. His adrenaline was through the roof, making it hard to think straight. But Scout had years of training to fall back on. So he took a breath and nodded.

"Yes. Serious danger."

Somehow, Kamran made the slightly old Mustang go that little bit faster. He nodded and glanced at Scout with a somber expression. "Then let's get you there in time, okay, cowboy?"

Scout nodded grimly.

He could beat himself up for letting Emery out of his sight. He could get deranged, imagining all the things that might be happening to him right now because Scout had fucked up.

Or he could trust that because Emery's signal was still moving, there was still a chance he was okay. Which meant Scout still had a chance to reach him before anything reprehensible happened to him.

He didn't need to say anything. He just looked toward Kamran, and that was apparently enough to encourage him to blow through a red light. It wasn't like there was anything coming the other way.

"This is fucking awesome," Kamran muttered with a grin. Then he glanced over at Scout and raised his eyebrows with a contrite look. "So long as we find your buddy in time, I mean."

"We will," Scout growled.

He had to believe that.

Because he didn't know what he was going to do with himself otherwise.

EMERY

In HINDSIGHT, EMERY WISHED HE AND SWIFT HAD GONE OVER how to escape from a locked, speeding vehicle. Or what to do when someone shoved a gun in your face. Because that sure would have come in useful right about now.

Emery was backed up against the car door, his fingers gripping into the material of the seat as his eyes frantically darted between the gunman and the driver.

Now he was paying acute attention to them both, Emery thought perhaps they looked kind of similar. They both had strawberry-blond hair in buzz cuts, square jaws and narrow, mean eyes. Although the gunman appeared to be taller and had blue eyes, whereas Emery was sure the driver had brown, he guessed they had to be related. Brothers or cousins, he was sure.

They were both smirking at Emery and each other, clearly very pleased with themselves. Emery, on the other hand, was amazed he hadn't peed his pants. He was so terrified.

"Where are you taking me?" he croaked.

By now he'd realized this was not, in fact, his Uber. How

could he have been so careless? He *always* checked the license plate. If he was being kind to himself, he might admit he had been deeply distressed and suffering from low blood sugar. But in that moment, all he could feel was rage and fear that he hadn't even checked the color of the car's paint job.

The brothers chuckled maliciously. "You'll see," said the gunman. "It's been fun tormenting you and all, but you're a tricky one to pin down, homo. Time to end this."

End this. How? Emery did his best to push down the wave of nausea that rolled over him. He had to focus, and he couldn't do that if he was paralyzed by fear.

"So. I'm guessing you're the ones behind all those 'ekleinhater' accounts." Emery licked his lips, stalling for time. It had never occurred to him that it could be more than one person targeting him from the same handle. "What do you want? Money?"

They both scoffed, and the gunman curled his lip. They were driving along one of the winding roads through the woods, heading out of town. Emery hadn't seen another car for five whole minutes.

"So fucking typical," the gunman sneered. "Yeah, part of what we want is money. Lord knows you don't deserve all you have, prancing around in your goddamned underwear like a fucking pervert." The loathing rolling off him as he spoke was disturbing. There was no question that these guys detested Emery for what he was.

The question was, what were they going to do about it?

"F-fine," Emery stammered. "I can give you money. Just take me to an ATM."

More laughing. "And give you a chance to run off or shout the house down?" the driver said.

"No chance." The gunman shook his head. "That's not how this is going to work. Just accept that you have no control here, faggot."

Emery winced at the slur and felt himself break into a sweat. It was grossly perverse and somewhat ironic that these guys were unwittingly using the very thing against Emery that he usually employed to calm down. Relinquishing control like he had only this morning with Scout usually made him feel safe and turned on. Now, he couldn't imagine anything more terrifying.

"Look, I don't know what I ever did to you, but-"

"What you did?" the gunman shouted, waving his weapon around and making Emery recoil in terror. "You were fucking born, that's what! Then you go around tricking hard-working Americans into throwing cash at you like some two-bit hooker. It's disgusting!"

The driver shook his head and mumbled in agreement.

"Why should you get all the free trips and free apartments and shit?" the gunman continued.

"Apartment? I paid for-!" Emery began, but he stopped when the gun was pointed back at his face.

"Don't fucking lie to us, okay?" the gunman growled. "We lost sponsors to your queer Chink ass channel. Viewers complained and got us shut down, just for having the balls to tell the truth. No one wants your gay agenda! It's because of people like you this country is going down the toilet!"

Emery swallowed. *Shit.* These guys were clearly psycho and had decided that Emery was the root of all their problems. They must be vloggers too – or at least, they had been, once. It sounded like they weren't anymore, and that was somehow Emery's fault.

Emery's instinct was to rage at them and lash out by mocking and insulting them to get some power back. But the reality was that harsh words were no match for a firearm.

"I'm so sorry if I inadvertently hurt you," he began slowly, "but I don't know you. Please. I'll do what I can to help make this right."

The gunman sneered, the forest speeding past through the window behind his head. They were going pretty damn far out of town. *Fuck, fuck, fuck.* No one was going to hear Emery screaming, that was for sure.

Come on, Scout, he begged silently, praying he'd seen the pin and was on his way in his car right now. Emery wanted to see his face so badly he could sob.

The brothers shared a scornful look. "He doesn't even fucking recognize us, does he?" the driver said disdainfully.

"Nope," the gunman agreed, popping the 'p' sound and tilting his head. "What a self-absorbed prick, I swear to god."

Emery waved his hands. "N-no," he stammered. "It's nothing personal. I have a terrible memory for faces-"

He was cut off as the gunman smacked him across the face with the cold barrel of the gun. Emery's lip split and hot blood gushed into his mouth and down his chin. He cried out and instinctively slapped his hand over his mouth to try and protect it from more harm.

The gunman scoffed. "You just expect everyone to remember your face because you're so fucking pretty, right? Goddamned fairy. Let's see how pretty you are when I'm done with you. You really don't remember at all? Dinner in Honolulu? A romantic table for two? Ring any bells?"

Emery blinked as a memory resurfaced. "The waiter. You – you were our waiter?" The asshole one who had made Emery feel like shit – not that he was going to say that out loud and aggravate him any further. *Holy shit!* No wonder he hadn't seemed like any of the other lovely members of staff.

The gunman shook his head. "And *you* didn't eat your damn meal, too busy tap-tap-tapping away on your fucking phone. You're what's wrong with this generation. Never spent an hour outdoors like a real man."

"What did you do to the food?" Emery asked, horrified.

The gunman chuckled. "Just sprinkled a little something

on there to make you groggy. We tried to grab you then, but your fuck buddy kept getting in the way."

"He found our present under his car too quickly, too," the driver added bitterly. "All that effort. Who knew all it took to finally get him away from you were a few photos?"

"Hang on," Emery said, staring at the reflection in the rearview mirror. "You were the angry manager from the camping shop who was there after the explosion! It was *you* who put that bomb there, wasn't it?"

The gunman rolled his eyes in disgust. "And I thought Asians were supposed to be smart. Jesus Christ. I'm embarrassed it's taken us this long to get our hands on a dumb fuck like you."

The driver shook his head. "We weren't set up properly before, though. It's better this way."

The gunman nodded sagely as Emery looked between them. "S-set up? With what? What are you going to do to me?"

Their combined chuckle was the darkest one yet.

"Oh," said the gunman. "You'll find out soon enough. The thing is, we were thinking too small, just trying to get something to blackmail you with or trying to beat the shit out of you until you paid up. But then it hit me. You're going to give us *all* of your money. Willingly."

The driver hummed gleefully. Emery wiped the perspiration from his forehead. He was struggling not to throw up for the hundredth time since he'd had a gun shoved in his face.

"I said I'd pay you," he told them in a small voice, jumping out of his skin as they ran over a pothole. They were definitely getting off the beaten track now. "There's no problem here. No one has to get hurt."

The gunman gave him a withering look with his watery

blue eyes. "You're not going to get out of it that easily, you little fucker."

Emery wanted to beg. *Please don't hurt me. Please don't kill me.* But as desperate as he was, he wasn't going to give them that satisfaction.

How much further did they have to go? How much longer did Emery have on his pin location? There was no way of knowing either of those things, but Emery pleaded to the universe all the same.

Find me, Scout. I need you. Please.

He may have held his tongue, but he couldn't seem to stop the twin tears that escaped from under his eyelashes and rolled down his face. He gritted his teeth and cursed silently. The last thing he wanted to do was appear vulnerable in front of these monsters.

Sure enough, the gunman sneered. "Now, now. None of that. We've got to have you looking pretty for the camera, haven't we?"

Emery sniffed and rubbed the tears, sweat and blood from his face. "Camera?" he repeated in confusion.

The brothers looked the most smug they had the whole drive. They were so deep in the forest now Emery would be lucky to have signal on his phone at all. Would his pin keep broadcasting?

"Surely you love any chance to get in front of a lens, you whore," the gunman jeered. "It's all you're good for, after all."

"So we're going to put your so-called skills to good use for once," the driver chipped in.

Dread filled Emery, and he gripped harder on to the car's upholstery. He honestly had no clue what these guys had in mind, but whatever it was, it probably wasn't going to be good.

And Emery was going to have to face it all on his own.

23

SCOUT

"How many minutes left?"

Kamran grimaced, his hands wrapped tightly around the steering wheel. "Three."

Scout let out a string of profanities that would have earned him several Hail Marys as a child. Emery's car was still moving, and there was no sign of him anywhere on this twisting woodlands road.

To be fair, Kamran hadn't been joking. He certainly knew how to handle himself, and they'd made incredible time catching up to Emery. But the clock was ticking, and unless they reached him before the signal dropped out, it would all be for nothing.

Dusk was creeping in, and the dense tree line wasn't letting much of the setting sunlight through. Scout squinted through the gloom for any hint of flashing headlights, but there was nothing. He chewed his thumbnail and resisted the urge to ask Kamran to go faster.

Scout didn't care that he was probably going to get fired regardless of what happened now. He had let his emotions get the better of him by allowing Emery to get into a stranger's car unaccompanied. He deserved to lose his job.

But he'd never be able to live with himself if any harm came to Emery. He'd gladly hand in his notice to Christopher on the spot so long as he could get Emery safe and back in his arms. There was still time. He couldn't give up hope.

Not much time, though.

Kamran gritted his teeth and glanced at Scout's phone. "One minute," he growled, putting his foot down. Ordinarily, Scout would have reprimanded him for dangerous driving. But all he did now was pray no one met them coming the other way and no wildlife chose this moment to cross their path.

"Come on, come on," Scout muttered under his breath, glaring at the tiny blue dot on the screen. "Stop fucking moving. *Stop.*"

It did stop.

By vanishing altogether.

"God fucking *damn it!*" he roared in horror and frustration.

Kamran smacked his thigh. "Can it and let me drive. The quicker we get to the last location it was broadcasting, the quicker you can get out of the car and try looking and listening manually. Don't bail on me now, cowboy."

Begrudgingly, Scout nodded, knowing Kamran was right. He felt eternally grateful that out of all the Uber drivers who could have been nearby, it was him who had shown up. "Thanks," he grunted.

Kamran snorted. "Thank me when you find your man." He arched an eyebrow at Scout's expression. "What, you didn't think I'd actually believe he was just your client, did you?"

Scout crossed his arms and grumbled. "He *is* my client... as well..."

Kamran grinned. "Yeah, yeah. I bet all your clients will jump into your arms and – *shit* – here we go!"

He screeched the Mustang to a halt on the deserted road. Scout was opening the door before Kamran had even fully applied the brakes. Scout jumped out onto the asphalt as Kamran killed the engine. Scout strained as hard as he could, but all he could hear was the rustling of trees and the start of the evening chorus of wildlife chirping.

No, no, no. They'd been so close!

"Hey, look here." Kamran held up Scout's phone as Scout looked back into the car. Kamran had opened up the maps app, and there was now another blue dot representing where they were. "This road goes on for another mile before we hit a fork. Shall we at least try driving until then and see if we can't find something?"

Gratitude washed over Scout. "Thank you for this," he said as he dropped back into the passenger seat.

Kamran fired up the engine and shook his head. "I can't believe I'm doing this off the clock. This fella of yours better be rich."

"He is, actually," Scout said weakly.

Kamran beamed and threw the Mustang into drive. "Oh, goodie."

They rocketed along the road once more, but Scout had to admit he wasn't all that hopeful they would find a sign of which way to go before they reached the fork. Kamran must have been thinking something similar, as he bit his lip and threw a serious look at Scout.

"If we reach the fork and there's still nothing, let's call the cops. They might be able to track your friend's phone via satellite."

"Really?" Scout said "How – *stop!*"

Kamran slammed the breaks without hesitation, once more killing the engine as Scout jumped out onto the road.

On the map it may have shown there weren't any turn-offs until the big fork half a mile away still. But on their right, there was clearly a dirt track with two grooves in the ground, indicating many vehicles had driven down it.

Scout's heart was racing, but he did his best to strain his ears over it and the sounds of nature around him. The dirt track curved away into the gloomy tree line, so Scout couldn't see anything useful.

But then he heard it.

He gasped as a faint cry rang through the air.

"Emery!" His reply hadn't even been a shout. However, what he'd just heard sounded like someone screaming their lungs out from pretty far away.

But now Scout had a direction to run in.

"Fuck!" Kamran yelled as he started the ignition once more. "Come on, let's go!"

But Scout shook his head. "They might hear us coming. I'll go on foot. You call the cops and get some reinforcements here. Pass me my phone, and I'll head that way."

Kamran was already thrusting Scout's cell into his hands. "I got this, cowboy. Now run! And don't let that asshole give you any shit! The douche driving the car – not the boyfriend – oh, you know what, just fucking run!"

Scout didn't need telling again. He resisted the urge to say thank you once more. Instead, he nodded, then broke into a desperate sprint. It would have been nice if he hadn't been on a treadmill for the past hour, but this was no time to whine about it. His legs knew what they had to do because there was no alternative.

Every second wasted was another second Emery was in danger.

God fucking damn it, what Scout wouldn't give to have his gun right now. He prayed that the cops arrived soon with theirs. Really, they should have called them sooner, but they hadn't had a location to send them to. Scout just had to hope he wasn't walking into a complete ambush.

He hadn't had much experience of this particular line of protection. He wasn't ex-military or police like a lot of Christopher's guys were. Scout knew how to check an area was secure and how to put down an aggressor quick and easy. But charging into a kidnapping situation like he was Rambo or some shit – that was out of his wheelhouse.

But he'd had basic training, and there was no other option. He was on his own here. So he continued running down the dirt track, sticking to the increasingly shadowy tree line for cover.

He hadn't heard anything since the far-away cry, and he thanked god they had arrived at the dirt track at just the right time. It wasn't often Scout considered himself lucky, but right then, he had to be grateful for that stroke of fate.

"Hold on, Emery," he muttered to himself. His legs threatened to tremble as he pounded across the ground. "I'm coming. Just hang in there."

He rounded another bend, and all of a sudden, a small log cabin came into view. Scout skidded to a halt and threw himself behind a tree, breathing heavily. There had been lights on inside the cabin.

Carefully, he peeked out from behind the trunk and surveyed the scene. He couldn't see anyone outside the building, but he did spy the car parked out front.

A silver Toyota Prius.

"Got you, you sick fuck," he snarled.

Treading lightly, he began to make his way closer toward the cabin, using the trees for cover. Mercifully, the foliage ran all the way up the track and surrounded the back of the property as well. There was every chance he could make it up to the building undetected.

Then a thought occurred to him.

What if he was wrong?

What if Emery had ditched Scout for another hookup? It didn't seem likely after all the threats he'd endured, and it didn't make sense for him to then send his live location to Scout. But what if he wanted Scout to catch him making out with another guy? Or what if he was going to a secret hookup, but he'd sent the pin by accident?

As unlikely as that seemed, Scout couldn't entirely shake the thought away. He had to be prepared for anything.

As he neared the log cabin, his heart beat faster, and his hand itched for the gun he'd left back in the rental car's glove compartment. Whoever was inside the cabin hadn't bothered pulling any blinds or curtains – it wasn't fully night yet, after all. They probably thought they were safe all the way out here in the middle of nowhere.

The result was that as Scout got closer, he started to see shapes silhouetted from the light source within. It was pretty damn bright just for regular lamps. He frowned but, so far, couldn't make out anything all that unusual. Just someone's living room. Quite possibly someone over eighty, from the glimpses of floral and chintz he was getting.

He approached the side of the house, but there still didn't seem to be anyone walking patrol. Whoever this guy was, Scout was guessing they were civilian. Good. In theory, the odds were that whoever it was wouldn't be a match for Scout if he could just get up close.

The front door was a bad idea. He needed to sneak in if at all possible, and to go in the front, he'd have to run up the steps and cross the front porch. So he headed out back, soon finding a bathroom with its lights turned off. Perfect. Scout could peer into the lit-up living room and see inside while still remaining mostly in the shadows. He could only see a slice of the living room, but luck was on his side again.

Sort of.

He restrained a gasp as he saw Emery pushed into his line of sight. Jesus. Scout almost wished he *had* walked in on another hookup. Emery had blood on his face, and he'd clearly been crying. Scout's heart felt like it physically broke in two.

But he had less than a second to dwell on it because the bathroom light suddenly switched on. Without hesitating, Scout dropped to his knees to avoid being seen.

Because there wasn't just another man behind Emery as he stumbled inside the bathroom. There were two. "Come on, you little fucker," one of them growled, his voice muffled through the closed window. "Hurry up and wash that sorry face of yours."

Scout didn't understand why they would be shouting at him to get the blood off his face, but he didn't care. Because just as he'd dropped out of sight, he'd seen the taller guy right behind Emery clearly, if only for a split second.

He'd also seen the gun he was pointing directly at Emery's head.

And there Scout was with nothing but his fists to fight with.

He clenched them. They would have to do. Because Emery had looked terrified, and he was counting on Scout to save him. There was no way in hell that Scout was going to let him down. Not after getting this far.

He just needed a plan.

24

EMERY

Emery had tried. He really had. The moment they'd exited the car, he'd bellowed *"GET OFF ME!"* at the top of his lungs and shoved the gunman in the split second of confusion that had caused.

But there were two of them against just one of Emery. And even though the gunman was taller than the driver, they were both still bigger than Emery. So as he'd pushed the gunman and spun to try and make a dash for it like Swift had taught him, the driver had leaned from the car and delivered a sucker punch right into Emery's gut.

He'd gone down like a sack of potatoes.

"Who the fuck do you think is going to hear you out here, pretty boy?" the gunman had snarled, grabbing Emery by the scruff of his neck and hauling him back to his feet. "Grandma was a prepper, god rest her soul. She went entire months without seeing another living being."

"Unless you counted the critters she shot and ate," the driver had added with a dark chuckle.

Emery hadn't protested any more as they'd shoved him up the porch steps and inside the front door of the old, creaky log cabin. Twilight was falling fast around them, and as the light faded, so did Emery's hopes that he'd get out of this mess unscathed.

They entered directly into a living room that had clearly belonged to an old woman, judging by the décor. There were floral patterns on the furniture and doilies under all the china knick-knacks littering the many dark wood coffee tables and bureaus. Multiple photos hung on the wall. At a glance, they looked to be the two strawberry-blond brothers from when they were growing up. There were also numerous heads of dead animals proudly mounted, an ancient-looking confederate flag preserved in a frame, and three different antique shotguns. Normally, Emery abhorred guns, but in that moment, he wondered desperately if any of the weapons were loaded.

Not that he'd know what to do with any of them if they were.

As he was marched through the living room, he realized that all the furniture had been pushed to the side and one of the walls stripped of any paraphernalia. Pointing at the blank wall was a phone on a tripod, and behind that was a circular LED light on another tripod with an aluminum foil reflector board propped against it. These guys had some vague idea of how to make a video at least, but it didn't fill Emery with any kind of confidence. Instead, he eyed the chair positioned in front of the phone and the coil of rope placed on the seat.

He licked his dry lips and tried to swallow around the lump of fear in his throat. "So, you want me to do a makeup tutorial?"

The gunman shoved him toward the bathroom behind the tripods, flicking on the light. It might have been Emery's imagination, but he could have sworn he saw something move beyond the window. It was probably just deranged hope making him wish for a savior, seeing faces where there were only trees.

"Come on, you little fucker," the gunman snarled, still waving his handgun around. "Hurry up and wash that sorry face of yours."

Emery wished he had the guts to quip something like 'Without moisturizer, I don't think so!' But he was ashamed to admit he didn't want to be hit again. Instead, he clenched his jaw and turned on the faucet with a trembling hand. He watched as the water spluttered, coming out a rusty brown color for a few seconds, then running clear enough he felt able to touch it without fear of contracting a disease.

He'd barely rubbed the drying blood from his face when the driver lunged forward and slammed the faucet off again. The gunman thrust a crusty towel into Emery's face. He only just caught it before he was being frog-marched back out into the living room.

"Sit," the gunman barked, digging the barrel of his gun into Emery's lower back and snatching the rope from the chair. How trigger happy was this guy? Emery's imagination ran wild as he pictured the gun accidentally going off and blasting a hole through him.

He managed to dry his face as he sat down on the chair in front of the phone before the towel was unceremoniously ripped from his grasp. "Enough," snapped the gunman. "That'll do."

He then busied himself behind the phone tripod, the gun always pointed at Emery. The driver took the rope from his brother and began to tie Emery's wrists to the arms of the chair.

He couldn't stop himself from quaking in fear. *Oh, god.* He was going to die. These guys weren't going to let him go free after they'd done this to him. He'd seen their faces!

How was this happening? Emery's life was ridiculous, but

he'd never in a million years thought this was where he'd end up.

No victims of crime probably did, though, did they?

He wanted to be brave. He wanted to spit and scream and lash out. But all he could do as the rope got tighter was grit his teeth as hot tears slid down his face. He might not be so bitterly angry if these assholes hadn't forced his hand and made the last words he'd said to Scout ones of hate. He couldn't bear the thought that if he had to go, Scout would think he didn't adore him.

Love him, maybe.

The driver picked the towel off the dusty wooden floorboards and roughly wiped Emery's teary face. "Stop it," he grunted. Then he threw the towel back down and stood up, retrieving several sheets of brown cardboard from atop one of the dressers that had been pushed to the side of the room. On them were large words written in the same chicken scratch that Emery recognized from the backs of the photos they'd sent him.

They were cue cards.

The gunman narrowed his eyes at the screen before turning to flick the bathroom light back off. Then he propped the reflector board on another chair and angled it toward Emery. That seemed to satisfy him that the shot was now right.

"Okay, fairy boy. You're gonna read the cards *exactly* as they are. We'll do it until I'm happy you've done it right."

"Sound sad," the driver said with a malicious grin as he held up the first card for Emery to read from. "You're remorseful."

"For what?" Emery bit out.

"For a life of fucking sin," the gunman snarled. He didn't seem as concerned at pointing the gun Emery's way now he was tied up. In fact, he placed it on the bureau next to him so he could use both hands to adjust the tripod fractionally.

Emery quashed the small thrill of hope that gave him. Just because the gunman had put his weapon down didn't make him any less in danger.

"What happens after you're happy with the take?" Emery asked through clenched teeth.

"Depends on how well you read the cards, whore," the gunman shot back, and the brothers chuckled.

What the hell was going on? If these guys wanted money, why were they making Emery record a video? He shifted anxiously in his seat.

"Stop moving," said the gunman. "It's a tight closeup. So quit with the wriggling and start fucking reading."

"Look sadder," the driver barked. "Unless you want another gut punch."

Emery took a few breaths and tried to relax his face. It wasn't difficult to look upset with everything whirling through his mind.

"I can't do this anymore," he began to recite. "I'm a fraud. I – are you fucking *serious?*"

The gunman picked up his firearm again and pointed it at Emery's head. "I can edit this, but we need clean takes of all the words. It's not our fault you're a queer fucking pervert. *Get on with it.*"

Emery winced. It took him a moment to tear his gaze away from the gun barrel and focus on the phone lens again. He opened his mouth but froze once more. Was that…had something moved in the bathroom? He didn't hear anything in the silence, and he didn't dare look, so he blinked and glanced at the cue card. It was probably just wishful thinking again.

"I have lived a life of sin, mocking god and the good

people of America. I have tricked you into giving me thousands of your hard-earned dollars. There-"

Tears threatened to spill again as the driver revealed the next cue card. Oh no. *No, no, no.* So this was their cunning plan to get his money.

The gunman jerked the firearm and arched his eyebrows. Trembling, Emery didn't see he had any choice but to continue.

"There is no Over The Rainbow Foundation. I lied about sending kids to college and taking them off the streets. That money was mine, and I spent it all. But it's gone now, and the guilt is killing me. I beg your forgiveness. At least now..." Oh...*shit.*

At least now I won't hurt anyone else. I'll be at peace, and only god can judge me.

It was a fucking suicide note.

They didn't want to just rob him. They want to ruin him. Tarnish everything he'd built. Rip away the beacon of hope he'd offered to all those people who had written to him and countless others who hadn't but felt the same. If these assholes made people believe he was a fraud, an embezzler, how many other lives would they ruin? All those kids who got through the day because Emery told them tomorrow would be better. What about the scholarships he'd set up? Would those kids be kicked out of school?

Normally he tried to downplay his importance and let self-doubt eat away at him. But in that moment, it became crystal clear to him. If Emery did what they wanted, who knew how many other lives they would hurt? How much would it set back LGBT activism if his foundation went down in a scandal? How much fuel would his disgrace give to bigots who hated him and his community?

He couldn't let that happen.

"No," he snarled, tugging so hard against the ropes his

skin started to bleed. But he thrashed again, kicking his legs. "No – I won't do this!"

"You should have tied his legs!" the gunman moaned at his brother. "Sort it out! And you! Shut up!"

But something insane had taken over Emery. He struggled and rocked the chair, kicking and thrashing like he'd been possessed by the devil himself. "Kill me!" he shrieked. "Kill me and take my money, you fucking cowards! But you won't destroy my legacy! I've made this world a better place, and I won't let you shitheads change that!"

The driver tried to get near him, but Emery kicked and screamed. The chair legs scraped and banged on the floorboards. The driver hadn't thought to cut the rope when he'd tied Emery's wrists with it, so he was trying to grab the end to tie it around his ankles but Emery was flailing it about too much.

"Pack it in!" the gunman roared.

"Get off me! Let me go, you assholes!" Emery screamed back, deranged with fury. He knew there was still a gun being pointed at him, but he wasn't going to get shot until these guys got their video. Besides, the driver kept getting in the way as he dove for Emery's thrashing legs.

Emery would rather die than betray the thousands of people he had helped over the years. He wasn't going to say he'd embezzled money. The only thing he had to leave on this earth was his reputation. He wasn't going to call himself a sinner or a dirty queer. He wasn't going to give these bastards one penny.

They were just bullies, and Emery had been standing up to those his whole life.

"Fuck you!" he howled as the driver finally tackled Emery and shoved his chair against the wall to give him less room to flail.

As he did, Emery banged his head, stars exploding in front of his vision.

He almost missed what happened next.

From the shadows of the bathroom, a figure came hurtling out. Emery must have been concussed because there was no way this could be real.

Delusional or not, he couldn't stop the words that screamed from his raw throat.

"Scout! He has a gun!"

But it didn't make any difference.

SCOUT

The sound of the three people talking inside the cabin became muffled as they moved back into the living room, partially closing the bathroom door behind them. Although 'talking' wasn't really the word. It was more snarling and yelling.

Scout clenched his fists and weighed his options. Risk running in there and getting them all killed, or waiting for the cops to arrive and let them handle it? Except, how did he know the kidnappers wouldn't hurt Emery more before the blues and twos showed up? This wasn't Chicago. Who knew how long a small force like Pine Cove's would take to mount a rescue.

Scout needed a weapon. It didn't matter that he could use his fists when one of those guys had a gun. They both might, for all Scout knew.

He crept away from the cabin and began scouring the forest floor, looking for anything he could use. A large rock or a sturdy branch. It wasn't long before he found a fallen log, not so big he couldn't wield it easily enough, but heavy enough that it had some clout.

Scout gave it a few practice swings, testing the weight. Yep, that would do. It would have to.

As quickly and quietly as his bulk would allow, he slipped back through the trees toward the bathroom. The light had been turned off. Scout peeked through the edge of the window again. The door had once more swung partially closed. Its hinges must not have been properly aligned if it kept doing that by itself. Well, it made Scout's chances better for not getting seen, so he was grateful.

His lucky streak continued, though, when he saw that the thugs in the living room had their backs to him. But the tall one was still waving his gun around, and Emery wasn't in his line of sight. It kind of looked like the two guys were fiddling with some equipment. Scout wasn't sure what they were getting up to, but it needed to end. Now.

He placed the log on the ground and prayed his luck would give him one last win. Unbelievably, it did. As he pressed his palms against the glass and carefully pushed up, the window juddered and creaked, but it budged. It wasn't locked. However, it was stiff.

"Come on, come on," Scout muttered, gently easing the old wooden frame up millimeter by millimeter. Grubby white paint flecked off, sticking to Scout's damp skin.

Around him, dusk had fallen into night, and the wildlife was just as noisy as before, the steady chorus of chirps masking the sound of the groaning wood. At least, that was what Scout hoped. It might not have mattered, however, as through the glass he could detect more yelling. He was pretty sure he could hear Emery giving as good as he was getting, even if Scout couldn't make out the exact words.

Scout prayed he was being careful. As proud as he was that Emery wasn't rolling over without a fight, Scout knew how infuriating his sass and attitude could be, and that was coming from someone who cared deeply for him. Would he push someone with a gun just as hard, or did he save his teasing for the people he also cared about?

Scout was about to find out.

With a sudden lurch, the window jumped up a few inches, opening a small gap. Scout froze, but the taller man was shouting again, so it didn't seem like he'd been heard.

"…we need clean takes of all the words. It's not our fault you're a queer fucking pervert. *Get on with it.*"

Jesus, Mary and Joseph. He was pointing the gun with purpose now, not just wildly waving it about. He had to be aiming it at Emery's head.

Scout tried the window again despite the moment of quiet from the living room. Now it had broken free from the bottom of the frame, it slid upward nice and easy. Even when it was fully open, though, the gap wasn't all that big. Scout would just have to try and fit through. It was that or the front door. He didn't have the time to go around the cabin and look for any more unlocked windows.

First, he carefully picked up his log and reached his arm into the bathroom, carefully resting it against the sink. He could hear Emery talking now, saying something about money and kids. Then…

"…I beg your forgiveness. At least now…"

Emery's voice choked off, causing Scout to pause just as he had been about to haul himself through the window frame.

Emery started screaming.

"No! No – I won't do this!"

Scout's heart almost stopped in terror. It took everything he had not to yell out himself. The thugs started bellowing back, and the sounds of some kind of furniture clattering filled the house. Scout was never going to get a better chance. He heaved his body inside the cabin, only just squeezing through, then tumbling awkwardly into the bathtub.

With them all yelling, the words were all a jumble as Scout scrambled out of the tub and snatched up his log. But Emery was screaming his head off and sobbing as Scout cautiously approached the half-closed bathroom door. As he peeked out from the dark room into the living area, he saw the shorter guy shove Emery – who was tied to a chair – up against a wall, cutting off his tirade as he smacked his head against the wood.

Red mist descended over Scout's vision.

The taller guy still had his gun, but he was closest to Scout, and both of the thugs had their backs to Scout.

So he charged.

As he raised the log, Emery screamed, wide-eyed with terror, *"Scout! He has a gun!"*

Not anymore.

Scout smacked the taller guy cleanly on the side of his head, sending him spinning and the gun sailing through the air, clattering onto the floor. The shorter guy snapped around just in time for Scout to arc the log back around and smash him in the face too. He rebounded off the wall and crumpled to the floor. Not moving, but he looked like he was still breathing.

"Scout!" Emery yelled. "Look out!"

The taller thug was still conscious and scrambling back up to his feet. Emery yanked against the rope holding him in the chair, his wrists raw and bloody. Rage filled Scout as he flung the log to the floorboards and barreled over to the thug, fists raised.

He managed to land a couple of punches to the ribs, but for all the guy lacked in skill, he made up for in scrappiness. He was obviously used to brawling and employed a few tricks to leverage his body weight and twist free of Scout's grasp, landing a few hits of his own. It was dirty fighting. They crashed into the furniture, dislodging china ornaments and sending them smashing to the ground. Picture frames shook as Scout threw the thug against the wall with a primal roar.

The thug wasn't giving in, though. He shoved himself back off the wooden wall with a snarl. "Why didn't you just blow up like a good little goon?" he taunted, wiping blood from his mouth. "You're a man, for fuck's sake! You're not like this sissy! What the hell is wrong with you?"

"Says the psychotic kidnapper?" Scout said incredulously, taking another swing.

The thug might have been scrappy, but he wasn't trained. Scout fooled him with a feint, then landed a punch square across his jaw, force exploding through his arm. The thug stumbled backward into the tripods, sending both the camera and the circular light flying. He got tangled up in the legs as he and the equipment tumbled to the ground.

But Scout had made a critical error.

The thug was now considerably closer to where the gun had fallen.

He thrust the tripods off himself and tried to crawl for the weapon, but Scout bellowed and lunged for him, dragging him back by his hips. The thug gave a nasty kick that connected with Scout's thigh, forcing him to release his grip for a second. The thug used the chance to turn onto his back and smash his fist into Scout's nose.

Pain exploded in his face as stars filled his vision, and blood spurted down into his mouth. By the time he'd shaken himself and wiped his face, the thug was crawling out from under him, his fingers reaching for the gun.

Emery was screaming, but Scout's ears were ringing from the blow, and adrenaline was making the blood rush too loudly for him to pick out what he was saying. But if he was screaming, that meant he was still alive, and right now, that was all Scout cared about until he put this bastard down.

How *dare* he hurt Emery. What the hell was this sick set-up with the camera? What had they done to Emery in the car ride over here? After all the emotional torment he'd put Emery through – from the disgusting messages, the break-in, the car bomb, and all the rest – Scout had had enough.

It ended now.

The thug touched the handle of the gun, pulling it to him. Scout smacked his arm away as he swung around, the deafening bang of the trigger being pulled tearing through the air. Emery stopped yelling, probably in shock. Scout's ears were ringing again.

But he was used to recovering quickly from all his years in boxing. Luckily, it looked like the bullet had only blown a hole in the wall and not any people. So Scout was already lunging for the thug, grabbing the arm holding the gun with both hands and slamming it against the floor, forcing him to release his grip. The thug snarled as the gun dropped from his grasp, trying to scramble from underneath Scout. But Scout shoved him down before pushing the gun away, sending it skittering under one of the bureaus.

The thug scratched at Scout's cheeks and chest, but Scout straddled him and punched his face. Then he punched again.

And again.

He didn't know who this man was, but it didn't matter. To Scout, he'd become faceless, just another bully. He was the jock who picked on the nerds at high school. He was the sexual predator lurking in a back alley. He was the husband who beat his wife and kid while the rest of the world thought he was a charming motherfucker.

He was the man who had tried to hurt the person Scout had come to care about more than pretty much anyone else in his life.

He punched him again, his face becoming bloodier.

But then something pierced through his fury. A voice was

calling to him. Scout stilled his hands, his breaths heavy and his body trembling.

"Scout!" Emery yelled. "Don't kill him! He's not worth it! Stop! Come back to me!"

Scout blinked, looking down at his knuckles, red from not just the thug's blood but his own as well. He took a shaky breath, then another one.

"Yes, Scout!" Emery sobbed. "You've won! Don't do anything stupid. Listen! The cops are coming!"

Scout grunted and shook his head. Sure enough, those were sirens he could hear wailing in the distance. God bless Kamran. He'd called the cavalry.

His senses were slowly coming back to him. The thug was groggy underneath him, but he looked to be mostly out of it. Still, Scout wasn't taking any chances. He staggered to his feet and lurched for the rope binding Emery. He had tears running down his face as he watched Scout begin to untie him. There was nothing Scout wanted more than to hold him, but he just had one last job to do.

Once Emery was free, Scout stumbled back around and quickly bound the thug's wrists, then his ankles.

It was over.

A sob broke from his chest as he spun back around and pulled Emery to him. They sank to the floor, and they gripped each other for dear life. Emery was emitting a high-pitched whine as he dug his fingers into Scout's back and buried his face against his neck.

"I didn't mean it!" Emery shrieked between sobs. "They had photos of you, of everyone! They were going to hurt you! I was just trying to get away! I didn't mean any of what I said. I love you, Scout. Please believe me!"

"Shh, shh," Scout soothed. Many forms of relief washed through him. Emery was okay – physically speaking, anyway.

They had caught his stalkers. The cops had to be almost there from how loud the sirens were getting.

But most importantly, Scout and Emery were together, and Emery didn't hate him.

"It's okay. I understand," Scout rasped, rubbing the back of Emery's head and pressing their temples together. "I've got you. I'm not going anywhere. I'm so sorry. I should never have left you alone-"

"If I hadn't been such a jerk-"

Scout kissed him hard on the lips, cradling his face. "It's over," he murmured into his mouth. "There's nothing to be sorry for. Everything's going to be fine. It's over."

Emery took several shuddery breaths, then nodded, staring into Scout's eyes. "Yes," he said, gradually calming down. "Yes, it's over. We're okay. You stopped them."

Scout's heart ached. "You were so brave. I heard you fighting back."

Emery nodded, suddenly looking completely exhausted. Scout sat down, his back against the wall. He opened his legs and pulled Emery gently between them, his back to Scout's front. Emery helped by scooching over, snuggling into Scout's embrace. Scout rested his chin on top of Emery's head and hugged him tightly.

"I've got you," he murmured. "You're safe. I won't let anything else happen to you."

"*Police!*" a voice bellowed from outside.

Scout shuddered and grinned in relief. "We're in here!" he yelled back. "It's clear!"

The front door wasn't locked, so it burst open easily, and several uniformed cops came pouring through, their guns raised as they surveyed the scene. Scout looked up weakly at the slim brunette woman in her early forties leading the charge. Her hair was pulled into a ponytail, and she wore a grim expression while taking the scene in before her in less than a second.

"Detective Padilla," Scout said weakly. "I think it's just those two," he informed her, jutting his chin at the thugs lying on the floor, "but I didn't check any of the other rooms."

The cops were already fanning out through the cabin, calling "Clear!" as they entered each room.

Padilla placed her hands on her hips and nodded as each of the thugs were cuffed by uniformed officers. "Jesus, Duffy. Did you have to go full Schwarzenegger on these guys?"

"Yes," Emery spat savagely. He sat up and glared at the taller guy who was still just about conscious. "The camera should still be recording. It's all there. They admitted they were behind all those 'ekleinhater' accounts. They tried to frame and disgrace me and steal thousands from me, and from the suicide note they were making me read, I think they were going to kill me."

"Kidnapping, grievous bodily harm, harassment," Scout added, still holding on to Emery and nodding. "I'm pretty sure you can throw the book at them."

Padilla arched an eyebrow down at them. "With pleasure," she said as half a smile curled at her lips. "You boys did good. Let's get you seen to." As one of her colleagues carefully plucked the phone from its tripod, Padilla pulled her radio out and clicked it on. "All clear here. We have civilians in need of medical attention. ETA on the EMTs?"

The radio crackled. *"A couple of minutes out."*

Padilla nodded to herself. "Roger that, see you in a sec."

"Whoa."

Scout, Emery and Detective Padilla all turned to the figure leaning against the doorframe, looking over the scene with pure delight.

"Cowboy!" Kamran cried in glee. "You did it!"

"Sir, this is an active crime scene," Padilla snapped firmly.

Scout waved a hand. "It's okay. He's with me."

Padilla narrowed her eyes at Scout. "I don't care if he's the Queen of England. He can't come in here."

Kamran cackled at the taller thug as he was cajoled out of the front door by two armed officers. "No, it's cool, ma'am. I'll wait on the porch like a good dog. I just wanted to check on my buddy here."

"Can we go sit on the porch, too?" Scout asked.

Padilla huffed, then gave him a small smile. "Sure. Just try not to hurt yourself any more and…don't let him touch anything, okay?"

Scout nodded, then kissed the side of Emery's head and looked him in the eye. "You feel up to standing?"

Emery nodded back sleepily. "Who's your friend?" he asked as Scout helped him across the wrecked living room and out into the cool night air. He inhaled deeply. The realization that this was actually over, that Emery was safe, was finally sinking in. He smiled down at him, his heart bursting with affection.

"Emery, I'd like you to meet Kamran, the best driver in all of Pine Cove."

"Damn right," Kamran agreed with a grin. He stuck his hand out at Emery. "Well, you sure as hell look like shit. Good thing your man here is a one-man task force. I'm really glad you're not dead."

"That makes two of us," Emery replied with a weak smile.

Scout hugged him as tightly as he dared. He'd be happier once the paramedics had seen to Emery. "And Kamran, this is Emery, my…"

"His boyfriend," Emery snapped, pumping Kamran's hand hard. "I'm his boyfriend, and he's my boyfriend, and I'm not letting him go, even if it means tying him to a chair." Scout looked down at him, mildly horrified. "What?" Emery gave him a very tired grin. "Too soon for dark humor? If I don't laugh, I'll cry."

Kamran wagged a finger at them and laughed. "You got yourself a fireball there, cowboy. I reckon he'd have been just fine without you."

But Emery's expression dropped, and his lip wobbled as he flung himself against Scout's side. "No, it's okay," he said in a small voice. "He helped a little."

Scout chuckled. He could feel himself crashing from the fading adrenaline. "A little," he repeated fondly.

The flashing lights of the paramedic unit caught their attention, and Scout sighed in relief. Kamran touched his arm.

"Seriously, man," he said. "Nice job. I'll be waiting here. My ride's just behind the cop cars. I'll hang around and take you guys wherever you want to go."

Scout sagged in gratitude. "Thank you. I mean it."

"Yeah, yeah." Kamran grinned and jogged backward down the porch steps. "You owe me a beer, is what you mean."

Scout chuckled, nuzzling his cheek against Emery's hair, feeling him warm and tight in his embrace. A beer was the very least he could owe Kamran for what he'd done. Scout was pretty sure he'd never be able to repay him for the part he'd played in saving his boyfriend's life.

Boyfriend.

Well, that sounded like Emery was interested in working something out. Thank god, because there was no power on Earth that could have made Scout walk away from this incredible man.

Not now. Not ever.

EMERY

EMERY DIDN'T THINK HE'D EVER ENJOYED A SHOWER SO MUCH, largely thanks to who he was sharing it with. The crazy thing was, he and Scout weren't even having sex. He was pretty sure they weren't planning on it, either.

Emery couldn't think of an occasion when someone *not* wanting to have sex with him had been so damn romantic.

As soon as they'd made it home in the early hours of the morning – thanks to a ride from Scout's new friend Kamran – Scout had gently pulled Emery into the bathroom and carefully stripped them both naked. Now he was sponging Emery's aching body and combing his fingers lovingly through Emery's wet hair.

Emery was pretty certain the horror of what had happened that evening wasn't going to leave him anytime soon. But with all the lights in the apartment on, Sonic snuffling happily in his cage, and Scout's promise not to leave Emery's side until the morning, he was beginning to feel more human again. This was his life. He could start to put the Mercer brothers' torment behind him, for good.

Before she'd let them go, Detective Padilla had confirmed

some details to Emery about the men who had made his life hell for the past few months, particularly over the last week. As he'd guessed, they were two brothers named Larry and Chuck. Larry had been the taller gunman and was a couple of years older than the shorter driver, Chuck.

They hailed from Salt Lake City, but it seemed their dear old grandma had been a resident of Pine Cove her whole life. According to Padilla, Larry had become quite animated with vitriol when describing how much she'd hated the increasing popularity of the town's 'resident queer,' obsessively following him on social media.

It was a shame Grandma was dead because Emery would have loved the opportunity to tell her that literally no one had been forcing her to pay attention to anything he did. He wasn't hurting her. She'd only been hurting herself.

In any case, when Chuck and Larry's own vlog had been shut down due to increasing reports of hate speech, Grandma had convinced them it was people like Emery who were to blame. That was it. Emery hadn't directly stolen any sponsors or viewers from them. They probably would never have been aware of him if it hadn't been for their grandma's bigotry.

To think he'd almost died because some old woman was so full of hate. Life really was that random sometimes.

But sometimes the randomness worked in your favor. Sometimes it brought you down a path you'd never imagined but now couldn't fathom any other way it could possibly be.

Emery turned and slipped his arms around Scout's wet torso, resting his head on his chest. "Thank you," he said softly over the running water. "I knew you'd come."

He hadn't, though. In the moment, he honestly hadn't believed he'd been worthy of saving. He didn't know how Scout could possibly have gotten to him in time, even though he'd sent the pin location. A sob rose in his throat as he threatened to start crying again. He was just beyond happy that he'd arrived when he had.

"Shh, baby, it's okay." Scout just hugged him for a while. Then once Emery's hiccups subsided, Scout switched off the water. He touched his finger and thumb to Emery's chin, tipping his head back for a gentle kiss. "Come on. Let's get you into bed."

Emery was bone tired, so he didn't put up any resistance as Scout helped him step out onto the bathmat and began to carefully towel dry him. Once he was reasonably water-free, Scout wrapped him up in a fresh, warm bath sheet, then quickly rubbed himself down. Emery sat on the closed toilet, watching him. They were both kind of a mess. Luckily, they hadn't needed to go to the emergency room, but there was going to be a lot of pain killers and packs of frozen veggies in their immediate future.

He felt a million times better after a shower, though. Even better when Scout led him into the bedroom and dressed him in his softest, comfiest pajamas. Scout had a pair of sweatpants lying around that he slipped on. Then they pulled the bedcovers back and got into the bed where they'd already made love several times.

There was nothing sexual about the way Scout held him then, however. Emery realized he was trembling again, but he didn't seem to be able to stop himself. Scout didn't put any pressure on him to calm down, though. He just held him, gently stroking his back and kissing his hair. Eventually, Emery began to relax.

"I think I might need to find a therapist after this," he said, breaking the silence. There was a beat, then both of them laughed. It was pure relief making them slightly hysterical. It felt good after so much awfulness.

"Yeah," Scout agreed with a sigh. "I might give it a try, too. We were doing pretty good with the old communication thing. Might not be a bad idea to have a bit of professional help, as well."

Emery bit his sore lip and looked up at Scout. He didn't want to keep so many walls up anymore. He'd thought he was all alone in this world, no more so than when he'd been tied to a chair, facing death. But he wasn't alone. He'd meant what he'd said. He wanted Scout to stay with him. But more than that, what those assholes had done had made him clearly see that actually, Emery was damn important to a hell of a lot of people.

It was time to stop shutting them all out.

"I was telling the truth," he rasped, his gaze meeting Scout's gorgeous green eyes. He was beautiful, even with a shiner and a busted lip. He'd be beautiful to Emery anytime, anywhere, he was absolutely sure.

Scout rubbed his arm. "Truth about what?"

Emery crushed any doubts that might have tried to surface in his mind. If tonight had told him anything, it was that life was too damned short. "About wanting you to be my boyfriend. I don't know how we'd make it work, but-"

Scout cut him off with a very delicate but tender kiss. It was just lips touching lips. They were both still hurt, after all. But Emery sobbed, it was so compassionate.

"I'd love nothing more." Scout beamed down at him and caressed the back of his neck. "In fact, I…well, I'm pretty sure I love you, too."

Emery knew he was still very bad at processing deep and genuine emotion. This was why he needed a damn therapist. So his initial reaction was to laugh. "No, you do not love me," he scoffed. "It's literally not even been a week. Romeo and Juliet had a longer relationship than that."

But it appeared that Scout only needed a week to know Emery well enough because he didn't take offense. He actually laughed back and rolled his eyes. "Well, you started it, brat. Don't tell me you love me if you don't want to hear it back."

"I didn't-" Emery began to splutter indignantly. But Scout arched an eyebrow at him. "Oh, yeah. I did. In the cabin. Okay, fine," he grumbled, snuggling back against Scout's side. "I love you, too, you big loser. Happy now?"

Scout kissed his hair. "Yes, very."

Emery made some protest noises, trying to hide his grin against Scout's chest. He didn't think he did a very good job, but he didn't really care.

Scout played with Emery's hair as it dried. "I was going to take some time off work," he said after a while, making Emery look up. His expression was thoughtful. "But after tonight, I think I might just hand in my notice."

"What?" Emery cried. "Why? You did an amazing job!"

Scout shook his head. "I fucked up. I'm not sure I could trust myself with another client. Besides…" He glanced away and pulled at the bed sheets. But then he looked back at Emery, holding his gaze. "I'm sick of traveling. I'm sick of motel rooms. I thought…well, if it's not too full on or anything, I thought I might sell my empty place in Chicago and look into getting an apartment in town. Here. In Pine Cove."

Emery scrambled up to sit in front of where Scout was propped up against the pillows. "You'll do no such thing!" he cried, absolutely incensed.

Scout's eyes went wide. "I mean, I could go back to Chicago. But I thought if we were going to try dating-"

Emery waved both his hands, then placed them one over the other on top of Scout's mouth, careful of his busted lip but enough to shut him up. "You'll move into this place with me! Dear lord, why do you have to be so difficult? And *I'm* supposed to be the brat?"

Scout blinked, then carefully pulled Emery's hands down

by his fingers, avoiding his sore wrists. "You'd want me to move in? Already? But…but we barely know each other."

"And yet I'm rather fond of you," Emery said, pretending to sulk because he was tired of crying, and it was easier to make a joke out of it.

He knew it was fast. He knew their relationship so far had been bat-shit crazy. But after being reminded very forcefully of just how short life could be, he had no intention of dithering around.

"Don't let it go to your head. But I'm only fond of a very few people. So, you know, be honored and shit."

Scout let his head drop back as he belly-laughed. Then he bundled Emery against him, kissing him all over his face. "This is just because I'll do the dishes, isn't it?"

A smile played on Emery's face. "Maybe," he said because it was easier than admitting the truth. For now, anyway. If he got on with some therapy, perhaps one day he'd be able to explain to Scout how it felt like his ice palace was melting. Like he was floating on air, freer than he'd ever felt in his whole life. "You don't have to worry about working for now," Emery said. "I'm doing well despite everything."

"I'm not going to be your kept man," Scout grumbled, but there was no malice to it. "My ma raised me better than that. I'll think of something. I'm sure a guy like me can fit into a town like this."

Emery turned and cupped either side of his face. "Of course you can," he said sincerely. "You're kind and hardworking, and you don't take any shit. If you want to stay…if you want this to be your home, it will be."

The warm look on Scout's face made Emery's heart hurt. For a minute, Scout just held his shoulders, gazing into his eyes. Then he kissed Emery's lips reverently.

"I've never had a home," Scout said, his voice hoarse. "Not really. When I was a kid, home was a scary place. Then I just lived out of motel rooms, bouncing around the country, occasionally dropping into my empty apartment."

Emery crawled on top of him, hugging his big warm body and burying his face against his neck. "I'll be your home," he promised. "You don't have to be alone anymore."

Scout held him firmly. "Neither do you." Then he laughed, obviously equally unable to maintain a serious moment. "Even if you're a brat. You're my brat."

Emery knew what he really meant, though, despite his playful tone. He was as grateful as Emery felt that the universe had brought them together. Emery took a deep breath and decided he wanted to try being brave, speaking from the heart for once.

"I'm so glad our paths crossed. I'm so glad you remembered me and didn't give the job to anyone else. I'm so glad you gave us a chance. You...you make me so happy, Scout Duffy."

Emery wasn't sure, as he blinked several times, but he was pretty certain Scout's eyes glistened with tears. "You make me happy too, Emery Klein," he mumbled.

For a while – how long Emery didn't know, but for a good long while – they just lay there in bed, safe in each other's arms. They kept all the apartment lights on all night. Emery only dozed, his body not able to fully switch off just yet with the remnants of fear still lingering in his system.

But Scout never left him. They twisted and turned in various positions as they drifted in and out of light sleep, but Emery stayed in Scout's arms until dawn. As the world came to life once more around them, Emery finally gave in to sleep. The sound of the traffic below, the dawn chorus, and the bright sunshine made him feel like the terror was finally behind him. The Mercer brothers were in custody, and Emery would testify against them. Scout gave him the strength to know he had survived this and would continue to survive. Thrive, even. Flourish.

Emery had told himself he'd been safe with all his walls up, keeping love out. But in the end, love made him stronger, and he didn't need those walls anymore.

He was free.

SCOUT

THREE MONTHS LATER

"IT'S GONNA NEED A HELL OF A LOT OF WORK." KAMRAN whistled and looked around the space, shaking his head. "Yep. It's a real fixer-upper."

Scout frowned and leaned in to murmur against Emery's ear. "I didn't think it was *that* bad."

"*Shush!*" Emery hissed. "Let the nice man haggle for you."

They were standing in a pretty dirty and long-vacated space in Pine Cove's warehouse district. Which, in a town this size, was three warehouses close together next to a lumber mill. It wasn't perhaps the ideal location, but it was a decent enough place to start out. Or at least, that was what Scout had thought when looking online and when he'd swung by last week to meet with the owner. But then his boyfriend and new best friend had reacted with horror that Scout might make an offer without their approval, so here they all were.

The owner was a fairly large man in his fifties called Bryce Brooker. His family business apparently owned several of the commercial buildings in town, such as the warehouse they were standing in that had been broken up into smaller ventures in the early nineties, a bottling plant, and the local newspaper as well as its printing press.

Bryce Brooker was not a fool. But Kamran Amir was still trying his luck.

"It's practically falling down," Kamran announced, throwing his hands out and shaking his head. "It's going to take a month alone to get rid of all the pigeon nests and the spider infestation."

"Spiders?" Emery hissed in alarm.

"There might be a mouse," Scout whispered back. "One. I had a good look around. I'm not a total idiot."

Scout shook his head fondly from where they were standing by the glass front of the space, which was pretty much just a large room with some amenities out back. He was actually very touched his friend wanted to get the best deal for him, but Scout already knew this location was perfect.

A blank space. Just what he needed.

The old guy shook his head and arched an eyebrow. He seemed to know he was being played, but he apparently didn't mind all that much. One-thousand-eight-hundred a month," Bryce said. "That's my final offer."

Kamran scoffed and put his hands on his slim hips. "Are you crazy! Fifteen."

"Seventeen"

"One-thousand-seven-hundred is *great*," Scout jumped in. He meant it. That was a hundred dollars less than he'd been prepared to pay, and he didn't want to swindle anyone out of a fair rent. "One point seven. Shall we shake on it?"

Bryce chuckled and peered over his bifocals. "Sure, then we can sign a whole load of legal documents, too. Just for kicks."

Kamran huffed and crossed his arms. "You spoil all my fun, cowboy."

Scout grinned at him, though. "I'm sure there are a few things around here I can let you smash up or burn. Look at all that junk in the corner." He pointed to one of the nooks behind one of several pillars that had apparently become the trash pile when the previous tenants had vacated.

Kamran danced on the spot, wiggling his fingers. "Okay, you're forgiven. Besties again."

Scout laughed, shaking hands with the owner of the near-empty space, then watched as he went to presumably go fetch a contract, and Kamran ran off to investigate the heap of debris from old cabinets and bookcases.

It was funny how a bare room could bring Scout so much happiness. He squeezed Emery's hand. "What do you think?"

Emery beamed as he turned this way and that, his eyes shining with delight. "I can see it," he whispered.

So could Scout. He led Emery to the middle of the space, rubbing his knuckles with his thumb. "We'll put the ring here. I can hang the bags from that beam there. Over there, we can build lockers and individual changing stalls. That way, they don't have to be gendered."

Emery smiled harder. "Excellent idea," he praised, making Scout feel warm and flushed.

"The bathrooms will need refitting," Scout continued, "but the plumbing is all there. I might need help making it look, you know, nice. Fancy. I was thinking we could make it a bit like the place in Hawaii? You know, with the framed photos on the wall, and hang up some gloves. I've been talking to some of my old buddies from back in the day, and a whole bunch of them want to help. So-"

Emery stood on his tiptoes and placed his lips against Scout's, cutting him off mid flow. "It's going to be *awesome,* hon. Swift said he'd help promote classes at the Aspire. He was really excited. Your own boxing gym. I'm so fucking proud."

Scout couldn't help but smile bashfully. Leaving private security had been the best move he could have made. To begin with, he'd done some part-time contract work here in town. One of Emery's best friends, Robin, had a cyber-security business he'd been getting off the ground, so Scout had worked a while for him advising on camera installs and the like. But one day he'd been back at Aspire talking with Swift about the possibility of getting a real punching bag installed instead of just the free-standing one Scout had been using at home.

His and Emery's home. Moving in together had been the other best decision he could have made, and he hadn't had a single regret.

Swift had raised his eyebrows. "Only if you're going to teach a class. I have no extra time these days."

It was like a lightbulb going off in Scout's mind. All the memories from his youth had come flooding back, of how the ring had given him a place to escape his old man, a home away from home. He'd made so many more friends there than at school. He'd felt in control of his body for the first time in his life, and therefore, his own destiny.

He wanted to give that to other people.

He didn't want to just attract guys. He was already planning on running classes for kids and teens, for women, and possibly even promoting LGBT-focused time slots. The town had a far bigger queer community than he'd realized when he'd first arrived. He wanted everyone to feel safe and welcome here at his new gym.

He'd been approved a loan by the bank and also had the money from the sale of his place in Chicago that he was tapping into while he was getting started. Emery was refusing to let him pay even the tiniest amount of rent right now, so Scout was just contributing to the running of their home. It was frightening starting up a business in this economy, but he was so passionate about this venture he knew he had to try everything he could to make it work.

Besides, Pine Cove was his home now. He wasn't going anywhere. So he felt more than confident putting down some real, solid roots.

And with Emery by his side, he felt like he could conquer the world.

It was almost impossible to believe that for all those years, Scout had felt being alone would make him stronger. Together, there wasn't anything that he and his talented, intelligent, beautiful boyfriend couldn't do.

"What?" Emery said playfully as he caught Scout staring.

Scout smiled and hugged him to his side. "Thank you for supporting me. For believing in me."

Emery rolled his eyes, but then he bit his lip and huffed. After they'd both found very good therapists to start working on their issues with, they were getting better at saying what they meant and not playing around.

The games were still plentiful in the bedroom, of course. But Scout preferred not arguing thanks to misunderstandings outside of it.

"You were one of the only people who truly understood my work and how important it was, other than my friends," Emery said. "You've never once made me feel like I should get a real job."

Scout gave him a stern look. "You have a 'real job,'" he insisted. "I don't get credit for using my brain."

"Shut up and let me praise you," Emery said, his words full of lust.

"Hey! You two!" Kamran barked from the pile of junk he was inspecting like it was a treasure trove. "At least let the rest of us escape the building if you're planning on christening it!"

Scout and Emery snorted. That wasn't a bad idea, to be

fair. Sex in unusual, semi-public places was definitely one of their kinks. But only once they were alone.

Scout was prepared to share Emery with the world in many ways, but not like that.

"So…" Scout said. "Now this is settled, Mom mentioned having us visiting her next week for Thanksgiving in Chicago. What do you think?"

After a couple of pretty difficult sessions with his therapist, Scout had decided to end communication with his father for the foreseeable future. They hadn't seen each other for years, and his phone calls were always toxic, leaving Scout feeling grubby. He'd let his dad convince him he owed him some kind of relationship, simply because they were related. But Scout had drawn a line under it now.

As a result, he and his mom were already getting closer again. In fact, she'd hinted once or twice that she'd always considered the Pacific Northwest for her older years. She seemed prepared to give Scout a chance to properly settle down, but he had to say, he liked the idea of having his mom closer to him.

She'd started talking about grandbabies again, and even though he'd rolled his eyes and told her 'one thing at a time,' he didn't completely dismiss the idea. He'd love the chance to be a better dad than he'd ever had.

Emery looked pleased as punch. "I'd love to. And you know, I think my folks might want her and you over for Christmas dinner. If that's not too much?"

If he was honest, Scout had never shared Christmas with anyone else, and for a second he did feel kind of overwhelmed. But why shouldn't they get their families together? Why not start intermingling their lives? Emery's friends had embraced Scout with open arms, after all. And by friends, that mostly meant the Coal family, who apparently enjoyed adopting their kids' friends and partners. Nothing was too much trouble for Deb and Joe Coal.

Scout had always regretted he didn't have a big family like he knew a lot of Catholics did. Now it was as if he was bursting at the seams with found siblings and parents and aunts and uncles. Even Emery's conservative folks were cautiously starting to accept that their son was in love with a man and that man wasn't going anywhere.

Which was good because Scout was madly in love. He'd never have imagined anyone could keep him on his toes like Emery Klein did, and not just in the bedroom. He made his life better in every aspect, and Scout just hoped he did the same for Emery, too.

He got the impression he did. Emery had mentioned a couple of times that he might have hinted to his followers that there was a special man in his life. Scout was in the process of deciding if he wanted to show his face to the masses. Seeing as he was no longer in the security business, he was leaning more toward 'why the hell not?'

He often thought of Emery's words from the night of the attack. He couldn't agree more with how grateful he was to the universe for bringing their paths together again and again when there had been so many times they could have lost each other to the randomness of life. It was clear to Scout that he and Emery were meant to be together, and he was going to do everything he could to make sure they stayed that way.

They were just getting started on their shared lives. Luck had been on their side several times before. But Scout had a feeling that they didn't need it to ensure their journey lasted for many years to come. They had each other, and together, they were stronger than anything the world could throw at them.

Nine Months Later
Emery

EMERY STIRRED HIS RASPBERRY VODKA AND LEMONADE AND looked out from the kitchen door to where Scout was sitting looking over some businessy things that he was so very good at. God, he was as gorgeous as the day Emery had first laid eyes on him. More so. He almost didn't believe he was capable of loving someone as much as he did Scout Duffy.

He took a sip of his drink, then glanced down at the fluffy husky puppy sitting at his feet. Fenrir – so named after some badass wolf in Norse mythology – tilted his head and looked up at Emery. *You can do it, Daddy!* Emery imagined him saying. Emery bit his lip and raised his eyebrow.

What if something goes wrong? he asked back in his mind.

Fenrir whined and yipped, chasing his tail in a circle, then smiling up at Emery. That clearly meant *You'll never know if you don't try!*

"Smarty-pants," Emery murmured under his breath and took another sip for Dutch courage.

It seemed like Scout hadn't noticed he was being watched yet. Emery needed to move before he lost his nerve.

There were very few things in life that scared Emery anymore. After his ordeal with the Mercer brothers, he'd really put that theory to the test, but after going to court and helping put them both away for many years, Emery's confidence had bounced back tenfold.

He knew he could be a sassy, arrogant brat a lot of the time, but it was just a delightful game. Scout knew him inside and out, when they were playing and when they were serious. Emery knew he should be serious now, but he was genuinely scared, and it was too easy to fall back into his old persona. He was much braver when he was Emery Klein, Influencer and LGBT Activist, than just plain old Emery the Boyfriend.

So he gulped down half his vodka lemonade in one and placed the glass down on the kitchen counter. The place was generally so much tidier now with Scout living here too. He understood how certain chores made Emery feel, and they now shared the load, making the house into a home. It was one of the many things Emery loved most about Scout. Other boyfriends might buy their guys flowers or chocolates, but Scout knew the way to Emery's heart was to do the dishes and help ease his depression worries. That was way more romantic as far as he was concerned.

He was a lucky guy.

Emery gave himself a shake, then twirled and sashayed his way into the living room. He moved over to Scout's armchair with Fenrir galloping on his too-big paws beside his feet. From over in his cage, Sonic gave a snuffly snore, wriggling sleepily in his wood shavings.

"Dar-ling," Emery said in a sing-song voice, straddling

Scout's lap and removing the boring papers from his hands. Scout huffed in exasperation, but he knew better than to protest. Emery beamed and placed the papers carefully on the coffee table. "There now. That's better. Tell me, do you know what day it is today?"

Scout arched an eyebrow and rested his arms on the chair. Emery would have thought he'd hold his waist, playing along with Emery's seduction. After all, he was only wearing the smallest pair of denim shorts he owned, a crop with the Cher quote 'Mom, I *am* a rich man,' and some lip gloss. He knew he looked fucking hot. However, a flicker of worry went through Emery's mind, but he continued to smile. If he pretended this was all going to plan, maybe it still would.

"Yes," Scout said patiently. "I know what day it is. Because I value my life. It's our anniversary. Which is why I'm taking you out for a fancy dinner, then dancing at Aquarium, and then back home to give you the ridiculously expensive present I've bought you."

Emery licked his lips. "Well, I haven't *bought* you anything, because you're lucky enough to have me. *However,* I do still have something to give you."

Scout looked up at him, as did Fenrir. "Is that so?"

Nerves fluttered through Emery's chest, and he did his best not to second-guess himself. "Yep."

"And what is this free gift I'm getting?"

Emery preened. "Me."

Scout sighed and gave Emery a smile that was pure indulgence. "You just said I was already lucky to have you."

Emery walked his fingers up Scout's chest, feeling his delicious muscles under the thin cotton of his tank top. "Yes, you are. But I was thinking of a more permanent arrangement." He took a shaky breath, then plastered his cutest smile on his face. "Scout Duffy. Will you marry me?"

Scout regarded him for a second that seemed to last an eternity.

"No," Scout said clearly.

For a fraction of a second, Emery's world almost came crashing down. He was so wrapped up in the moment he'd forgotten the rules they'd had since the very start. But of course Scout hadn't. He was beaming up at Emery, biting his lip as he smiled so hard it looked like he was going to burst.

"No," Emery repeated, arching an eyebrow. "Not 'guppy'?"

Scout lifted his hands to cup either side of Emery's face. "Not 'guppy,'" he affirmed.

"You *scoundrel*," Emery howled as happy tears spilled down his face, and Fenrir barked joyously. He beat Scout's chest as he doubled over laughing in the chair, hugging Emery to him. "You brute, you *monster!* So that's a yes? You're saying yes, you will marry me?" Still laughing, Scout stood with Emery in his arms. Emery wrapped his legs around Scout's waist as they kissed frantically, and Fenrir scampered around their feet. "Answer me, goddamn it! I hate you!"

"I hate you, too," Scout said fondly as they entered their bedroom, closing the door on their excitable puppy. He dropped Emery on the mattress. He bounced before sitting up and dangling his legs over the edge. He watched indignantly as Scout walked over to his sock drawer, shaking his head. "You just can't wait for anything, can you?"

His expression was nothing but love as he glanced over his shoulder. Then he opened the drawer and retrieved something.

A small box.

Emery gasped, his hands flying over his mouth.

He knew, deep down, that he'd been afraid this might not happen. So he'd taken charge and decided to ask for what he wanted, when he wanted it. But as Scout walked back to him at the edge of the bed and got down on one knee, he could never have imagined how happy this moment would really make him.

Scout opened the box to reveal a dazzling band of diamonds. He wasn't kidding earlier about the expensive gift. That had to have cost a fortune. But Emery didn't care. He didn't need a ring at all. Because the truth was, Scout wanted to spend the rest of their lives together just as much as Emery did.

"Yes!" he screeched, bouncing up and down on the bed and waving his hands. "Yes, yes, yes!"

Scout laughed and gave Emery the long-suffering look he was well used to by now. "I haven't even *asked* you yet. I had a whole big speech prepared about how you're the best thing that ever happened to me and how you make me the happiest man alive."

Emery sat on his hands. "Okay, yes, I want that, please."

"Yeah, well, you can't have everything, you little brat." Scout reached up and brushed Emery's hair back, cupping the side of his face. "But you do get this: Emmerich Klein. You're perfect in every way, even when you drive me totally crazy. I love you, and I..." He grinned as tears spilled from his eyes. Emery slapped his arm, then cradled his own hand against Scout's face.

"Stop it," he said with a hiccup. "You're setting me off."

"No, I won't stop," Scout said with an even heartier laugh. "I used to think being alone was the only way to survive. But now I know I could never live without you. Emery, sweetheart, brat of my life. Will you marry me?"

Emery wailed and threw his arms around Scout's neck, dragging them both to the floor. "Worst proposal ever," he said between sobs and the kisses he was peppering on Scout's tear-stained face. "I love you so much, you awful man. And I don't want to waste a single moment. So yes, I'll marry you, and I'm going to spend every day reminding you how grateful you should be."

Scout seized him around the waist and rolled them over so Emery was underneath, the open ring box near his head, the band sparkling within.

"I wouldn't have it any other way," Scout said with a sigh before kissing him sensuously. When they broke apart, Emery looked up at him fondly. Then he reached out with grabby hands.

"And now I want my bling-bling." Scout laughed and shook his head but obediently plucked the ring from its box to slide on Emery's finger. It fit perfectly. Emery admired it for a moment, his heart bursting with happiness. Then he fixed Scout with a stare. "And now I want my sexy times. Really good ones."

"Oh, is that so?" Scout asked in a disapproving tone while grinding his groin down on Emery's. Emery moaned and ran his hands up Scout's toned arms, over the wolf tattoo that had in the last year become a pack. He nodded.

"I want you to fuck me while I'm wearing nothing but your ring, baby."

Scout grinned. "I'll fuck you anytime you want, *fiancé*. Starting now."

Emery kissed him deeply. "Fiancé," he said with a sigh. "I like the sound of that. Of course, husband sounds even better."

Scout hoisted him off the floor and threw him back onto the bed. "You know there are *some* things you're going to have to wait for, right?"

Emery grinned and kissed the tip of his nose.

"Some things are worth waiting for." And he meant it.

It felt like he'd waited his whole life for Scout to appear, and now he had him, he was never letting him go.

THANK you for reading **Scout and Emery's** story! The next **Pine Cove** book is coming out on September 17th, 2019. To pre-order right now, click here! getbook.at/PineCoveHomewardBound

If you would like to be the first to know when my new releases are available, as well as read several awesome and totally FREE stories, please sign up to my newsletter! Emails will only be sent occasionally and you can unsubscribe at any time.

If you enjoyed reading Troubled Waters, I would very much appreciate it if you could share your experience with others online. Reviews, recommendations, fan works and general love is the best way for me to reach new readers.

If you'd like to meet with other HJ Welch fans, why not join our Facebook group? Helen Juliet Books. We're very friendly!

Thank you to: my beta reader, Mum; editors Meg and Tanja; cover artist AngstyG; cheerleaders Ed, Amelia, Cara, Lucy, Susi and Piper; loving husband; and fur babies Arya and Tyrion.

After Micha Perkins finds himself wrongly implicated in a crime, the last person he wants coming to his rescue is his secret crush Swift; his older brother's best friend. But when Micha returns to the town that never felt like home, he discovers Swift's young daughter is in trouble as well. If Micha can help them both in any way, he knows he will.

Self-defense coach Swift Coal never realized he was a father until he gets custody of five-year-old Imogen and her cranky cat. His neat and tidy life is about to come crashing down, but to his surprise, Micha Perkins is there to save the day. He's so damn good with kids, and just as cute as Swift remembers. When Micha moves in to help look after Imogen, Swift struggles to repress the feelings he's kept hidden.

Micha's always been a misfit and Swift's life was always orderly.

Micha may have taken the fall to protect those more vulnerable than him, but who will save him when his past comes back to haunt him? Was Swift a fool to risk the safety of his daughter around a bad element like Micha? When their chaotic worlds collide, perhaps love and family are the middle ground they both need to become stronger together.

Homeward Bound is a steamy, standalone MM romance novel with a guaranteed HEA and absolutely no cliffhanger.

Coming September 17th, 2019. Click here to preorder on Amazon today!

Robin Coal wonders if asking his straight housemate Dair to be his fake boyfriend for his high school reunion will be the worst thing he's ever done…or the best. But there's no way he's going home to face his abusive ex alone, and former Marine Dair is just the protection he needs. So long as he doesn't find out about Robin's secret crush, everything will be fine.

Mechanic Dair Epping never expected to spend a week sharing a bed with his adorkable friend, however pretending to be bi is easier than he imagined. He knows he'll do anything to keep Robin safe from his ex-boyfriend, but as the chemistry between them grows, the line between fake and reality begins to blur.

Could Dair *actually* be bi? Even if he was, would an ex-Marine really be interested in a computer geek like Robin? When his ex's intentions turn dangerous, how far will Dair go to protect the man he's falling for?

Safe Harbor is a steamy, standalone MM romance novel with a guaranteed HEA and absolutely no cliffhanger.

Click here to get Safe Harbor on Amazon today!

ABOUT THE AUTHOR

HJ Welch is a contemporary MM romance author living in London with her husband and two balls of fluff that occasionally pretend to be cats. She began writing at an early age, later honing her craft online in the world of fanfiction on sites like Wattpad. Fifteen years and over a million words later, she sought out original MM novels to read. She never thought she would be any good at romance, but once she turned her hand to it she discovered she in fact adored it. By the end of 2016 she had written her first book of her own, and in 2017 she achieved her lifelong dream of becoming a fulltime author.

Safe Harbor is the first book in her Pine Cove series. She also writes contemporary British MM romance as Helen Juliet.

You can contact HJ Welch via social media:
Newsletter (with FREE Homecoming Hearts material and original stories) – https://www.subscribepage.com/helenjuliet
Website – www.helenjuliet.com
Email – helenjulietauthor@gmail.com
Twitter – @helenjwrites
Instagram – @helenjwrites
Tumblr – @helenjwrites
Facebook Page – @HJWelchAuthor
Facebook Group – Helen Juliet Books

succeeded with Below Zero. But when the record label throws the band aside, Joey ultimately has to face the shame of returning home.

Gabe Robinson loves his town. As a firefighter, he'd do anything to protect it. He even tries to help the prickly, fallen-from-grace Joey Sullivan. Gabe is nursing his own broken heart though, so his immediate attraction to Joey can't be anything other than a rebound.

An unexpected road trip forces Joey and Gabe together and the sparks fly between them, but it can't last. Their worlds are too different. Joey plans to get as far away from home as soon as he can, yet Gabe can't imagine any other life. But when Joey hits rock bottom, Gabe is the only one who can save him. Protect him. Keep him warm.

Gabe's saved lives before. But can he rescue hearts?

Burn – Homecoming Hearts #3

Raiden Jones never thought he'd need a bodyguard. His life as a songwriter has been tame to the point of boring compared to his popstar days. But when a malicious hacker starts destroying his career and threatening his life, he finds himself desperately in need of protection.

After leaving the Marines, Levi Patterson takes a place with his uncle's private security firm. The last thing he expected was a dumb babysitting job for the bratty, privileged Raiden. However, the two men have no choice but to get to know each other as they are forced on tour with one of Raiden's remaining clients.

Levi has never told anyone of his secret, occasional hook-ups with guys from his unit, and Raiden's never thought about going with another man before. But it's obvious the increasing chemistry between them is becoming more than physical, and there's only so long they can resist.

As the hacker becomes bolder, Levi finds himself in a race against time before Raiden is taken from him forever. He's no stranger to combat, but with his heart on the line, he finds himself in the fight of both their lives.

Steam – Homecoming Hearts #4

Bad boy movie star Trent Charles is more famous for his outrageous behavior than he is for his acting these days. After one scandal too many, his manager sends him home to the snowy ski slopes of Wyoming to get his life together. No parties, no fast cars, and certainly no women.

Ashby Wilcott is done with bad boys. His heart is broken from his last relationship disaster. A few weeks of peace and quiet in the mountains is just what he needs. He is absolutely not interested in moody Trent Charles, even if he is hot enough to melt snow with his rippling muscles and mysterious ways. Good thing Trent is straight.

But the two men can't seem to stay apart. Trent finds himself pretending to be Ashby's boyfriend, a lie that gets Ashby invited to a wedding as Trent's guest. Regardless of Trent's protests that he's not interested in the beautiful Ashby in that way, the chemistry between the two steams up. With only a few weeks together, what harm can they do having a little fun?

As outside forces threaten to tear them apart, Trent realizes Ashby means more to him than just a fling. In fact, he'll do anything to protect him.

Blaze – Homecoming Hearts #5

International pop sensation Reyse Hickson has it all. Or so it seems. Thanks to his homophobic label, he never expects to find love. But when he's saved from a mugging by a gorgeous stranger, the chemistry between them is undeniable. Reyse can't help but fall into his savior's arms…and his bed.

Corey Sheppard is nobody's hero. He got himself out of the foster system and stands on his own two feet. He could never be anyone's closeted lover. But there's so much more to Reyse Hickson than the world sees. Corey just can't stay away.

When Reyse's dad suffers a stroke, Reyse insists on going home. In desperate need of a friend, he asks Corey to join him. A short time together is better than none. With Reyse's lifestyle, they know it's the best they can manage.

But for the first time in his life, Corey finds a family with Reyse. And Reyse doesn't think he can hide how feels for Corey, even though his label threatens to drop him if he ever comes out. Can Reyse and Corey walk away from the best thing that's ever happened to either of them? Or is this love worth going down in a blaze of glory?

Firefighter Remi Washington never told anyone he's bi, let alone acted on it. But when he temporarily offers his spare room to his best friend's younger brother, he's drawn to the twinky, beautiful Kris in a way he can't ignore. How long before he gives in to this temptation?

Soon Kris stands accused of having started the fire and he has to fight with all his strength to clear his own name. Will Remi risk outing himself to stand by Kris's side, or will that closet door remain closed forever?

Welcome to Hidden Creek, Texas, where the heart knows what it wants, and where true love lives happily ever after. Every Men of Hidden Creek novel can be read on its own, but keep an eye out for familiar faces around town! This book contains a daring rescue, a meddling mommy matchmaker, and enough sparks to start a wildfire.

Masterpiece – Men of Hidden Creek

"I want to trust you."

Koby Duvall always knew his place at school. Art nerds like him were just target practice for guys on the football team. NFL star Vince Russo may never have bullied him, but the two men are still nothing alike. Except when Koby is asked to create a sculpture of Russo, they find themselves stuck together.

Vince is only home for a few weeks over the holidays while he recovers from a head injury. Face to face with his former classmate, he finally has a chance to prove to Koby that he's more than just a dumb jock.

However, sparks fly and Vince realizes he and Koby may have more in common than they thought. But all Vince knows is football, and coming out in the NFL is career suicide. When a violent grudge comes back to terrorize Koby, though, Vince knows he'll do anything to protect the man he loves.

Welcome to Hidden Creek, Texas, where the heart knows what it wants, and where true love lives happily ever after. Every Men of Hidden Creek novel can be read on its own, but keep an eye out for familiar faces around town! This book contains a steamy modeling session, big families with even bigger food portions, and enough chemistry to melt steel.